*To take her mind off the nausea,
she focused on him. . . .*

He hadn't shaved in a day or so, judging by the dark stubble. She could smell the faint odor of sweat, feel his body heat. His hair was so long that it brushed against her fingers.

He waited. "Okay now?"

No, she wasn't. Not this close to him. "Yes."

**"Readers are not going to leave a page
unturned. This is the kind of joyride
for which bedside lamps were invented."
—Judith Gould**

Paradise Island

GENA HALE

AN ONYX BOOK

ONYX
Published by New American Library, a division of
Penguin Putnam Inc., 375 Hudson Street,
New York, New York 10014, U.S.A.
Penguin Books Ltd, 27 Wrights Lane,
London W8 5TZ, England
Penguin Books Australia Ltd,
Ringwood, Victoria, Australia
Penguin Books Canada Ltd, 10 Alcorn Avenue,
Toronto, Ontario, Canada M4V 3B2
Penguin Books (N.Z.) Ltd, 182–190 Wairau Road,
Auckland 10, New Zealand

Penguin Books Ltd, Registered Offices:
Harmondsworth, Middlesex, England

First published by Onyx, an imprint of New American Library,
a division of Penguin Putnam Inc.

First Printing, April 2001
10 9 8 7 6 5 4 3 2

PUBLISHER'S NOTE
This is a work of fiction. Names, characters, places, and incidents either
are the product of the author's imagination or are used fictitiously, and
any resemblance to actual persons, living or dead, events, or locales is
entirely coincidental.

For Christine M. McCoy
artist, SuperMom, and best friend,
forget-me-not.

Acknowledgments

My thanks to
five people
who made this book happen:
My editor, Cecilia Malkum Oh,
for your enthusiasm, talent, and insight.
(I owe you at least a crate of Godiva by now.)
My agent, Robin Rue,
for all your efforts and endless faith in me.
(Better make that order for two crates.)
My friends and critique partners in crime,
Marilyn Jordan and Debbie Andrews,
bless you for every wonderful Wednesday.
(Marilyn, I'll remember to order white, too.)
And Catherine, for everything.
(Oh hell, I'll just go and rent a truck.)

Chapter One

Luke spotted it through the binoculars.

"What the hell ...?" He squinted. Groaned. Closed his eyes.

It was a hallucination. Had to be. Maybe from the heat. No, it was cool inside the house. The A/C was still working. Okay, not the heat. It was an optical illusion. A mirage. The onset of psychosis. Anything but real. He opened his eyes.

It was still there.

For something that could conceivably drive him to homicide, it wasn't very big. Not that size made a difference.

"This can't be happening."

It continued to rock gently on the dappled surface of the cobalt blue water. He watched it float in with the tide, foot by foot. Maybe it wasn't that bad. It could have come from anywhere, been drifting for days. But what was he going to do with it?

He squinted again. "Oh, Christ."

It wasn't empty. Luke could just make out a flut-

ter of white fabric and what appeared to be an arm
and a leg draped over one side.

There was someone *in* the damn thing.

He dropped the high-powered lenses from his
eyes and swore savagely. His big hands, scarred
and callused from years of working on deck,
clenched into even bigger fists. Luke continued to
run through what profanity there was in the five
languages he knew as he stomped out of the house.

The glass-paneled door leading out to the beach
slammed behind him with enough force to shatter
the delicate beveled panes. Luke didn't bother to
look back. The damage was already done.

The sea was calm today. A light breeze came up
from the south to tease the palm fronds. They rus-
tled above their trunks like so many grass skirts
atop curved brown legs. Overhead the July sun
was hard and polished, its powerful rays heating
the sand to scorching degrees. Light glittered in a
thousand diamond flashes off the gentle crests of
the inlet waves.

Dragonflies chased each other through the fringe
of hibiscus and sea grape that bordered the U-
shaped beach. Their iridescent wings whirred
madly while they hovered. The air was a sultry,
tangy blend of salt, drying seaweed, and flowers.
Paradise Island had always been Luke's personal
retreat.

One that was now over.

Three years. Three years he had worked, surveying the sites, gathering data, and completing

his analysis. *Shuiba* was the culmination of all that work. The project had required meticulous investigation. Considerable discretion. Not to mention over a thousand days of his life, sweat, and unwavering dedication.

His mouth flattened as he thought of all the months spent tying up the loose ends, collecting evidence, and covering his tracks. The island provided the solitude he needed. Recent events had placed a catastrophic deadline on the project. One the State Department wanted Luke to beat. He was almost there. A few more weeks and he would have nailed them.

Now everything was blown all to hell.

As he walked to the water's edge, Luke saw that the inflatable was sagging low into the water. There was one of those toy-sized outboards on it, the kind that droned with an annoying, high-pitched buzz. Right now it was silent, hanging off the back of the long oval of black and yellow rubber. Probably snagged on the reef. The coral was high at the inlet's shallow midpoint. Whoever was lying inside was apparently asleep.

Probably some nitwit tourist, out fishing or working on a tan. Either the idiot had forgotten to secure the tie-lines, or had let the outboard run out of gas. Some blithely unconcerned fool who had drifted off into some of the most treacherous waters in the Atlantic Ocean.

He peered through the binoculars again, this time toward the horizon. No sign of a larger craft.

So where had the idiot come from? Could the boat have capsized? Would there be other survivors? And wouldn't that be icing on the cake?

He cupped a hand over his mouth. "Ahoy there!"

Luke would have a few more choice words to say to the occupant, once they were face-to-face. Unless it was someone who had *deliberately* come to the island. If that was the case—he pushed the possibility aside. Right now he had to find out what moron was intruding on the most critical thirty days of his life.

"Hey! Ahoy the raft! Wake up, stupid!"

The raft gently rocked on the incoming tide. The person inside didn't move, didn't make a sound.

Maybe the fool was drunk. Luke hoped not. He wanted him sober enough to appreciate the beating he planned to give him.

He stripped off the binoculars along with his shirt, and dropped them on the sand. After he kicked off his shoes, he waded in and dove under the waves. The surf temperature was barely cooler than bathwater. Luke wouldn't have been surprised to hear it boiling off his skin. He couldn't remember a time he'd been this pissed off. Not even when Fischer had beat him to the *Atocia*.

He crossed the distance easily, avoiding the sharp branches of coral beneath his kicking feet as he reached the reef. Grasping the side of the raft with his hands, he shook his head and blinked to clear the water from his eyes.

"Hey, I said . . ." He stopped, stunned.

The occupant of the raft was a woman.

An unconscious, sunburned woman.

Was she still alive? He reached to check for a pulse, causing a small flood of seawater to spill over the side. Yes, there it was. Strong and steady.

Her flimsy white robe had fallen open, revealing a pastel blue bra, matching panties, and a horrible sunburn. Good thing she was unconscious. The lingerie she wore looked like someone's idea of a sick joke. Spindrift dusted her limbs and face. How long had she been drifting?

Then Luke saw the blood.

"Jesus." He put his palm on her dark hair and turned her face toward him. She had a shallow, two-inch cut on her forehead. There was more dried blood matted in her hair and on her neck.

"Honey? Can you hear me? Can you open your eyes for me?"

She didn't respond to his voice. He couldn't see any other injuries, but he couldn't be sure. He had to get her out of the water and back to the house. Fast.

"Hold on, sweetheart."

Luke let go of the side to stop the flow of any more water into the raft. He groped around the bottom of the raft until he found the remnants of a short length of rope tied to an oar ring. Too short. Cut, from the look of it. It took several attempts before he freed the bottom of the raft from the coral. The woman made no sound except for the barely audible whisper of her breathing.

He swam back toward the shore as fast as he could, towing the raft and the woman behind him..

When she came out of the darkness, she saw a cloud above her.

No, that isn't right.

Not a cloud. A canopy. It was made of white crocheted lace draped over carved, dark red wood. Hard to see the pattern clearly. Her eyelids felt weighted and wouldn't open all the way.

A wave of agonizing, scalding pain washed over her, accompanied by unbearable thirst. It was so sudden and unexpected that it shocked her.

What had happened?

She tried to groan, but someone had lined her throat with sandpaper. Her tongue felt thick, seemed glued to the roof of her mouth.

With tremendous effort, she raised a hand to her face, but stopped before touching herself. Her dry, gritty eyes finally widened a fraction as she saw her fingers. They were bright red. So was the back of her hand. And her forearm.

Burned? Had she been burned? She let her arm go limp and drop as she tried to understand. She felt battered and sluggish. Why? How? An accident?

"You're awake," a man's voice said.

She wasn't alone, thank God. Someone was

close. A doctor? She moved her eyes toward the sound.

He was right there, beside the bed. A tall, deeply tanned man with wet, fair hair. She didn't know him. Whoever he was, he didn't look like a doctor.

Where am I?

The guy didn't dress like a doctor, either. A black T-shirt stretched over his linebacker's chest, the sleeves ripped off to bare muscular arms. Damp shorts clung to his hips and thighs. Her gaze moved back up to his face. Handsome, but not happy. The expression, combined with his stillness, made him appear more statue than human. If she hadn't seen his chest move, she would have mistaken him for a well-developed mannequin.

One with an attitude problem.

Why was he wet? Water beaded his dark skin, dripped from his hair, saturated his clothes. As though he'd been swimming and had neglected to dry off properly. That made no sense. Not that much did.

"Don't move."

His voice was a lot like his face. Masculine but don't-mess-with-me. His green eyes caught the sunlight as he gave her the once-over. Something was going on behind that look. Something that disturbed her more than the sight of him or this strange place. Even more than the pain crawling through her.

Why was he looking at her like that?

His large, calloused hand touched her mouth, and she felt a blessed coolness. He was applying something, she realized, using his fingertips to rub it on her cracked lips. Whatever it was soon numbed the pain. At last she was able to open her mouth. Now she could get some answers.

She tried to speak, but nothing wanted to work. She tried to pucker her lips, but still nothing. The horrible thirst only made the problem worse. The man turned, then brought a glass of liquid close to her face. She felt the edge of a straw against her teeth.

"Drink."

She struggled to get her numb lips around the straw. Her first sip tasted cool and delicious. The effect on her parched mouth and throat was instantaneous—relief followed by even more voracious thirst. With a weak gasp, she took another longer drink.

He immediately whisked the glass away from her and set it aside. "That's enough."

She looked up at him in stunned disbelief. Was he *kidding*?

He shook his head. "You'll puke if you take too much too fast."

That made her angry. She had to have more, now! An instant later her stomach cramped. His prediction was about to come true. No, it wasn't. She gulped in air until the nausea passed.

He watched her without reaction.

Where in God's name was she? she wondered,

frowning at him. The canopy above her didn't fit. What kind of hospital draped their patients' beds with antique lace? And if this guy was a doctor, he needed a refresher course in Bedside Manner 101.

"Wh—where . . . ?" It came out a thin croak. She gagged on both the effort it took to speak and the sickening feeling that returned at once.

His fingers touched her lips again, silencing her. "Don't talk. Don't move. Just take deep breaths. Nice and slow."

The nausea ballooned, and fighting it back demanded all of her attention. She closed her eyes and focused on her breathing. When she looked at the man again, he was busy doing something beside the bed.

He caught her watching. "I have to treat your sunburn," he said.

Sunburn? That was it? That was *all*?

"Do you understand?"

Mr. Congeniality was frowning down at her, waiting for her to nod? Applaud? What? That was when she saw a pair of scissors in his hand. He wanted to treat her sunburn with scissors?

He made an impatient sound. "I'm going to cut your clothes off."

And didn't he look thrilled about that? "Wait . . ."

"Hold still."

Oh, sure, do nothing while a strange man used

scissors on her. She wondered if yelling would bring someone else. She wondered if she *could* yell.

He bent over her, and she heard the snick of the scissors, felt the damp material on her body fall aside. He cut her clothing away with efficient speed, but that didn't make it any easier. Especially when the cold metal of the scissors brushed against her.

Wasn't there a nurse around here who could do this?

Fresh pain swept over her when his arm eased under her waist and lifted her. She couldn't hold back the groan as he carefully pulled the remnants of her clothing out from under her.

"Easy now." He lowered her back to the bed.

Her dry eyelids stung as her burned skin reacted to the movement. No tears came. Too dehydrated, she thought wearily, and squeezed her eyes shut.

The sound of water penetrated the pain and her eyes flew open. He was touching her, sponging her off. In spite of his care, the gentle pressure was the equivalent of being skinned alive.

She bit her bottom lip. She wasn't going to whimper. Screaming might be a problem, though.

"Almost done," he said.

The man put aside the sponge and applied a soothing lotion. His broad palms moved quickly and lightly over her. It didn't matter. Being carved alive would have been pleasant in comparison.

Something rushed in her ears. An acid, coppery taste collected on her tongue.

I am not going to throw up.

"There," he said.

That odd sound, she realized, was sobbing. She was sobbing. She'd bitten her lip, too, hard enough to draw blood. But she hadn't screamed, or even whimpered. The man drew a soft sheet over her. Things got fuzzy as she fell into an exhausted doze.

When she opened her eyes again, he was still there. Still standing over her. Still frowning. He pressed something against her right temple. He pulled it away, and she saw crusted, dark red stains on a gauze square.

What the hell is that from? "B—blood?"

"It's not too bad," the man said as he pushed a handful of her hair away from her face. He used another pad, and the sharp odor of antiseptic accompanied the stinging jab she felt as he cleaned the wound. "What did you hit your head on?"

Didn't he know? She frowned, trying to remember. Sunburned . . . a head injury . . . how had she managed . . . ?

Her anxiety grew.

She couldn't remember what had happened. She was getting scared. I was on the boat, she thought, with . . . there was a gap. With what? Blankness where there should have been, well, something. As she focused, the fear got worse. So did the nausea.

They would kill her.

She struggled to prop herself up. Where had that come from?

The man swore as he clamped a hand on her shoulder to hold her down. "Don't move—"

"No." More pain. She fought it, and him. "Have to, oh God, have to get away—"

Getting those words out drained the last of her strength. She sank back down, breathless and aching from the effort.

"You aren't going anywhere, sweetheart."

Her gaze flew to his. *Sweetheart?*

"Well, at least not for a few days." A strange expression crossed his face. "Or weeks."

She had to remember what had happened. *Right now.* There was the image of the boat. A peculiar, frightening feeling made her heart pound. Her mouth became terribly dry again. Her insides promised more unpleasant things to come. No, she wouldn't think about that boat. Not until she could do it without wanting to vomit.

"What's your name?"

Didn't he know? Hadn't he even bothered to look at her chart? Unbelievable . . . her eyes widened as she realized there was a considerable gap in her memory.

No, not a gap. An *abyss*.

"My name?"

"Yeah. What is it?"

"Do you . . ." She had to swallow and speak slower in order to get the words out. "Do you . . . know . . . my name?"

He didn't answer her, but his lips turned white. He put the pad to her head again. Despite the pain, she reached up and caught his wrist with her fingers. He looked at her.

"Tell me." She had to know.

He let out a breath and tossed the gauze in a basin. She watched him rub his fingers over his eyes. She waited. His hand dropped. Whoever this guy was, he certainly didn't like her.

That was why what he said next shook her down to her heels.

"I don't know your name," he said. "I've never seen you before."

When he returned to the kitchen, Luke poured himself a cup of coffee. The dregs of the pot tasted bitter and muddy. Not that it mattered. A plate with the congealed remains of breakfast still sat on the table. The wall clock told him he'd missed lunch, too. That didn't matter either. His appetite was gone.

The woman, on the other hand, wasn't going anywhere.

He had packed the medical supplies, thinking he'd never use them, outside of minor first aid for himself. Luckily he'd tossed in what was needed to treat her sunburn. A habit left over from his expeditions, when there had always been some fool student or rookie researcher who'd spent all day topside and ended up fried to a crisp. The migraine pills he'd brought had come in handy, too. If Luke didn't suffer from occasional tension headaches, Madame X wouldn't be sleeping now.

Luke thumped the coffee mug down on the table. He could see the headline now: BEAUTIFUL NAKED CASTAWAY SAVED FROM CERTAIN DEATH—EXCLUSIVE RESCUE PHOTOS!

It had to be a setup.

Luke tossed out the coffee and headed into the den. The shortwave ICOM HF radio, set into a wall unit beside his desk, crackled to life as he tuned in the frequency he needed. He eyed the laminated KORNOR map over the console. Of all the latitudes and longitudes covering the forty-one million square miles of the Atlantic, Madame X's raft just had to float into his. No, not an accident.

"WID714 to Marathon WAX237, over," he said into the microphone.

Mike Anderson's baritone voice came back over the slight crackle of static. "Good morning, old buddy, over."

Anderson ran a successful food service business for the Keys. He was Luke Fleming's best friend, had been since high school. He was also the only person besides Madam X who knew where Luke was. In their glory days, Mike had blocked any defensive lineman trying to sack quarterback Luke Fleming. Now he did the same thing, just with the rest of the world.

Mike had ferried Luke over to the island, stocked his supplies, and kept in weekly contact with him over the shortwave radio. They'd argued about the boat—Mike had told him he was out of his mind to stay on the island without means to get off. Luke didn't want any visible signs that he was there. Boats were a dead giveaway.

Luke had eventually won the argument, but only after resorting to blackmail. "Quit bitching at me, Anderson, or I'll tell Laurie what *really* happened with you and the Roselli twins after the prom."

The side of his mouth hitched as Luke recalled his threat. "Happen to mention to anyone where I'm spending my vacation, Mike? Over."

"Not me, old buddy. You know better than that. Got a problem, over?"

Luke threaded his fingers through his hair, scrubbing them over his scalp. "Just me and the little lady here." That was specific enough to warn Anderson of the circumstances. "So what's the latest news? Any storms headed my way? Looking out for any missing boaters, over?"

Anderson, who monitored transmissions ranging from simple fisherman's reports to emergency calls, also acted as an unofficial liaison with the local Coast Guard station. He had a line on everything that happened, in and around the Keys.

There was a minute of silence. Luke knew Mike was consulting his clipboard, on which he kept note of official bulletins and other pertinent news to broadcast to the outlying islands.

"A tropical wave coming off the coast of Africa. Could turn into something interesting. I'll keep you posted on that. No local fronts or lost tourists,"

Anderson said, then chuckled. "So how is the little lady, over?"

Luke hesitated for a moment. If he reported rescuing the woman, someone would have to come out to get her. Even if Anderson came to pick her up personally, a report would have to be filed at the hospital. He couldn't ask Mike to lie for him. You didn't fool around with the Coast Guard. Luke knew how they worked—if they even smelled a cover-up, a cutter went out. He would be recognized. One word would lead to another boat coming out, just for curiosity's sake, and then another, and another . . .

If Luke didn't report her, he would be stuck with her. She'd probably keep up the amnesia act. He had no other way to get her off the island.

Mike interrupted his thoughts. "Old buddy, you going to respond, over?"

Luke blew out a frustrated breath. "You remember I.C.B. Emily, over?"

The girl he'd referred to had long ago invited herself along on a weekend fishing trip with the two of them when they were all teenagers. Emily's nickname referred to her formidable profile *and* her appetite for sex—"built like an intercontinental ballistic missile, and about as persistent," Mike had said. She'd been Luke's first "groupie."

"Oh, no." His best friend laughed. "One up, over," Mike added, meaning to change frequencies. Luke checked the list of preselected channels they both had agreed on using.

They both switched to the next channel on the list, going to the next one down, in direct contradiction to Mike's instructions. A code from the old days, when they were just a couple of kids fooling around with UHF radios.

"How did she find you, over?" Mike wanted to know.

"This type always finds a way. Over."

"You got trouble, *mi amigo*, over."

"Tell me about it. Three down, over." They switched frequencies once more.

"What are you going to do, over?"

"Nothing until the first of next month," Luke said. "You know that as well as I do. Two down, over."

They changed channels again.

"If I hear anything, over?" Anderson asked.

Luke knew Mike was concerned about the authorities. He and Mike would both land in boiling water for concealing a missing person.

"Let me know. We'll figure something out." Even as the words left his lips, Luke silently cursed himself. "How's the weather shaping up for the next week, over?"

He listened to Anderson's report but neither bothered to chase around the frequencies, now that their subject was "safe." Luke ended the transmission after hearing Mike's latest joke about thong bikinis and city commissioners. He switched the radio power off, and closed the door of the wall unit, effectively concealing it. He regarded the empty mug in his hand.

"Good move, Fleming. Now you're really stuck with her."

Whoever she was.

She looked to be in her midtwenties. Small, too, barely over five feet. When he had carried her into the house, she'd felt like a child in his arms. But she was no kid. The lingerie, and what was under it, proved her adult status without a doubt.

That luscious little body packed one hell of a punch, too.

Once he'd checked her head wound, which turned out to be thankfully minor, he'd only been interested in getting her cleaned up and treating her sunburn. Until he'd cut off her clothes and un-covered those high, firm breasts.

The instant knot in his gut should have been a warning, but he was too busy with the fantasy that had popped into his head. Putting his mouth to the tight little nipples, one after the other. Running his tongue over them, sucking them. For hours.

He was not going to think about her breasts. Ever again.

She was slender and fine-boned. Her smooth belly was flat, no scars or stretch marks there to indicate she'd had a child. When he'd cut off her panties, the dark brown curls at the top of her thighs had brushed the underside of his forearm. They weren't wiry, but soft as silk. He wished now he'd never found out. His arm still tingled.

Her legs were long for a woman of her size. Luke had been admiring them as he pulled the clothes out from under her. Then she'd convulsed, and her thighs had parted. Luke had looked away a second too late. She was pink and beautiful down there, too.

His shorts had instantly shrunk two sizes, and he'd been forced to turn away to adjust matters. Not that it had helped. By the time he'd turned back and looked at her again, he'd nearly forgotten the reason why he'd cut her clothes off in the first place. And his shorts had felt *three* sizes smaller.

Treating her sunburned body, however, had been like dousing himself with a bucket of ice water. Despite his care, he'd hurt her. Toward the end she'd been shaking under his touch. Luke had finished, shocked to find his own hands shaking badly. As necessary as the treatment had been, he hated causing her more pain. The underlying lust only added self-contempt to the list.

The fact remained, he had intimately stroked or touched virtually every inch of her. She was a beautiful little lady, and he hadn't been with a woman in months. Despite her condition, and his disgust with himself, Luke couldn't stop fantasizing about touching her all over again.

Hell, he wasn't a pervert, he told himself, ignoring the painful kick from his conscience. Who could see a woman put together like that—much less touch her—and not want her?

Her skin was unblemished under the fierce sunburn. Once that and the swelling faded, she'd have a very pretty face. Luke had left off washing her dark hair for the moment, but could see it was thick and long. How would it feel in his hands? Would it gleam, spread across his chest? His thighs?

He abruptly got up from his chair. He didn't want to play with her hair. He wanted to *strangle* her with it.

Anger swelled in his chest. She was damn lucky she wasn't dead. What had she been thinking, heading out on a raft dressed like that? Her sexy little outfit had caused most of the damage. The fact that she had drifted into the cove was a bona fide miracle. Heron Island was the sole inhabited island within a fifty-mile radius.

She had no purse, wallet, or personal effects—nothing but the clothes on her back and a jade ring on her right hand. The ring looked like an antique gold filigree, with a square-cut stone.

As for the raft she'd arrived on, there was nothing else in it except a single oar. No radio or survival gear, not even a compass. The outboard motor's tank was empty. She'd either neglected to fill it, or had used the motor until it ran out of fuel.

Had she done that, searching for him? She'd have been lucky just to find a map that showed the island on it. Maybe she'd done some research on the mainland and uncovered the old records about the island. Made an educated guess he'd hide out here. Staged her ploy to be washed up on his beach.

She hadn't done a very good job of that. If the currents had swept her away from the island, she could have easily died from exposure. From her general condition, Luke guessed she'd only been drifting for a day, two at the most. She was dehydrated, but the cut on her head didn't need stitches. With luck, she'd be fine in a few days.

Then he'd have to decide what to tell her.

Four lousy weeks, and I'm finished. If she's part of a setup, Mike can pick her up and drop her at the nearest police station. Luke's attorney had a barracuda attitude; he'd make sure she got a hefty fine for trespassing.

Normally he would have leveled with her, but her "amnesia" was just a bit too convenient. Did she really think he was that dense? Wherever she came from, she—

"Damn it."

She couldn't have left the mainland on that little raft. She'd either chartered a boat to drop her off, or brought her own. He'd put his money on the first possibility. There were plenty of shady skippers on the mainland who'd do it, given enough cash. Once they hit the open water, they wouldn't care where they dumped her. Maybe the deal had gone bad.

If not a charter, then a partner could still be waiting out there somewhere. If that was the case, whoever had gone along with her stupidity would eventually turn up. Then Luke would have to handle that, too.

He didn't want to believe she was telling the truth. That would make things even worse. A police report would be filed. She was too young and attractive not to be missed. If not by a partner, then by a mother, father, brother . . . husband.

Luke frowned. No wedding ring on her left hand, but that meant nothing. He didn't like the idea of Mister X showing up to find Madam naked in Luke's bed. For some reason, he didn't like the idea of her having a husband, period.

His mood grew more foul as he speculated on how long he could keep her under wraps. He'd stuffed the deflated raft in a storage shed next to the dock. Mike wouldn't say a word, but if her family put out a missing persons bulletin—Luke's hand fisted. The problems her presence created were endless.

There was only one course of action.

He had to take care of her. He had to give her a free month of vacation on a tropical island. If she was everything she appeared to be, no harm done. However, if she was lying . . .

It was decided, then. No choice. She was staying.

She was awake, sitting up and looking around the room when the big man walked through the door. He was carrying a tray with a pitcher of juice and a bowl of cereal. She tried to smile, but her chapped lips made the smile into a smirk. He didn't smirk back.

Maybe he wasn't a morning person.

Was it morning? Through a large window next to the bed she could see either a sunrise or sunset. The open jalousies allowed a corrugated view of the myriad of colors in the sky: azure blue and amethyst cloud, streaked with orange-crimson light.

Sunset. It must be beautiful here. Wherever here *was.*

The sound of the tray distracted her. The man thumped it down on a side table next to the bed. She watched as he poured what looked like watered-down fruit juice into a glass and added a straw. Her hand trembled as she held it out to take it from him.

"Take it easy," he said, cupping his fingers around hers until she was steadier.

She nodded, making a face as she remembered what had happened the last time. For several minutes she simply sipped, paused, and breathed deeply. She was relieved to find her stomach much more cooperative than before.

"How are you feeling?"

She sipped again from the straw before she answered. "Better." Her voice sounded stronger, clearer now, although her throat still felt a little sandy.

The man pulled a straight-back chair up next to her bed and straddled it.

She studied his face. A watchful face, hard, suspicious. His thick, tousled hair seemed lighter now.

Probably because it was dry. His clear eyes had a mesmerizing effect.

Stop gaping at him and say something.

"Who are you?"

Inexplicable dislike made his face look even harder. "Oh, that's cute."

"Excuse me?"

He folded his arms over his chest. "You know who I am."

"No, sorry, I don't." Something about him nagged at her, like an itch she couldn't reach. Maybe it was his personality. Mosquitoes probably took lessons from him.

He looked at her skeptically for several moments, then shook his head. "Okay, you *don't* know me."

Then why was he being such a pain about it? "So what's your name?"

"Luke."

"You're a doctor, right?"

He didn't answer that, his gaze on her arms where they rested outside the sheet. The lotion he'd used had helped, she saw when she glanced down, but they were still very red. Would the sunburn start to blister?

"You'll heal fine," he said, accurately reading her thoughts.

"If you want to make me feel better, tell me you've got a medical degree." He shook his head. "Okay, then how about a nurse?"

"I don't have one of those, either."

How reassuring. "What happened to me?"

"You tell me."

"I wish I could." Her voice cracked on the last word, and she took another sip of the diluted juice. "I can't. I don't remember a thing."

Luke's brows drew together, and he said something she couldn't make out.

"Excuse me?"

"Okay. I'll play along." He pointed to the window. "I found you out there yesterday morning, floating in with the tide. You were unconscious, and the raft you were in got snagged on the coral reef. I had to swim out to bring you in. You're lucky." He sneered, not a good thing on that hard face. "If you'd hit another current, we wouldn't be having this little chat."

Processing all the bizarre information he was tossing at her was like trying to catch twenty fast balls with one glove. The mental overload team was winning, too.

"I was on a raft, you said? Caught on a reef?" He nodded once. She rubbed her temple with her fingertips. "Where am I?"

"East-southeast of Marathon," he said.

Now her brows drew together. "What marathon? Boston's?"

"It's a place, not a race. You know, in the Keys. The Florida Keys."

Florida itself meant nothing to her, except a vague impression of theme parks, beaches, and hotels. As if she'd only visited here. She shook her head.

"Great." Luke thrust a hand through his hair.

Now he looked pissed-off. Why? She wanted the answers even more than he did. "I'm sorry, but none of this sounds familiar. I've never heard of Marathon, and as far as I know, I've never been to the Keys or Florida."

She finished the juice and handed him the empty glass. He dropped it on the tray, hard enough to make her flinch.

She didn't like that. Why was he being so snotty? It wasn't her fault she couldn't remember anything about being in Florida. "Look, I'd tell you if I knew something."

"All right, honey. I've had enough. Game's over. Time to start talking. I want to hear the whole story."

"What game?"

"How did you find me?"

"*Find* you?" She blinked. "If I was unconscious, like you said, how could I have even been *looking* for you?"

He muttered something else. Something fairly vile.

"Why do you keep swearing like that?"

He ignored that. "You don't remember your name. Do you know how old you are?"

She thought for a moment, then shook her head. She had no idea.

"Where were you born?"

Nothing came to her. She was a complete blank.

"What's today's date?"

The same thing happened. Unable to tell him, she lifted one shoulder.

"What's your favorite TV show? Ice cream? Food? Color?"

She rubbed her hands over her face as she groped for a shred of memory, anything that would answer his rapid-fire questions. She found nothing. "I don't know."

"That's not good enough."

"It's going to have to be," she said.

"Damn it, I want some answers."

"What do you want me to do? Make something up?" That only made him more angry, she saw. The hell with him. She didn't know what had him so pissed-off, but it wasn't her problem. It wasn't a crime to forget what kind of ice cream she liked. Anyway, why was *he* getting so upset? How did he think *she* felt?

"You have a bad sunburn, and you're a little dehydrated," Luke said. "The bump on your head isn't that bad. Neither is the cut." He paused. "That's all." When he saw she didn't follow, he clenched his teeth. "Sweetheart, it's over. Forget the amnesia act. If that was the plan, it wasn't a very good one."

Amnesia act? The *plan*? He thought she was faking it. "That's crazy. Of course I didn't plan this."

"Oh yeah?"

Unbelievable. "What makes you think I did?"

His temper finally blew. "You showed up! Out of nowhere! In a *bathrobe*, for Christ's sake!"

"Where?" she yelled back.

Luke got up so fast he knocked the chair over backward. With another curse he jerked it up and slammed it back down.

He was starting to scare her. "Where am I?" She checked the window again. "It's not some kind of secret, right?"

"Fine. That's the way you want to play it, honey. No problem. Just forget about it."

The way he dismissed what had happened to her was infuriating.

"I'm not going to forget about it. I think I've done enough of that, don't you?" He gave her another nasty look. "Look, I'm not *pretending*. I don't *know*."

What he'd told her meant nothing—except that he didn't like what she said. Maybe he had the right to be angry. That didn't mean she was going to lie here and let him yell at her. Not until he came up with some kind of explanation.

"Would you mind telling me why you think I'm pretending to have amnesia?" He didn't say a word. Her fingers tightened, wrinkling the sheets. "For heaven's sake, why would I lie about this?"

"Christ." Luke shoved the chair out of his way and stalked over to the window.

According to him, he'd rescued her. She was injured and suffering from memory loss. He wasn't a doctor, and he obviously didn't want her here, so why hadn't he simply called 911?

Maybe he didn't want to.

"Luke." She kept her voice calm, and looked around for something she could bash over his head. "Where is this place? Am I in some kind of danger here? Did someone try to kill me?" He didn't respond. Might as well go for broke. She could hit him with the tray, if necessary. "Are you involved with whoever did this?"

"God Almighty." He turned around. "Here's the deal: there's no danger. No one's trying to kill you. Especially not me."

But he was tempted, wasn't he? She touched the cut on her head. "How do you explain this? *Someone* did this to me."

"You're on an island. *My* island." He produced another sneer. Not at all an appealing one. "There's no one else here, but you, and me. We're stuck with each other, honey."

"I'm on an island. Great. Just great." This was getting more bizarre by the moment. "And what do you mean—*stuck*?"

"I don't want you here. Believe me, if it was up to me, I'd take you back to the mainland right now."

"Right now sounds excellent. What's the holdup? Let's go."

"We can't go anywhere," Luke said. "I don't have a boat, and we're a good fifty miles from civilization. My next supply drop will be in four weeks."

Chapter Two

Four weeks! Stranded on the proverbial island, just her and Prince Charming.

"I can see you're as thrilled about that as I am," Luke said. "What, they give you a deadline for this plan of yours?"

Only the Prince was about as charming as her sunburn. "You can't be serious. I'm really going to be stuck here for four weeks?"

Luke leaned back against the wall. "Yeah."

"And you're sure there's no other way to leave? We just wait for this supply boat to show up? That's it?"

"Yes."

"How could you expect me to just accept that? This is *insane*."

One of his eyebrows arched. "You being an authority on the subject?"

Outrage replaced her fear. "You think this is *funny*?" She counted off her fingers. "I can't remember my name. I can't remember what happened to me. I can't remember who hurt me. And now, you're telling me I won't be able to get proper medical treatment for a month? What if I need more than a sponge bath and some lotion?"

"I'll deal with it."

"Oh, that's comforting. You think I did this to myself? That I crashed this damned island because I have some kind of crazy plan? That I'm *faking* this? Excuse me if I don't have a whole lot of confidence in how you'll deal with it."

"But I will." Luke gave her an awful smile. "You should be worried, baby. If I find out you're lying, I'll press trespassing charges. And that's just for starters."

"Trespassing charges?" She stared at him. "You're still harping about your precious privacy? And don't call me baby." She felt her dry lips crack. Not good. "Why are you living on an island by yourself, with no way to get off?"

"I like being alone."

Obviously. "What if you had some kind of accident? You couldn't even get help for *yourself*. Wait, don't you have a radio? You've got to have a radio."

He swung back to look out the window, and lifted his hands to press them against the frame above his head.

"Did you hear me? I said—"

"I have a radio. Too bad, but it doesn't work."

She sank back against her pillows. "Wonderful. Can't you fix it?"

The shaggy blond head shook. "No parts."

"I see. No boat. No way to get help. No way to leave. How *convenient*."

"Not for me," he said.

Wasn't there a movie she'd seen, about an injured man at the mercy of a deranged woman? She got the vague image of a hatchet, and winced, at once blocking off the memory. She looked at Luke's white knuckles. Could he be some kind of lunatic?

No, that was a bit extreme. He might be upset, short-tempered, and sarcastic, but he *had* been gentle and taken care of her. In reality, Luke might be nothing more than what he appeared to be: a crabby hermit.

"If you're right, why would I come here? If I knew you, wouldn't I know you wanted to be left alone?"

"Maybe you couldn't resist."

Her jaw dropped. "Good Lord, you think you're so gorgeous and irresistible that I couldn't help myself?"

"You wouldn't be the first."

"Just how many women have washed up on this island?"

He ignored the question and came over to put the tray on her lap. "Eat some of this. Stop if you feel sick." He poured her another glass of juice from the pitcher.

She sighed, then picked up the spoon. The tasteless oatmeal went down only with the help of more juice, but her stomach continued to accept it without protest. Luke returned to his position by the window and kept quiet. He did watch her, though. Incessantly.

She finished as much as she could, then realized she had to go to the bathroom. She moved the tray to one side, eased her legs over the side of the bed, and managed to keep the sheet to her chin. Everything hurt.

"I'm sorry for whatever trouble I've caused you," she said. It would be best not to antagonize him. She could be polite—for now. "And I'm grateful for what you've done."

"Yeah. Sure."

"Do you have a robe I can put on?" At his frown, she added, "I need to use the bathroom."

Luke walked out of the room without a word. He returned a few minutes later carrying a lightweight cotton shirt with long sleeves. One of his, she thought. Something to wear when he got tired of ripping sleeves off T-shirts to flex those manly biceps.

"Use this."

She eyed that thin shirt. "You don't own a bathrobe?"

Luke dropped it in her lap. "Forget about making a fashion statement and put it on."

"Right."

"The bathroom is in there." He inclined his head toward the other side of the room.

"Thank you." She held on to the shirt with her one free hand and gave a hint by looking at the door.

He finally got it and turned his back on her again. His voice took on a distinct edge as he said, "Hurry up."

Would it have killed him to leave her alone for a minute? Well, she couldn't wait any longer, or she'd have an accident. As she got up and tugged on the shirt, her knees got shaky. She grabbed for a handhold.

At once Luke was there, holding her up, taking care not to squeeze her.

"Easy," he said. "I've got you."

She held on. Yelling at her one minute, treating her like spun glass the next. The man was as unpredictable as her knees.

There was an awful lot of him, she thought as she looked up. She'd seen the differences in their sizes, but right next to him, she felt like a midget. The contrast didn't scare her. On the contrary. She felt secure for the first time since she'd opened her eyes to this place.

Whoever wanted to hurt her would have to get through Luke first, and that wouldn't be easy.

Luke kept an arm around her and helped her to the bathroom. There he waited with his back to the open door as she took care of her immediate problem. When she washed her hands, she saw her reflection in the mirrored wall cabinet for the first time.

"Jesus. I'm a tomato."

Her face was as bright red as the rest of her. The raw gash by her hair was scabbing over, but still looked ugly. She held on to the edge of the porcelain sink, shocked not by her sunburn, but by her face.

She didn't recognize *her own face*. The woman staring back at her could have been someone else, a stranger looking through a window at her. How was this possible? How could she have forgotten *her own face*?

"Finished?"

"Yes."

She was now seriously scared. The bad dream was now appallingly real. She was a stranger to herself. How could she not have known what she'd look like? What had happened to her, to cause this? It had to be more than a bump on the head—her entire identity was gone. All of it.

Thinking about how that could have been done made the suffocating nausea return full-force. Staggering a little, she reached out for support. Luke's arms quickly came around her.

"Do you need to throw up?" She shook her head and simply held on as he picked her up. "Time to get back in bed."

"Wait." She wasn't so sure now, and put a shaky hand on his shoulder to stop him. "Wait a minute." Carefully she took slow, deep breaths.

To take her mind off the nausea, she focused on him. He hadn't shaved in a day or so, judging by the dark stubble. She could smell the faint odor of sweat, felt his body heat. His hair was so long that it brushed against her fingers.

He waited. "Okay now?"

No, she wasn't. Not this close to him. "Yes."

Luke carried her over to the bed and carefully lowered her onto the sheets. "You want another pain pill?"

"No. I'm so tired now I can sleep no matter what hurts."

"Okay. Get some rest." He removed the tray and bent to pull the sheet back over her. "I'll check on you later." Before he straightened, he smoothed a tangle of hair from her cheek.

Maybe he wasn't a complete jerk, she thought as her eyes closed. Soon she was fast asleep. In the darkness she felt the tug of a dream, and slowly moved into it.

Wherever she was, it was bright and beautiful. Hot sunlight streamed over her. Clean, crisp air filled her nose. An undulating landscape of glittering turquoise spread out before her eyes.

Water?

A vibrant concoction of sound, rhythmic humming, laughter, and splashing waves rushed against her ears. Swift, streamlined gray forms leapt in the air around her. For some reason this made her laugh.

She went still as the light abruptly disappeared.

Shadows pressed all around her. Someone called her, and the urgent voice compelled her forward. A blurred face appeared, then an outstretched hand. She had to help him. Now she ran, faster and faster, desperate to get to him. Just before she reached the hand, something hit her.

The terrible blow struck her without warning. Deeper, endless darkness. She was being lifted, then, suddenly, she was falling. Saltwater splashed her face. Instinctively she curled into a ball. Pain and fear tore at her with hard, jagged teeth.

"Go! Hurry!"

"Tell me, Goddamn it!"

"I don't have it!" another voice said, but it wasn't hers. *"Please, you've got to believe me—no!"*

There was someone else there. Someone as terrified as she was. She couldn't see anymore. Then she saw the knife.

"I'll cut you to pieces!" a voice said with vicious pleasure.

The other, desperate voice followed her, too. *"Help me!"*

Something hit the water. She couldn't make a sound. So much blood—

She woke to the sound of her own screaming.

"No!" She sat straight up, oblivious of the eruption of pain the sudden movement caused. They would kill her. Her hands clawed at the sheet where it tangled around her legs. They were coming for her. She struggled to get off the bed and fell forward. They would find her. She slammed into the hardwood floor with a heavy thud. *Run.* Agony exploded all over her.

She gagged on her own tears, terrified by the looping images that kept replaying in her head.

The man with the knife—was it Luke? Had *he* done this to her? Lied to her? Beaten her? Tried to kill her?

She wasn't going to wait to find out. She grabbed the side of the bed and pulled herself to her feet. Her heart was pounding so hard and fast she could almost hear it.

Have to get out of here, now—

He caught her just outside the room, and she screamed again.

"What the hell—"

"No!" She hit him as hard as she could. "Let go!"

"Hey." He forced her arms down as he locked his around her. "Calm down."

Caught in the nightmare, she fought him, frantic to break his grip. "Let me go!"

"You're not going anywhere." He held on. "Knock it off!"

"It was you! You did this—didn't you? You had the knife! You hit me!" Every movement she made scraped the sunburn until she knew her skin was being flayed from her. It didn't stop her. Nothing would stop her. She got a hand free and struck him hard in the face.

"I didn't do it. I *found* you. That's all." Luke dodged another blow, then gave her a single rough shake. "Settle down."

The raw sunburn and weakness soon made her sag against him. She cried, clutching his shirt as she sobbed. Slowly she calmed down.

He wasn't hurting her.

Luke was strong. He could inflict considerable pain—probably wanted to—but instead he was holding her very carefully. Tears slid down her hot face and made round, wet spots on his T-shirt.

He could have hurt her before, many times. He hadn't. He wasn't hurting her now. No, he wasn't the one.

"Okay now?" Luke asked, and she nodded. He let her sag against his chest. The steady, heavy beat of his heart under her ear felt good. The secure feeling came back.

It couldn't be him. If he'd done this to me, no way would I feel this safe.

"Hey," he said, and she lifted her face. "What brought this on?"

"I just discovered I have a canopy phobia. Sorry."

"Try again."

"I just realized that you didn't do this to me. I know that now. I can feel it."

"Okay. What else?"

"I'm not sure. I was dreaming. There was a man with a knife. And blood. I was trying to get to someone, then the man hit me."

"That's all you remember?"

He didn't sound like he believed her. "It meant something." Pain filled her ears with a noise like swarming bees.

"Like what?"

"I wish I knew." Her vision grew blurry. "I feel strange."

Luke said something, but she couldn't make it out. Her panic and the pain were too much. She dropped gratefully into darkness.

A thousand miles away from Paradise Island, two men faced each other over a long, polished table in an executive conference room on the top floor of the Shandian Corporate Building.

One of them, a silver-haired Chinese man, radiated the physical vitality of someone half his age. His tailored suit, Rolex watch, and manicured hands discreetly proclaimed his affluence. The black eyes beneath his white brows were flat and deceptively mild.

In contrast, the younger man, an American, appeared far less polished. His own expensive suit seemed at odds with the graceless frame it covered. Thick fingers above scarred knuckles silently drummed on the table's surface. His meticulously groomed hair couldn't quite make up for his rather ordinary features. His small, pale eyes were steady.

"Thank you for seeing me, Mr. Chang."

"Your message indicated it was an urgent matter," Chang Yu-wei said. "I trust Mr. Carter delivered everything as promised."

"No, sir. Carter is dead." The American shifted in his chair, avoiding Yu-wei's incredulous gaze. "We've searched his boat and condominium, but found nothing."

"You were sent to pay him off. How is it that he is dead?"

The younger man briefly explained the circumstances, then added, "We may still be able to salvage the situation."

"Indeed." The Chinese man regarded him without expression. "How do you propose to accomplish that?"

The younger man's discomfort grew visible. "There is evidence that Carter met with someone before we got to him."

Yu-wei's silver eyebrows rose. "Evidence?"

"We found this." The American produced a folded paper from his pocket, which he spread out on the table between them. "Too much for one man on a three-day fishing trip."

Yu-wei took the document and studied it in silence.

"We worked on Carter for hours, but he wouldn't talk. He must have had a partner on the side. Probably dropped him off on one of the islands before we intercepted the boat." The younger man sat back and smoothed a hand over his hair. "The partner knows what's involved. He'll contact us. Then we'll deal with him."

The Chinese man refolded the paper and handed it back. "You will go back and find this partner." Yu-wei's black eyes glittered. "At once."

"Sir, if we sit back and wait, I'm positive that—"

Two smooth hands reached across the table and

grabbed hold of the American's lapels. A brutal jerk brought the younger man's upper body across the table. Only inches separated them now. "I cannot sit back and wait. You will return to Florida, find Carter's accomplice, and bring him to me."

The younger man began to bluster. "Mr. Chang—"

"If you fail me again, I will have your head removed from your body. Slowly."

The American looked into that unequivocal gaze and managed a nod. "I'll see to it personally."

"Keep me advised of your progress." The manicured hands released him. "Now get out."

Yu-wei waited until he was alone before he began to swear in his native language, crudely and at length. He had a deadline to meet, and this unforeseen complication threatened his success. Failure was unacceptable. He had never been thwarted, not since he had clawed his way out of the slums of Taiwan.

A light tap at the door to the conference room cut short his tirade. "What is it?"

The silent figure of his assistant appeared. "General Sung wishes to speak with you, Mr. Chang."

A former party official and now Director of Biotechnical Research, General Sung had personally formulated Yu-wei's rise to power within the Shandian hierarchy. Now close to retirement, the old man depended more and more on Yu-wei to assure the comfort of his remaining years.

Normally Yu-wei would have sent one of the legion of men working for him to oversee the situation in Florida. Unfortunately the particular circumstances involved indicated his direct supervision would be required.

"Tell the general I have left for the airport." Yuwei rose from the table and adjusted the line of his tie. Given the amount of money at stake, he would have to oversee this situation personally. "Assure him that you will relay his message to me as soon as I arrive in Miami."

Luke checked in with Mike over the shortwave to make sure there were no new missing boater reports. There weren't. Anderson updated him on the unusually large tropical depression heading west from the African coast. According to Mike, it was gaining strength and moving rapidly across the Atlantic.

"NOAA is deploying one of their P-3's later today to take a look at it," Anderson said. "Last time they sent one out this early, we got Hurricane Andrew in our face a week later."

Luke wasn't worried about the storm. No hurricane would ever demolish the house on Paradise Island. Jacob Fleming had seen to that.

His grandfather had been a native of the Carolinas. A shrimper and adventurer, Old Jake had sailed up and down the Atlantic Coast at the turn of the century. Eventually he'd reached the southernmost point in the U.S., and fallen in love with the Florida Keys.

Jacob had won Paradise Island, literally, in a poker game with the previous owner, a land speculator named O'Riley. It could have ended in disaster—it was one thing for a rootless drifter to win a game of chance, quite another to take a man's property. Luke's grandfather had insured his winnings, and general longevity, by courting O'Riley's daughter, Tamara. They had married, and Jacob had built their home on the island with his own hands.

He'd done a good job. From the outside, the house appeared more bunker than residence. The flat roof had a less than artistic appeal which nevertheless had survived countless storms. Three-foot-thick structural walls had enabled interior rooms to stay cool long before modern air conditioning had been installed. Solid cedar flooring defeated countless generations of hungry native insects.

It would take a bomb, not a hurricane, to destroy the house, Luke thought after he signed off with Mike. Out of habit he marked the last reported coordinates of the tropical depression on his KORNOR map. Even if a storm hit, they'd be safe.

They. Luke's hand dropped from the map. Where had that come from? She didn't belong here, and she wasn't staying once the month was over. There was no *they* about it.

Luke had set up his temporary office in the den. It was in a state of organized chaos. His reference materials crowded the many bookcases; geological sample containers littered the floor. Rolls of survey maps were stacked in the seat of a comfortable armchair. More maps, these much older and crumbling at the edges, were piled against one wall like so many wallpaper samples.

He crossed over and sat down at his desk. Behind him, a row of sophisticated computer equipment crowded an antique credenza. He frowned at an area on the chart he was working on, then swiveled in his chair to tap out a query on the keyboard.

A moment later, the monitor began scrolling a list of figures in response. Luke turned back to mark the locations on a second map, then compared the two.

The site locations were *identical*.

"Good," he said. "That takes care of the *Mao*, the *Haixing*, and the *Sha Chengbao*." He drew a line through the names on his clipboard. He was close. Very close. He restrained the urge to shout, knowing it would wake her up. She needed to sleep, especially after that bad dream she'd had.

His smile faded as he recalled the wildness in her eyes. Someone or something in that dream had terrified her. She'd fought him like a wild thing, too, even though she hadn't a prayer of getting away. He'd eventually gotten through to her, and she'd calmed down. She'd even tried to joke about it.

She was scared, but she wasn't a wimp. The things she'd mentioned—something about a man with a knife, and blood. Was that how she'd gotten the head wound? The thought of a man using a knife on her made him sick. He'd have to find out more when she woke up.

Luke glanced at the clock on his desk, and cursed. He'd wasted the better part of an hour brooding over her. It had to stop. He didn't have time to worry about her, or fall for her story. He had to take care of business, and forget about the woman.

He picked up his clipboard, and turned back to the computer. The project was more important than Madam X—than either of them. And if she kept Luke from finishing in time, it wouldn't matter what he did with her, or with the data he'd collected.

The Gates of *Shuiba* would slam shut forever.

She'd slept through most of the second day and night. Luke kept her fed and dosed her twice more with pain medication. She was too drowsy to object. At least the pills kept the pain and the nightmares at bay.

Her thirst was endless. When she woke, she automatically reached for the carafe of water he'd left for her on the side table. Each time she opened her eyes, she saw it had been refilled, even during the night. He was keeping a close eye on her, an odd but comforting thought.

She was safe here.

The third morning came with the low cries of seagulls from outside. She woke up and began to stretch, before she remembered the condition of her skin and halted in midmotion. Carefully she propped herself up into a sitting position. Her arms and legs were stiff. They ached, but the sunburn was rapidly healing.

Because she had nothing else to do, she examined the contents of the room. Across from her bed an armoire of old mahogany glowed against one white wall. Beside it squatted a large cedar chest, ornately carved and decorated. A neatly folded nine-patch quilt sat on top of it.

To one side of the bed, a porcelain pitcher and basin rested on a wrought-iron stand. Beside that was a bookcase stacked with leather-bound volumes. From the spines she could make out several names: Dickens, Twain, and Shakespeare.

"If Luke reads Shakespeare, I'm the Tooth Fairy," she said. "God, for all I know, I am the Tooth Fairy."

The most fascinating object in the room was the portrait of a smiling woman near the door. She wore an old-fashioned pale green gown. In her arms was a huge bouquet of large white flowers.

Gardenias. They smelled glorious. She knew because she had seen a whole hedge of them once. She remembered heat, the lazy drone of insects, and the heady, sensual fragrance. She'd been in a hurry, and brushed past them to . . .

"Oh!"

She cried out as the memory slipped away from her. Her head began to ache. She squeezed her eyes shut against the tears.

"Come on, get yourself together, you dimwit." She rubbed her eyes. "What if Luke comes in and here you are crying again? He may throw you and that raft back into the sea."

She got up slowly, and her legs felt steadier. Carefully she slipped his shirt on as she walked over to the window. Shading her eyes with one hand against the sun, she looked out.

Immaculate white sand, dozens of swaying palm trees, gorgeous flowers growing wild. Even the ocean and sky looked postcard-perfect. Luke had good taste in islands. This place was paradise.

The bedroom faced the west side of the island, where Luke had said he'd found her. The beach was a narrow horseshoe of amber sand against the blue water.

A few pelicans perched on the rails of an empty pier stretching out into the sea. She saw no sign of the raft Luke had said he'd found her on. This underscored the fact that unless someone showed up unexpectedly, she was stuck here for another month. She doubted anyone who knew Luke would pay a surprise visit.

A vision of him standing on the beach wielding a shotgun made her smile. The official Grouchy Hermit welcome for any poor slob who might stop by his island. Knowing Luke, she figured he'd fire off a warning shot and threaten to press charges.

That weird sense of déjà vu returned. Luke, standing next to the ocean. It seemed almost, but not quite, familiar. Did she really know him, in that past she couldn't remember? How? Who was he?

She spotted some bright blue crabs sunning beneath the tangled upper roots of mangroves. She laughed as they scuttled away from the lapping waves.

"So that's where Luke gets his pleasant disposition. He's been alone with you guys too long."

"I don't have to feed them."

She turned her head. "Ever hear of knocking?"

"It's my house," he said, and set the tray down beside the bed. "Anything coming back to you yet?"

"Just that I like steamed crabs." She edged past him. "Want to go catch some for me?" She sat down on the bed, and groaned. "A couple of muscle relaxers on the side would be nice, too."

"Here." Without ceremony, he carefully rolled her over on her stomach.

She lifted her head and looked back at him. "What are you doing? I can't eat breakfast like this."

"This will help." He began gently massaging her back. Relief made her press her face in her pillow and groan.

"Better?" he asked after a few minutes.

"Wonderful. I was starting to feel like a stale pretzel. Thank you."

He abruptly straightened and brought the tray to her. "Any time."

He'd brought her a mug of tea, a pleasant herbal

blend of cinnamon and rose hips. He'd made her breakfast as well; poached eggs, bacon, and toast. Her stomach growled.

"This looks great." She grinned at him. "Thanks."

No smile in return. "How do you feel?"

"Like this toast. Only more well-done."

That finally got a laugh out of him. "When you're finished eating, put this on your sunburn." Luke placed a small round jar on the tray. "Unless you need me to do it again?"

"No, thanks. I remember how to butter toast, so I think I can handle it. Anything else I should do?"

"Wash first."

That reminded her. "Could I take a bath? I feel sticky and my sunburn is starting to itch like crazy."

"A shower."

"I'd prefer a bath."

"Your skin is still raw."

"All right."

"Leave the door open."

Over her dead body. "It's not necessary. I'll be fine."

"Don't argue with me." His hand caught her chin and forced her to look up at him. "Stow the modesty. I don't want to kick in the door if you pass out."

"I guess there is that. Okay."

He released her. "When you're done, get back in bed. I've got work to do." With that, he left.

God, he was an arrogant piece of work, ordering her around the way he did. This whole mess, including something that vaguely felt like some sort of weird attraction, was getting on her nerves.

"I guess he's tired of telling the crabs what to do."

Eat now, she decided. *Figure out Big Bad Luke later.*

Her breakfast was a lot better than the tasteless oatmeal he'd been feeding her for the last two days. She was getting stronger, she could feel it. If only it would come with some clue about her identity.

She would give anything just to know what her name was.

Setting the tray aside, she took up the jar of skin cream and went into the bathroom. Luke had provided her with everything she needed, right down to a new toothbrush and small tube of paste. Unusually considerate for a man who regarded her as welcome as a bad case of heat rash.

When she got in the shower, she found out he was right. Her skin was raw, and the water and soap stung. She put up with it long enough to wash and shampoo her hair. Feeling clean again was more important than the pain.

Drying herself with the towel was another adventure in minor torture. She made a face as she quickly applied the cream. Some ingredient in the stuff took away the pain almost at once, and she pulled the shirt back on, feeling shaky but relieved.

At least I don't smell like three-day-old fish anymore.

If only she had something else to wear. He'd cut

off whatever she'd been wearing. He'd have to give her more of his clothes, once her sunburn was healed. And he'd probably gripe about that, too.

What about my face?

Abrupt dizziness made her grab the edge of the sink. *Don't pass out.* She made herself look in the mirror.

The swelling had gone down, and the sunburn was turning to a tan now. That didn't help. Nothing looked familiar, not the prominent cheekbones, dark blue eyes, or long, straight-as-a-stick hair.

Who are you?

A tiny mole was between her chin and ear on one side of her face. Her chapped mouth wasn't bad—not too wide, not too small. She had an unusual birthmark on one shoulder, the same size and shape as an almond.

She didn't dislike the face that stared back at her. It wasn't ugly. The face wasn't bad at all. It looked okay, even a little mysterious. She only wished she knew who lived behind it. She looked down.

Nope. Nothing familiar down below, either.

Her body was small and slender. Her breasts looked a little too voluptuous, compared to her long legs and narrow hips. The small, unburned triangles of skin over her breasts and lower abdomen were smooth and very fair.

I must not get out much, she decided, gauging the difference between the white and red areas. She put on his shirt. She was getting shaky again;

she'd have to sit down to get her hair untangled. She turned to see Luke beside the cedar chest, watching her. He had a nice, clear view of her through the open bathroom door.

She wouldn't let him embarrass her. "Not much to look at, am I?"

"Not bad, for toast."

"I thought you said you had work to do."

"Couldn't concentrate." Luke leaned back and folded his arms behind his head. "I kept thinking you'd fall and crack your skull open."

"Thanks."

"No problem." White teeth flashed. "I enjoyed the show."

Would he enjoy a few gaps in that annoying smirk of his, too?

Luke didn't leave, so she walked past him and sat on the bed. She'd stay cool and ignore him. Not do something to make him yelp.

With one hand she positioned the mirror on her lap, and tugged the comb through the ends of her hair. The teeth immediately caught on tangles.

"Ouch."

"Give it to me," he said, right behind her neck.

Give *what* to him? "I beg your pardon?"

He took the comb from her. "I'll do it." Luke sat down on the bed and pushed her around until her back was to him. His fingers pulled her hair over her shoulder, and went to work.

"I don't trust you when you're being nice. I don't think you *are* particularly nice."

"I can be nice."

"When? I want to watch."

"Just shut up."

One of his hands curled around her neck as he lifted another section of hair.

That feels good. More than good.

"Am I hurting you?"

"I'm fine." She'd shave her head before admitting how she felt.

This is a good opportunity. Talk to him. Find out what he's thinking. Find out who the hell he is, what he's doing here, and why he thinks I'm lying.

"Why do you live here by yourself?" Moments stretched into a minute. She was almost happy to hear the sneer in his voice.

"I don't live here. I'm on vacation."

As he lifted her hair, she took a deep breath. The way he was threading his fingers through it wasn't just untangling the knots. It was making all kinds of new ones. She liked it and wished he'd stop. "What do you do for a living?"

He paused in midstroke. "Survey work."

"That sounds interesting. Surveying what? Do you work for a construction company?"

"No." Luke smoothed back some hair from her cheek. On the way, one of his fingers brushed against her ear.

"Then what do you survey?"

"Oceanic topography."

Oh, didn't that just explain everything? "What do you do, measure waves or something?"

No answer.

Even Luke had to have a mother. "Does your family come here on vacation?"

"Sometimes."

"Must be nice, having your own private island."

"Not lately."

She rolled her eyes. *Here we go again.* "Anytime you want me to leave, just flag down a boat."

"Here." The mattress plumped up as he immediately stood and handed her the comb. "It's done."

She saw something lurking behind his blank expression. Something confined. Restless. Uncivilized. *He feels it, too. And wishes he didn't.* Recognizing that made her slide off the bed, then her knees suddenly buckled.

Luke caught her. Automatically she grabbed on and used him as support. He held her around the waist.

"Thanks." She looked up at him. Careful as his hold was, for a split second she thought he was going to throw her across the room. "Don't."

"What do you think I'm going to do?"

"Nothing, I hope."

"Christ, you're paranoid," he said, but there was no criticism in the words. In fact, he sounded almost, what? *Affectionate?*

He was staring at her mouth now. *Let go of him.* She couldn't tear herself away. *Back away.* Couldn't stop herself from leaning closer. *What are you doing?*

Couldn't keep her hands from spreading over his chest.

What was she doing? She took a step back. "Sorry."

"Take a nap. Maybe you'll wake up in a better mood."

"Okay." Like she was the moody one around here. "Thanks for combing out my hair."

"Anytime." The hands at her waist tightened. A muscle twitched along his jawline.

He wasn't turning her loose. "Um, in order for me to actually *take* a nap, you'll need to let go of me."

"What are you so worried about?" He cradled her face with one hand, and studied her. His thumb brushed slowly across her bottom lip, back and forth over the tiny dents left by her teeth.

"Lots of things." Like what he was doing to her, right now. "Under the circumstances, I think I'm entitled."

"Yeah." He wasn't listening to her. He was involved with what he was doing. His eyes were darker. His hand slid into her hair.

She was in trouble. "Maybe I should rest . . . now."

He didn't. His calloused fingers followed her hair down to her shoulder. She took a quick breath, and saw the smile lines around his mouth get deeper. He knew what he was doing to her. Liked it. Wanted to do more.

How much more?

"Luke." Her voice hovered just above a whisper. "I think—I want—"

"This what you want?"

His arm closed around her, dragging her into him until their bodies collided. The full-length contact made her senses explode into full awareness. Muscles hardened under her fingers. Her palms glided up the broad expanse of chest to rest on his shoulders.

He wanted her.

She held on and closed her eyes for a moment, dizzy with new knowledge.

"I like how your hair feels," he said, his breath warm on her face. one hand tilted her chin up. "So long, soft."

He was going to *kiss* her.

Suddenly she felt very small in his arms. Flimsy. Powerless. He lowered his mouth to hover a mere inch above her lips. Her breath caught as she felt the radiant heat from his skin touch hers. She wanted to kiss him. Wanted to hear him whisper her name.

But he doesn't know your name. Neither do you.

She had to put a stop to this.

She turned her head to one side and arched away. "I'm flattered, but I'd really like to take that nap now."

Luke lifted his head and stepped back. She sank down on the bed, wishing she hadn't stopped him, relieved that she'd had the brains to call a halt. Then she saw how furious he was.

"You're good," Luke said. "I like the innocent-but-horny act. If that's part of the plan, it's priceless."

He stomped out of the room.

Chapter Three

Michael Lawrence Anderson woke up, stared at the ceiling, and said, "I'm still alive. *Gracias, Amigo.*"

He'd made the same grateful miniprayer every morning since he'd been shipped back from the Persian Gulf. During the war, his platoon had been cut to pieces on a featureless Kuwaiti desert. Mike had gone down, positive he was going to die.

Miraculously, he'd woken up in a medical unit instead, his battered body being prepped for surgery. The doctors cut half a pound of shrapnel out of him, but were unable to remove one fragment lodged in his spine. That single chunk of twisted metal made all the difference.

Michael Lawrence Anderson would never walk again.

After they told him, Mike had quietly performed a personal examination. All his limbs were still attached in their proper places. He could move some of them. Everything else still worked. He could go home. So he did.

That morning Mike hoisted himself up by the

handgrips hanging over his bed, and spent the next half hour doing his usual workout. When he was through, he swung himself from the bed into his chair. He didn't even think about using it anymore. Over time his wheelchair had become merely an extension of his body.

The back of the warehouse had been modified for him, complete with railings, handgrips, and other specialized equipment that allowed a handicapped man to take care of his needs without assistance.

Mike didn't have much use for the term "handicapped." He was a large man, with arms heavily muscled from a decade of supporting the full weight of his frame. He could bench-press three hundred pounds, lift a full-grown woman with one arm, and haul himself up a cliff, if need be. He proved the first on a weekly basis at his gym, the second on numerous occasions at his favorite bar, and planned a trip to the Appalachias in the fall, to try the third.

"Hey in there," a strident voice called outside his door, followed by a series of sharp raps on the window. "Rise and shine."

"Laurie?" Mike propelled himself over to the door, opened it, and silently groaned. "What are you doing here?"

"Moving in." The tall redheaded girl sauntered through the door. She wore a wrinkled baby doll smock and retro bell-bottom jeans. In each hand she carried an expensive suitcase. "Mom kicked me out."

"Do you need an attorney this time?" Mike shut the door and reversed his chair in time to see her toss her luggage in his spare bedroom.

"Not yet."

Mike chuckled in spite of himself. "Will I need one?" As she reemerged, he eyed the brown bag she carried into the kitchen. "What's in there?"

"Muesli and low-fat milk." She opened a cabinet and took out two bowls. "I'm eating only natural foods now."

Last month she had boycotted red meat. Next month she'd probably become a vegetarian. Laurie's diet was as steady as her place of residence.

"Hey!" Mike yelled as she tossed his box of danish in the trash. "That's mine!"

She threw him a smile over her shoulder. "I can hear the plaque building up in your arteries from here."

He silently counted to ten. "How much is it going to cost me to get rid of you this time?"

"Millions." She gave him a speculative look. The shadows under her light blue eyes made Mike's aggravation evaporate at once. "Or the keys to the boat this weekend."

"I'll call the bank."

They ate her muesli for breakfast (which Mike had to admit was okay, even if it did look like hamster food). Laurie dodged Mike's questions about school and her mother, and left half a bowl of cereal uneaten. He studied the untidy auburn mane, and the wilted condition of her fashionable clothes.

All the signs were there—she'd screwed up again.

"How long were you at your mother's house?"

"About a half hour. Probably a world's record."

Laurie swerved away from the subject and began pestering him about taking out the Grady-White skiff. Mike wasn't about to hand over the keys to his brand-new boat without putting up at least a token resistance.

"Give me a break, Laurie, will you? I'm already putting my insurance guy's kids through Harvard. All four of them."

She scoffed over that as she cleaned up the dishes. "I won't wreck this one, I promise. Besides, Jeff will be piloting it. I just want to go skiing."

"Jeff, huh?" Of all her friends, Jeff Carr was probably the only one Mike trusted to keep his boat intact. "Okay, you guys can borrow it. But I expect a full eight hours from you in the office."

"No problem." Laurie grinned. She often helped out with the business when she stayed with him. "I'll take a shower, then call Jeff—"

"*Before* you get the boat."

She made a face, then sighed and sat back down at the table. "Slavedriver."

"What happened with your mom?"

"The usual." One slim shoulder lifted as she played with the small gold cross she wore around her neck. Her long, rangy body was coiled with tension. "She thinks I'll be living under a bridge unless I get a degree. I got tired of listening to her harp on it. So here I am."

"I thought you liked the new college. Don't you want to go back and . . ." Mike trailed off at her visible wince. "You got expelled? *Again?*"

Laurie instantly went on the defensive. "It isn't my fault the head of the science department has absolutely no sense of humor. Or that certain chemicals, when combined slightly out of sequence, become volatile."

"Laurie—"

"Don't worry about it. So how's your love life, handsome?" She waggled her eyebrows at him, obviously hoping to distract him.

"I don't have one," he said, frowning.

Mike's handicap had never bothered Laurie. "Why not?"

She must have gone from the airport, to her mother's, then come straight here. God, hadn't Meredith even let her daughter in the house? "I have *you.*"

It hadn't always been that way. Mike enjoyed women, had even married one. That had lasted ten years, ending on a roller-coaster ride after Desert Storm.

His ex-wife, oddly enough, had been a physical therapist. When he'd returned from the Gulf, she'd tried to help him. The strain his condition had put on his marriage, however, had only gotten worse. The experimental treatments. Endless arguments.

He'd been treated more like a patient than a husband.

When at last his wife had been forced to accept the fact that Mike was a paraplegic for life, she'd asked him for a divorce. She'd been waiting for him to get better before telling him she'd fallen in love with another therapist.

It hadn't been easy after that, but Laurie had kept him too busy to have time to be bitter. The carrot-topped little girl he'd taught to sail and swim had grown up fast. Too fast for Mike, who was still trying to recover from Laurie's high school escapades.

He sighed, then pulled his clipboard from the table. "Here." He handed it to her. "Let's go over the orders, and you can tell me about how much property damage you caused later."

A relieved Laurie reviewed the manifests one by one. Toward the end of the stack, she paused. "This order came in for . . . Paradise Island . . ." She flipped a few pages and looked perplexed. "No other designation than that. When do we ship—and to who?"

No one knew about Luke Fleming's private estate, not even Laurie. "That's for a friend of mine," Mike said. "Schedule to ship next week. I'll take it myself."

"You've never mentioned this friend or Paradise Island before."

Mike tried to look innocent. "Never came up."

"What's the friend's name?"

"You don't know him." He gulped down the rest of his coffee. The watery decaf was another of Laurie's continual attempts to poison him with her health food. She didn't know about the canister of regular grounds he had hidden in one of the lower cabinets. He hoped.

"You aren't getting involved with those Political Asylum people again, are you?" Laurie asked. Mike seized on the opportunity and pretended dismay. "Ah-ha! Gotcha!"

"Okay, Nancy Drew. I promised a friend I'd keep his location under wraps until the INS approves his visa. That's all."

To Mike's relief, Laurie let the matter drop and continued on to the next order.

When they had finished, Laurie obligingly left the dishwashing for Mike. Mainly because the sink and other kitchen appliances had been scaled down for use by someone in a wheelchair, or no more than four feet tall.

Before going in to take a shower, she paused by the bathroom door. "Are you sure you're telling me everything about this friend of yours?"

"Sure I am. The same way you are about your mother."

Laurie let the door slam shut behind her. A moment later, the shower went on.

"Luke, old buddy," Mike said, rolling his eyes, "you're so lucky to have a devious pal like me."

Laurie practically worshipped Luke. If she found

out he was on Paradise Island, Cuban gun boats wouldn't keep her away.

Mike took a minute to phone Laurie's mother, but was forced to leave a message on her machine. Then he went over to the office. A wide hallway led directly from Mike's apartment to his business, which allowed his chair to travel between the two with ease. Ramps, enlarged doorways, and a specially designed lift to the second floor warehouse level enabled him to go virtually anywhere on the premises as well.

His manager had left him a pile of messages from the answering service on his uncluttered desk. When Mike wheeled himself into his office, he took a few minutes to thumb through them. An unfamiliar name caught his attention. No phone number was listed.

"Laurie?" he called out when he heard her walk in. "You know someone named Morris?"

"Never heard of him," she said as she came to his door.

"No number. Service said he's coming by this morning." He put the message aside. "Couldn't wait for a call back, I guess."

Mike devoted the next hour to returning calls and taking orders, and forgot about the odd message. At precisely nine o'clock, Laurie ushered a man to Mike's office, then hurried off to answer the busy phones.

"Hi, can I help you?" Mike asked.

The man produced a slim wallet, and showed

his ID. "Special Agent Paul Morris, Federal Bureau of Investigation, Mr. Anderson." The man looked at the radio array behind Mike's desk. "I need some information."

Mike had already noted the bulge of a gun beneath Morris's jacket. The expensive suit was slightly flashy for a fed, he decided. But he'd withhold judgment until he heard what the man had to say.

He offered a hand across the desk, which Morris took after a momentary hesitation. Like most people, the other man was disconcerted to realize Mike was in a wheelchair.

"Have a seat, Agent Morris." Mike indicated the comfortable chair across from his desk.

Morris sat down and looked through the window at Laurie, who was busy taking an order over the telephone. "You've got a fine-looking secretary, Mr. Anderson."

"Yes, my daughter gets a lot of compliments."

The man's eyes narrowed. "She's your *daughter*?"

Mike turned around a desk photo of himself, standing beside his ex-wife Meredith, holding a much younger Laurie in his arms. "I wasn't *always* in this chair, Agent Morris." He enjoyed watching the man wince. "What can I do for you?"

"We recently apprehended a man in Key West who is directly involved in an international espionage case. There is evidence he made a connection with someone down here just prior to his arrest. My job is to find out if he did, and who it was."

"The Coast Guard should be in on this," Mike said. "The DEA, and the Monroe County Sheriff's Office, too."

"I'm afraid I can't sanction that, Mr. Anderson," the agent replied. "The case involves a matter of national security."

"Is that right?" If that was all there was to it, Mike would eat his wheelchair. "Why do you think I can help you?"

"The man in custody bought supplies from your company a week ago. According to the signature on this"—Morris handed him an invoice—"you personally delivered the order to his boat."

Mike quickly scanned the order. "Yeah, I did. I remember him. He seemed like a nice guy."

"They usually do." The agent's observation was dry. "Did you see anyone with him?"

Mike remembered the radio call from his friend, the joke about I.C.B. Emily, then made a quick, gut-instinct decision. "Not that I recall."

Morris looked genuinely irritated. "Are you sure about that? You didn't see anyone else on board?"

"No, just him." Mike pointed back toward the radio. "I can put the word out, if you like. See if anyone else knows something."

"No, this information has to remain confidential, Mr. Anderson. The man in custody has gone into our witness protection program. He's implicated several government officials as conspirators, and someone overseas has put a contract out on him." He gave Mike a congenial, nice-guy grin. "Basically what I'm trying to do here is protect our witness and keep the whole mess out of the papers."

"Wouldn't hurt to contact some people, see if they saw his boat, what he was doing, right? Without giving them the details, of course." Mike spread his hands. "It's the least I can do, under the circumstances."

"All right," Morris said.

"Leave a number where I can reach you, and I'll see what I can find out."

The agent stood, extended a card from a local hotel with his room number written on it, shook Mike's hand again, and left.

Laurie, who had been unashamedly eavesdropping the entire time, appeared as soon as Morris was gone. Her expressive face was as tight as the fists planted on her hips.

"Dad, what's going on? That guy was a *fed*, for crying out loud."

Mike laughed. "Don't worry, honey. I'm not in any trouble. He's just trying to locate someone."

"So I heard." Laurie wrapped her arms around herself as she glanced back toward the door. "He gave me the creeps."

Mike didn't take notice. "I've got to do some running around. I'll be back later tonight. Have Ray take care of anyone who comes looking for me, and hold my calls."

"Great. What am I supposed to do about dinner?"

"Get some take-out tofu. Here." He tossed her the keys to the warehouse pickup. "Just remember, if you wreck my truck, I put you up for adoption."

She was finally well. Luke continued to watch over her as he brought her meals to the room, and checked on her several times a day. He wasn't obnoxious about caring for her—on the contrary, he seemed resigned. He maintained a grim silence at first, but she made an effort to be pleasant and cheerful. The tension between them gradually eased.

Despite Luke's frequent visits, she spent a great deal of time alone. She'd already skimmed through most of the books in the bedroom. It gave her a small sense of satisfaction when she realized she'd read most of them before. That indicated she'd had a good education, or at least had been an avid reader.

Boredom was inevitable, however, and her restless spirit ached for something Dickens, Twain, and Shakespeare didn't offer. Fresh air. Exercise. *Freedom.* One morning she woke up and found herself counting the flowers in the lace canopy.

"If I spend one more hour reading about Becky Thatcher," she told the ceiling, "I'm going to lose it. And it won't be pretty."

She got up and dressed. Once she had been able

to stand wearing more than his shirt, Luke had given her a pair of women's pink slacks and an ivory linen blouse. No explanation of who they belonged to or where they came from.

Whoever owned these clothes had to be at least eight inches taller and, judging from the generous darts, built like a centerfold.

Guess Mom and Dad aren't the only ones who come here on vacation.

"So Mr. Solitude has a girlfriend," she said as she buttoned the blouse. "Wonder what *her* name is? Something profound, I'll bet. Like Bambi, or Candy."

In the nearly empty armoire, she'd seen a long strip of satin ribbon, yellowed with age. After she brushed and braided her hair, she used it to tie off the end.

That looked good. "Maybe I'm a hairdresser. Or incredibly vain." It would have been nice to know for sure.

Her hands were neatly manicured, as were her feet. She wore no nail polish or jewelry, other than the jade and gold filigree ring on her right hand. She had taken it off once to see if it had an inscription, but the inside was smooth.

It must have been given to her by someone she cared about. That might explain the loss she felt whenever she looked at it.

She got tired of waiting for Luke to bring her breakfast. She wanted to take a look around. She didn't need to get his permission for everything. Even if he expected her to.

She opened the door and looked out.

The long hallway was deserted.

"I have a terrible headache," she said, trying out the excuse. "No, that won't work, there's a bottle of aspirin in the bathroom. I must be sleepwalking. There was this gigantic spider hanging from the canopy . . ."

She walked past a series of doors. One was open—another bedroom furnished with more antiques. As she continued down the hall, she checked out four more rooms similarly decorated. A fifth must have been a nursery at the turn of the century. She saw shelves stocked with dozens of very old toys.

Still no sign of her keeper.

She finally found the kitchen. Here modern appliances replaced the antiques. Lots of polished oak cabinets and spotless almond formica counters. Her empty breakfast tray was sitting on the kitchen table, and the coffeemaker was ready to go but not started.

She switched the drip machine on and enjoyed the smell of the brewing coffee. Her empty stomach woke up, reminding her that woman did not live by caffeine alone. Neither did man.

Where *was* Luke?

A sound drifted faintly into the kitchen. Luke's voice, from the other side of the house. She'd come this far. Might as well go the distance.

She followed the sound. She heard Luke swearing. Loudly. With very strong, Anglo-Saxon words. She stopped, listening.

What had set him off this time? Did she really want to know? If only for future reference?

"Come on, let's see what's got him all worked up."

She followed the obscenities to a set of double doors. One of them was slightly ajar. Behind it, she heard Luke yelling at something he evidently considered about as valuable as a human waste product. She saw he was seated behind a huge desk, his back toward the door. He was pounding on something and directing most of the bad words in the English language at some kind of television screen. No, she thought. Not a television.

A computer terminal.

Some instinct she was only faintly aware of took over as she pushed open the door and went straight to the equipment. Her brows drew together. A looping scramble of data jittered across the monitor like blinking lights on a Christmas tree.

Right away she knew what the problem was. *Him.*

"Worthless piece of—" Luke continued swearing, until she reached out, caught his hands, and pulled them away from the keyboard.

"Wait a minute," she said, and pressed three keys simultaneously. The monitor's screen cleared at once. "Pounding on it won't help. You've got to restart the system, then—here." She used an elbow to prod him out of the way. "Let me do it."

She bent over the keyboard, reading the scrolling auto-executive prompts as they appeared. Once the screen cleared, her fingers rapidly entered the required access commands.

The start menu appeared at once.

She straightened for a moment, and considered what could have caused the failure. She said, "You probably missed a keystroke and initiated the monitor test program." She proceeded to do a quick system check on the permanent memory. "You're lucky, you didn't wipe out the hard drive. That happens a lot when you don't know what you're doing. Why were you messing around with those system files—"

Her hands froze. What was she doing?

Like a cripple who had just run a marathon, she removed her hands from the keyboard and contemplated them in bewildered wonder. Then she remembered Luke. He was staring at her in complete astonishment.

"What the hell are you doing?"

"I looked in, saw the computer, and knew I could fix it."

"You should be in bed."

"Not unless you tie me down on it." He was never going to believe the spider excuse, so why bother?

He got to his feet. "I could do that. What are you doing in here?"

"I'm sick of staring at old lace and reading books written by dead guys, okay? I heard you, and followed the sound. Then I saw the computer—oh, my God, the computer—" She stared at the monitor as an amazed grin spread across her face. "Luke! I work on computers!"

"You *work* on computers?" He made it sound like she danced nude on top of them.

"That's what I do for a living." A flood of memories suddenly infused her. It was all coming back now. She didn't just work on computers. She *designed* them. She was good at it, too—in fact, she was one of the best people in her field.

"Lucky for me," Luke said.

"Considering the way you were hammering on that keyboard? Yes, it is."

"Whatever." He swung a hand toward the terminal. "Is it fixed now?"

Mr. Congeniality's way of saying thank you. "Yes. Access your program main menu—if you can do that without using your fists."

She watched him insert a disk, type a password, and a preliminary menu appeared. Before she could read it, he clicked off the power switch and the screen went blank. He pulled the disk from the drive before the activity light flickered off.

"Don't do that."

"Why? It's fine. I didn't even have to kick it, like the last time."

No wonder the unit had scrambled. She pressed

the heels of her hands against her eyes. "God only knows what condition the drive heads are in."

"What did I do?"

"Listen to me." She dropped her hands. "You don't use your fists on the keyboard. You don't yank the disk out until the little green light stops blinking. And you never, ever, kick a computer. *Anywhere.* Okay?"

"All right, all right. The guy who designed this piece of crap for me said—" Luke cut himself off in midsentence and took her arm. "Come on. I'll fix you something to eat."

She found she had a new reserve of knowledge to draw on. That was how she knew the "piece of crap" he referred to was one of the most powerful machines available on the commercial market. It was designed specifically to accommodate programs with vast amounts of statistical data, and execute complex targeting computations. The same kind of hardware NASA used to plot flight courses for the Space Shuttle.

So what was Luke the Hermit doing with it?

She took a last glance at the room before the doors swung shut behind her. It was a maze of books and maps. His survey work? Luke had made it plain he didn't want her asking questions about that. That didn't stop her from thinking about them.

Maybe she didn't have to ask. Luke had no idea how simple it would be for her to gain access to his programs. There wasn't a security program in existence that could lock her out. She also had no intention of telling him that. For now, she'd have to wait until the right opportunity presented itself. Then she'd find out what the big secret was.

In the kitchen, he retrieved some bread and eggs from the refrigerator. She noticed again all those shiny appliances.

"How do you manage to have electricity on an island?" She opened cabinet doors until she located the dishes.

"Generators," Luke said and began scrambling some eggs.

"I guess you're not hooked up to the Internet." He gave her an even-I'm-not-that-stupid look. "Right, of course not. No telephone lines."

He was an experienced cook, judging by his quick, economical movements. She wouldn't have done as well. When she tried to remember if she knew how to cook, she came up empty—except for the faint memory of something burning, and her own voice, cursing.

While Luke cooked, she set the kitchen table for two. He'd probably been working since dawn, and hadn't even stopped for coffee. She caught the bread as it popped out of the toaster. She unearthed a jar of orange marmalade and a dish of butter to accompany the meal. The coffeemaker finished brewing, and she poured a cup for both of them. She added a spoon of sugar to hers but left his black.

Luke brought the frying pan to the table, eyeing the second plate and waiting coffee with a frown.

"I thought you might like to join me," she said.

"I'm not hungry." He reached over to put the pan's contents on her plate.

"Can't you take a break for a few minutes? I really don't like eating alone." He hesitated, shrugged indifferently, then divided the eggs between the two plates. "Thanks."

In spite of what he'd said, Luke had a good appetite. She was hungry, too. The orange marmalade was homemade, with a handwritten label.

"This is terrific," she said as she picked the jar up to read the elegant handwriting. "Put this up yourself, Luke?"

"My mother did."

"Didn't she teach you her secret recipe?"

"Dad thought batting practice was more important."

"Pity. She makes a great marmalade."

"Yeah, she does. Want more coffee?"

"Please." He wasn't used to making polite conversation, she thought, then rolled her eyes. What did she expect? The guy lived on an island by himself. She was lucky he still remembered how to *talk*.

He handed her the coffee. "How's the sunburn?"

"Almost gone." She cautiously sipped from the mug, and decided to let it cool off. "Do all the antiques belong to your mother, too?"

"They were my grandparents'." A crooked grin

transformed his expression, making her stare. "My granddad won the island in a poker game. He built this house, spent the rest of his life here."

"You're kidding." She looked around. "He did all this by himself?"

"From the ground up, with his own hands." He sat back. "Mom refuses to change a thing. Says Granddad's ghost would come after her if she did."

"I wouldn't change a thing, either." She started washing up. He'd done the cooking. Fair was fair.

Luke was quiet, as usual, as she worked. What was he thinking?

She stacked the dishes in the sink rack to dry. "Something on your mind?"

"Not particularly."

Forthcoming as always. "Your mom must love it here. Does she visit the island often?" It wasn't as if she could ask about the centerfold material.

"A few weeks every summer."

"Is she a housewife, or retired?"

"She's a teacher."

He picked up a dish towel and started drying the dishes. "She must like working with kids." An image of a sweet, gray-haired woman surrounded by a bevy of small children came to mind.

"She's a professor at the University of Miami. She teaches English literature."

The mental picture of the motherly teacher became a tall, elegant woman in a suit, carrying a briefcase. Not exactly the kind of woman who made her own marmalade. "Your dad must be proud of her."

"He was. He died a few years ago. Heart failure."

"I'm sorry. Do the books in the bedroom belong to her?"

"No, they're mine. Listen, ah . . ."

"This is a pain, not having a name. Why don't you call me Anastasia? They never found her, right?"

Luke put the dishes in the cabinet and hung the towel on a knob to dry. "You're not an Anastasia."

"It's better than *Hey, you*."

He glanced down. "Jade."

"What?"

Unexpectedly he gripped her right wrist, lifted her hand, and tapped her ring with his forefinger. The green, square-cut stone glowed with a mossy luminescence against the lacy gold setting.

"Jade," he repeated.

"Oh. Right." She bit her bottom lip as she stared at the ring. "I've been tempted to take it off. It makes me really unhappy every time I look at it. Besides, I'm not a Jade."

"Why not?" he asked.

"I'm not that exotic," she said. His eyes, she realized, were almost the exact same color as the jade. She saw her reflection, caught in them. As she was.

Next thing you know, violins will start playing. Grow up.

"You're exotic enough."

"Getting amnesia, a bad sunburn, and washing up on a deserted island qualifies?" Why was he getting so close?

"It's just a name." Luke abruptly let go of her hand and turned away.

"Choosing a name seems to be beyond my mental capacity at the moment."

"Call yourself whatever you like." He was all business again. "Gertrude. Agnes. Doreen. Who cares?"

"Whoa. Anastasia was funny. Gertrude is repulsive." She'd better pick something before he did. "Let's go with Jade." She wiped her hands on a towel and looked around with satisfaction. "There. All done. What else can I do?"

"Time for you to go back to bed."

"Oh, no."

"You should be resting."

"I've had enough rest to last me a year."

He didn't seem sympathetic, only aggravated, but he did hesitate.

"May I take a look around the house?" she asked, quickly adding, "I promise not to disturb whatever you're doing."

Luke rubbed his fingers across his eyes in a now-familiar gesture, then released a sigh. "All right."

"I won't break any of the antique stuff."

"Stay out of the den. That's where the computer is. I don't want to be interrupted."

"Of course. I think I'll go take a walk on the

beach, kick around some coconuts, maybe say hello to the other crabs on the island."

He didn't crack a smile, but it was close. "No, stay indoors. Your skin isn't up to the sun yet."

"Okay. It's a big house, I'm sure I can keep myself occupied. I'll do the crabs tomorrow."

"Stay out of trouble." With that, he walked out of the kitchen.

Stay out of the den—stay indoors—stay out of trouble. Like she was a puppy who needed more house-training. Training—the word seemed to echo in her head. Something like training . . .

Experimenting. She'd been involved with a design experiment. Something to do with crystals, and—

Her memory stopped short, just as she was on the brink of remembering. The experiment had been to solve something . . . a common problem . . . she'd discovered . . . what?

She couldn't dredge it back up.

Forcing it was useless. It only gave her a migraine. At least she was starting to remember. It would only be a matter of time now, and then she would know why she'd been on that raft.

As she wandered through the rooms, she found a victrola that still worked. Although she didn't attempt to wind it up, not wanting Luke to believe himself interrupted. She found records ranging from classical to big band. All of them were stacked neatly in a rack beside another curio—an old-fashioned radio.

"I'd love to crank you up," she said, running her hand over the dome-shaped case, polished countless times over the decades until the wood acquired a hard, glassy shine. "But Luke would probably have a fit and start yelling."

In the nursery she saw a large variety of hand-made and manufactured toys. In one corner was a tiny rocking chair, a child's seat with the back and arms carved to resemble a small bear. Some-one had collected tin windup figures; many still had a key inserted in the small mechanisms. She wound up a primitive-looking race car and watched with delight as it spun around her feet, clicking madly.

Eventually she wandered back toward the cen-ter of the big house, trying not to look out the win-dows, but the beauty of the island waited just beyond her reach. She found the entrance to the long, screened-in porch at the back of the house and saw the courtyard from the windows.

Just like that, she fell in love.

The courtyard surrounded a large, square swim-ming pool. The surface of the deck had been in-laid with cut coral rock and mollusk shells. The multicolored surface appeared glass smooth, evi-dently safe enough for bare feet. Clever landscap-ing framed the deck with a fringe of grasses and flowers. The entire effect made it appear as though the pool were simply a natural part of the scene.

Fruit trees had been planted beyond the perime-ter of the deck. Their branches bowed under the weight of tempting globes of yellow and orange citrus. *It must be heaven to live here,* she decided, *to be able to step outside and pick the fruit you wanted for breakfast right from the branch it grew on.*

Stay indoors.

That was practically impossible, now that she'd seen the courtyard. Never mind what he'd said. It wouldn't hurt her to go out for a few minutes.

Dark green shrubs planted in oversized pots were placed around the walk to the deck. The huge, roselike white blooms nestled among the leaves gave off a thick, sweet perfume. Gardenias, she confirmed as she leaned over to bury her nose in one palm-sized flower. Just like the ones in the painting.

Luke kept the pool spotless as well, Jade saw as she went to the edge and looked over. He must use it regularly. She didn't feel like taking a dip, though. At all. Maybe she should go back in now.

Across the pool, Jade saw a banana tree, and walked over toward it. The ripest bunch hung just above her head. She stood on her toes to pick one.

"Jade!"

She lost her balance. She flailed her arms to regain her balance, but lost the battle and fell into the pool. The shock of the cool water on her sunburn made her yell, and water filled her open mouth and nose.

She tried to reach her toes to the bottom. There

was nothing under her. The side was several feet away. She was in trouble. Big trouble.

She didn't know how to swim.

Luke jerked the back door open and walked out onto the porch.

"Jade!"

She turned, slipped, and fell into the pool.

Luke laughed. She deserved a good dunking, maybe she'd listen to him the next time. He stopped laughing when he saw her struggling and the way she looked at the side of the pool. Her head sank out of sight.

Christ, she can't swim.

"Damn woman." He yanked open the porch door and ran to the pool.

Jade resurfaced, in full panic. "Luke! Help me!" She went under again.

Luke kicked off his shoes and dove in. It took a few seconds to reach her. When she saw him, her eyes widened and she tried to grab on to him. He pinned her arms under his and kicked hard to push them both up to the surface.

Once they broke the surface, Jade choked and spewed out water. Luke waited until she'd gotten her breath back before he turned her around and clamped her backward against him. From there he hauled her to the edge, hoisted her up, and shoved her onto the deck.

He stayed in the pool while Jade coughed and rubbed at her eyes. He wasn't in a hurry to get out. He wanted to be sure he wasn't going to throw her back in when he did. The thought had too many merits.

She'd scared the living hell out of him.

He finally got out and rose to stand over her.

Jade looked at him through dripping hair. "Um, I just remembered I can't swim."

"Congratulations." He sighed. "You're a walking disaster area."

More hair was plastered to her head and shoulders—she was soaked through. Like a cat who'd been caught in a downpour, Luke thought, and his mouth twitched. He didn't want her to be cute right now. He wanted her to be in Chicago.

"You were supposed to stay *in the house*," he said.

She nodded. "I know. Sorry."

She looked like he'd just kicked her. Unless this was part of her act, too. Not knowing made Luke's voice stern. "What do I have to do? Tie you to the bed?"

Now she looked like she wanted to kick *him*. "I wouldn't recommend you try."

That was the problem. He wanted to. Badly. Luke's hands clenched against the need to touch her. That was it. She'd finally driven him completely out of his head.

"I only meant to come out for a minute," she said.

"Honey, do me a favor. Stay *away* from water."

"Don't call me honey."

He just shook his head at her. It was the bizarre circumstances. He didn't want to hear the sound of her voice, or feel the warmth of her laughter, didn't want her looking at him. It had to be the enforced celibacy. That was why, dripping wet, she turned him on. Nothing else.

"I'll get back to bed now. Thanks for the rescue." She reached up, and he automatically helped her up. "You should be a lifeguard."

"Around you? It's becoming my full-time job." Somehow she'd taken the edge off his temper. All he had left to handle was wanting her. He knew how to do that. "So now you remember you can't swim?"

"That, or I remembered how to drown."

"Come on."

He pulled her back into the house, determined to put some walls between them before he did something really stupid. "Get out of those wet clothes before you get a chill."

In his own room, he rapidly stripped and dried off. After he pulled on a dry pair of denim shorts, he remembered she didn't have any more dry clothes. He went to his mother's room. "Can't have her running around naked, now, can I?" he said as he sorted through her closet. "No, not a good idea. I can handle her feeling better and wandering around the house, but she's definitely got to keep clothes on."

Her body wasn't the only attraction. He'd admired her silent endurance during those first days.

She'd never bitched, no matter how bad she felt. She'd even joked about it.

What would Mom think of her? Jade had that quirky sense of humor that kept popping up when he least expected it—something his mother would probably find enchanting. His sister would probably give Jade pointers on the best ways to harass him. What was he thinking? She'd never meet his family. In three weeks she'd be just another funny story to tell Mike over a beer. Nothing more.

Luke didn't want to look at her legs, so he traded the dress for a long-sleeved jumpsuit. The more covered she was, the better. At least he didn't have to give her any of his own clothes. The idea of Jade walking around in his shirts and cutoffs was appealing.

So was being slow-roasted over hot coals.

Luke took the clothes to her bedroom and walked in. He thought the room was empty at first, then saw differently when he turned his head.

Jade stood in front of the bathroom mirror, rubbing a towel over her face. Her wet clothes were in a heap beside the bathtub. She'd already braided her hair into a long, damp cable.

She was stark naked, too.

Chapter Four

Diffused sunshine came in from the window, making her glow. Her sunburn had healed, leaving behind a dark golden tan. That contrasted with the white triangles left by the bra and panties he'd found her in. Like she was wearing a transparent bikini.

So much for keeping her covered up.

He'd seen her naked before, but she'd been hurt. Now she was fine. Now he could touch her.

He watched her shiver, saw how her nipples contracted, reacting to the breeze from the small open window above the tub. Just as they had that first day. He wanted to feel those tight pink buds against his lips, soothe them with his tongue. Then suck on them for a few hours.

Heavy, pulsating anticipation made his breath thick. Sweat beaded along the edge of his upper lip. He licked it away. Imagined Jade doing the same thing. Smothered a groan.

The subsequent images his mind supplied made him swell and harden. Lowering Jade to the bed.

His hands separating her thighs. Her reddened lips spilling his name again and again. The soft sheath between her legs, taking every rigid inch of him, slowly, while he watched her eyes . . .

So much for perspective.

She took the towel from her head and wrapped it around her. That was when she finally realized he was there.

Busted.

"Luke? What are you doing?"

He was moving toward her before he knew it.

Jade watched him with her mouth open. Yet she didn't say another word. All she did was take a few faltering steps back. The side of the bathtub stopped her as it hit the back of her calves.

He stopped three feet away. The clothes in his hand fell to the floor. "Tell me to get out."

But Jade didn't tell him to do anything at all. She seemed frozen, her hands holding the edges of the towel together. But she didn't scream. No outraged objections. Nothing. She wasn't making a sound. She just stood there.

Might as well not keep the lady waiting any longer. She might get a chill.

He was on her in under two seconds. Her skin was warm; she was trembling. The way she was looking up at him was going to drive him out of his skull. He tugged at the towel and it obligingly fell to the floor without a hitch.

Luke looked down at her naked body. She was small but God, she was beautiful. So perfect. The smell of her skin filled his head. Warm. Bewitching. All woman.

Now she'd start screaming.

Color washed up from Jade's breasts and neck into her face. Still she didn't resist him in the slightest. Good, Luke thought. He liked her this way. She must have liked what he was doing, too. Otherwise she'd be pushing him out the door, yelling at him. *Something.*

He pulled the ribbon out of her hair. Touching her hair was one of many obsessions that had been eating at him lately. Slowly he worked the plaited sections loose until he could fill his hands. Dark ribbons of burnished hair streamed down his arms. When it was dry, he knew it would be incredibly soft. Just like the sweet patch between her thighs.

"Luke."

He used the hair in his fist to tug her head back, and looked at her throat with hungry eyes. "What?"

She said something, but the pounding in his head made it impossible to make out. Luke kissed the skin below her jaw. She sucked in breath and clutched at his arms. She tasted clean and soft and female. He lifted his mouth and smiled as he saw the wet, dark red spot he'd left behind.

By the time he was finished with her, he'd probably eat her alive.

"Luke," Jade said again.

That brought his attention to her mouth. He wanted that, too. Luke bent his head and gently grazed her lower lip with the edge of his teeth. He watched her eyes darken, felt her quiver. Her response made him smile again. He buried his face in her damp hair, let it soothe his hot skin.

"Why don't we—" he heard her say as he caught her earlobe and bit down gently. She cleared her throat. "Why don't we take a breather?"

"You breathe. I'm busy."

"This is a really bad idea."

She was entitled to a token protest, he supposed, not liking it. Just as he was entitled to see straight through it. "So why did you leave the door open?"

"I didn't." Her hair danced over the back of his hand as he traced her collarbone with a fingertip.

"Baby, the door was wide open." They'd agreed if the door was closed, he'd knock first. Luke brushed his thumb over the birthmark on her shoulder. It was velvety to the touch, just as he'd suspected. How would it taste?

"The breeze must have done that."

"It's not that windy." He let his fingers follow the line of her sternum, his knuckles brushing against the inner curve of her breast. "You left it open for me."

"I didn't. Even if I did, you should have knocked."

"Uh-huh." He bent closer. "You'd still have been naked, though. No dry clothes, remember?"

She was staring at his mouth. "I had a towel on."

"That didn't work."

One quick tug brought her up against him. The first sensation from that skin-on-skin collision was shocking in intensity. He felt her breath rush out against him. Heard the faint, startled sound she made. Her breasts flattened, the nipples hard against his bare chest. The subtle scent of mutual arousal blended and rose between them. He wrapped her hair in his fist and lowered his head.

Mine.

Jade kept her mouth closed. For about three seconds. A whimper emerged from her as his fist tightened momentarily against her scalp. He wrapped one arm around her, securing the embrace. She was trapped. That was when her lips softened, then parted with a moan.

He pushed his tongue between them, taking what he wanted. If her lips were silk, her mouth was wet, sweet satin. Tender. Luscious. Delectable.

No woman had ever tasted like this. Not this good. Luke's entire body went on absolute alert. He couldn't clear his head. She permeated every inch of him, the lush scent of her skin and the feel of her naked curves dragging him down into a dark, wild whirlpool of need.

"Say my name," he said against her mouth.

"Luke."

"Yeah." He stroked the back of her neck with his thumb. "Say it again. Just like that."

"We have to stop."

"*Say it.*"

"*Luke*, we have to stop."

He laughed once and kissed her again. Wanting her crowded out everything, until nothing existed except Jade.

His self-control started to crumble as she returned the kiss. She was hesitant; her tongue barely touched his. With low, coaxing sounds he drew her in, urging her to do more than tease him.

Shy but hungry for more. He'd give her more. His free hand slid down her back. A lot more.

He let go of Jade's hair and encircled her with both arms. His hands spread over her firm buttocks, kneading the tight curves for a moment before cupping them to haul her up off her feet.

That got her attention, fast. "Oh, my God." She dodged his mouth. "Wait. We need to talk."

"About what?" Luke watched her face. Her eyes were wide, her pupils dilated. "This?" Deliberately he pressed her against him, so she could feel what she'd done to him. Her soft thighs naturally cradled the erection between his. Everything fit nicely. Would fit even better once he was inside her. "Is *this* what you wanted to talk about, sweetheart?"

She clenched her teeth. "Not exactly."

"Funny, but it's all I can think about right now." She looked drowsy, sexy, the way she did when she first woke up in the morning. "I want you. I've wanted you since the day I pulled you out of the water."

"I thought I was on a raft."

"Details."

A guttural sound rumbled in his chest as he deliberately tortured himself, lifting and moving her rhythmically against his erection. Her eyes reflected soft, inner heat, and Luke felt rather than heard the sound she made.

Jade melted over him, while her fingers held on with unexpected, fierce strength. Now she was moving on her own, nudging and sliding against him in feminine demand.

Good. She needed him as much as he wanted her.

Luke bent to the curve of her throat again, catching the fragile skin with his teeth. A second love bite made her writhe and whimper again. That womanly, pleading sound echoed through his head, destroying what was left of his sanity.

Too good. Too fast.

For a moment, he put her down and rested his head against her shoulder. His chest worked with deep, steady deliberation to draw more oxygen into his lungs. Every muscle he owned was in iron knots. Sweat ran freely down his face, stray drops falling on her skin.

Control. Luke needed to get a hold on whatever he had left. If he didn't, he'd take her on the tile floor. He felt Jade's hand hesitantly touch the back of his head, then she pressed, holding him against her with exquisite compassion.

To hell with the consequences. Luke had to have her. *Right now.* He pivoted and carried her out of the bathroom in three strides. When she hit the bed, he was already on top of her.

Her lips parted on another helpless, yearning moan as he filled both of his hands with her firm, hard-tipped breasts. Her hips rocked against his again in mute entreaty.

"That's it, honey. Show me what you want." With dark satisfaction he rubbed the confined ridge of his erect penis against the sable curls between her thighs. She responded by opening her legs wider and rolling her hips faster. "You're going to give me everything, aren't you?"

"Luke . . ." A broken sound left her lips. "Luke, I need . . . oh, God, please . . ."

The way she said that made him smile.

She was his.

"I know, sweetheart," Luke said, soothing her with his big hands and deep voice. "I'll take care of you. I'll give you what you need."

He kept one thigh between hers as he reached between them to release the tight restriction of his shorts. The zipper defeated his one-handed effort, then snagged hopelessly in his haste to force it open.

"Luke."

Jade caught his wrist, and guided his hand back up to her breast. For a moment he simply watched her eyes flutter as his palm massaged and shaped her, teasing the erect bead with subtle, repeated circles of thumb and fingers. He recalled he hadn't tasted her nipples yet, and decided to remedy that immediately. His head descended, and Jade arched her back to meet his open lips.

"Luke, oh . . ." Her voice was lost as his mouth trailed over the taut mound to envelope the crest. The textures of soft aureole and tight nipple against his tongue was maddening. He sucked it with a ceaseless, rhythmic pressure that sent her thrashing frantically under him. "Too much . . . please . . ."

Luke wanted to please her. He wanted to thrust his swollen flesh into her body and stroke her until she cried out his name and came to him, over and over. The feel of her on his hands, against his mouth, under his body wasn't enough. One jammed zipper wasn't going to hold him off any longer.

Luke pushed himself away from her and onto his back. He reached down with both hands to rip the metal teeth apart. Beside him, he felt Jade stiffen. Then she curled over and rolled away. A moment later he saw her scramble to her feet on the opposite side of the bed.

"Jade?" He got off the bed slowly.

She was panting, her breasts heaving with each breath. "No, Luke." Keeping her gaze locked on him, she tore the twisted sheet from the mattress and covered herself with it.

"What did you say?" She was aching and as half crazed with wanting as he was. He could see it humming in every rigid, luscious inch of her body. "Come here."

Jade shook her head. Luke started toward her. Like a wary animal, she backed up against the wall.

"I said no."

He stopped just before he touched her. Christ, she was acting like she was *afraid* of him. "What?"

"You heard me." She held the sheet around her like a shield, her knuckles distended with white tension. "No, Luke."

Jade knew she was in trouble. Luke towered over her, his expression fierce, his eyes hungry. Using her head was the only way to stop him. Now if she could only remember how to do that. She forced her lungs to slow, her features to simulate rigid indifference. She was going to be ice. Cold, solid, invulnerable.

He extended one strong hand. "Come here."

That low, rough command acted like a blowtorch. It would be so easy to give in to him. Let him take her back to that bed. Touch her. Take her. All she had to do was reach out and put her hand in his.

No, she wouldn't. She *couldn't*. She didn't know him. She didn't even know who *she* was. What if she was involved with another man? A man whose love she couldn't remember?

Luke didn't care about her. He'd made his low opinion of her only too plain. He'd even accused her of plotting to get to him. Allowing this to happen now would only confirm it in his eyes. And what about the clothes he'd given her to wear? What if there was a Bambi or Candy waiting somewhere for him?

She shook her head once more.

The big hand dropped to his side. "I don't understand," he said, the words quiet, menacing.

Jade saw how he was poised to spring. She didn't kid herself into thinking she was safe yet. One wrong move, one unguarded word, and he'd be all over her. *Ice. Be a block of ice. Freeze him out.*

"What don't you understand, Luke?" she asked. "The 'en' or the 'oh?'"

He was close now, only a few inches separating them. She blinked, and suddenly his hands were propped against the wall on either side of her head. She was trapped.

"Was this part of the plan, sweetheart?"

Not "the plan" again. She groaned silently. "Luke. For the last time, *there is no plan.*"

"There is now."

His head descended until their noses nearly bumped. She wouldn't let herself blink or breathe. She didn't want to think what would happen if she did.

"No, Luke."

She could smell the sweat gleaming across his chest, flowing down the sides of his face. His breath was touching her skin.

"You want me."

This had to stop. She had to get him out of here. "Look, I'm not having sex with you. Can't you get that through your head?"

He abruptly turned his back on her and walked away. Thank God he'd backed off. Round two would have demolished her.

"I'm sorry, I shouldn't have said it like that."

Luke slammed his fist into the nearest wall. The portrait of the woman tilted forward and fell to the floor with a crash. He turned on her. "Say whatever you want. Think whatever you want." Luke shoved the painting to one side. "You want me, and I'm going to have you."

Out he went. The door slammed behind him.

For a long time, Jade just stood there. It took enormous effort to walk over to where he'd dropped the dry clothing. She picked it up, her limbs stiff.

When she glanced at her breasts, she saw bright pink patches. Whisker burn. Darker spots where his mouth had worked so hungrily. With jerky movements she pulled on the jumpsuit and covered up the evidence of his touch. It didn't work. Jade could still taste him on her lips. Feel him against her fingers. Smell him on her skin. Phantom sensations.

She pressed a hand against her bruised mouth. *What am I going to do now?*

She should have seen this coming. They were both young, healthy, and attracted to each other. Both stranded here, cut off from the rest of the world. That eliminated the normal protection civilization afforded.

It wasn't merely physical attraction, either, a small voice behind her eyes said.

Oh yes, it was, she thought stubbornly. She knew little about him and even less about herself. Luke certainly didn't care about her. He didn't even *like* her.

Of course, it would have been good between them. A small, mocking laugh left her lips. Good? It would have been fantastic. Her still-pulsating nerves could attest to that. And Luke? He had practically punched a hole through solid concrete when she'd stopped him.

He had stopped, the voice reminded her.

Jade could acknowledge that much. It hadn't been easy for him, nor had he been polite about it, but he'd respected her refusal.

The fact remained: the only thing they shared besides this inexplicable, astonishing passion was the island they were marooned on. Surely even the most ferocious need couldn't maintain itself indefinitely. Jade despised the idea of being little more than a scratch for Luke's itch. Whoever she was, she instinctively knew that kind of empty intimacy was wrong for her.

But would it be so empty? that inner voice asked.

She cared about Luke. Too much. He'd saved her life, cared for her injuries, watched over her. He'd even begun to open up to her, showing her a side she'd never suspected he had. When he'd spoken of his mother over breakfast, she'd even felt jealous.

What would it feel like, to be the object of that easy affection?

More importantly, what would she do if Luke touched her again? Jade didn't doubt for a mo-

ment that he would. She had to make sure not to
respond. He was a man who kept his word. She
returned to the bed, burying her hot face in her
arms.

Oh, God, she thought. *Three and a half more weeks,
alone with him? I'll never make it.*

"Yeah, Mom," Laurie said in a monotone.
"Right. Your concern is touching. Be sure and write.
Bye."

She slammed the receiver back on the phone and
flopped on the narrow bed. Above her were the
uneven stars she'd painted on the ceiling when she
was eight. Mike had let her stay with him for the
whole summer that year.

This time she might be here until she was *eighty.*

Okay, Laurie admitted, so fooling around in the
chem lab had been a really stupid idea. But had
anyone cared that she'd been conducting a genuine experiment for extra credit?

No. Immediately condemned by her reputation
alone, the professor had marched her straight to
the dean's office. Twenty-four hours and several
stern lectures later, she'd arrived at her mother's
house.

The Chief Coordinator of Physical Therapy for
Monroe County Hospitals, Meredith Anderson
Barry was a busy, impatient woman. The fact that
she'd been forced to cancel two morning appoint-
ments in order to deal with her daughter hadn't
improved her normally brusque manner.

Her mother's auburn hair had remained in its glossy French twist as she shook her head. "When in God's name are you going to stop acting like a child, Laura?" She glanced at her diamond-studded watch. Again.

"Oh, I don't know," Laurie had drawled as she watched her elegantly dressed mother pace the length of the tastefully furnished living room. "Maybe after I get out of prison?"

"Stop joking about this!" Meredith's flawless makeup didn't conceal her dark flush of temper. "If you don't get a decent education, you're just going to end up like your father!"

That had cut to the bone. For years her mother had put down her father, to justify the heartless way she'd left him for another man. Laurie was sick of it. "It's better than turning into an upscale bitch like you!"

What followed had been ugly. Meredith had delivered an extended verbal thrashing, dragging up every piece of idiocy from the past. The final blow came when her mother had announced she was through dealing with what was obviously beyond salvaging. A moment later Meredith was on the phone, calling a taxi.

Laurie had been handed several hundred dollars in cash, her packed suitcases, then shown the door.

"Always a pleasure, Mom," she'd said as she walked out. "Thanks for your support."

"Don't come back until you grow up." Meredith's manicured fingers had curled until her knuckles were white. "And for God's sake, use that money I gave you to buy yourself some decent clothes."

She'd had no place else to go but her father's, and even Mike had been less than happy to see her. From the terse conversation she'd just had with her mother, Laurie knew better than to darken her door again for at least a decade. She sighed, and pulled a pillow over her head.

What am I going to do now?

Tonight Mike had gone to the gym for his biweekly workout, and Jeff had been tied up at his job, so she had nothing to do. The empty evening stretched out in front of her, as barren as her future.

Poor Laurie. Unloved and unwanted by all.

Oh, knock it off, she thought, and threw the pillow across the room. She had to find something else to do besides wallowing in self-pity, or she'd cry herself into the hiccups.

Eventually she wandered from the apartment over to the warehouse. Everyone else was gone for the day, so she let herself in and got started on the orders to be shipped out in the morning.

As she sat processing the invoices at her desk, another partial shipment caught her attention. The order itself wasn't anything unusual, just some nonperishable food items and computer diskettes. The ship-to address, however, was only two words.

Paradise Island.

Her father had claimed a similar order belonged to a friend of his. The friend with the visa problems, Laurie recalled, and frowned. The way Mike had acted when she'd questioned the order had made her suspicious. Combined with the visit from Agent Morris, the whole situation reeked of trouble.

Laurie knew in the past her father had sometimes helped smuggle political prisoners out of Cuba and Central America. What if he had somehow gotten involved with this man the FBI was looking for? She tucked a long red curl behind her ear. He'd never tell her a damn thing, either. Mike trusted her about as much as her mother did.

Too bad, Laurie thought, pursing her lips as she memorized the order. She'd find out what he was mixed up in anyway.

She went to her father's records first. She'd been nagging him to transfer them to a computerized system, but Mike had a tendency to resist change. Especially when it involved high-tech tutorials. The ancient filing cabinet was choked with records, and it took some time to go through the H drawer.

Nothing. Not a bill of lading, invoice, or single scrap of paper on Paradise Island. Yet the shipment was for an "old friend," her father had said.

Laurie then went to the purchase orders. Mike's military sense of order made him meticulous about details, and every order was noted with the name of the customer for whom it was purchased. She uttered a low cry of victory when she came across a dozen orders, all labeled "Paradise Island."

"Eureka!"

She took the papers back to her desk and studied them. Food, perishable and otherwise, more office supplies, diving gear and ordinary household goods had been purchased for Paradise Island. Exactly what someone would order, Laurie thought, if they were moving off the mainland.

Or hiding out from the FBI.

She went to the huge map on the office wall, which detailed the name and location of every land mass within one hundred square miles of Marathon. No Paradise Island anywhere.

"So it's not on the map," Laurie said, and pondered this as she replaced the purchase orders. "That can't be right. You can't hide an entire island. Unless . . ."

Could Paradise Island have been renamed?

She'd need to check the old survey maps. City Hall was closed by now, but the nearest Monroe County library was only a few blocks from the warehouse.

The lingering depression of the last two days fled as Laurie hurried back to the apartment to grab her purse and the keys for the warehouse truck.

"Nancy Drew," she said as she climbed in the battered cab, "eat your heart out."

*   *   *

Jade remained in her room until twilight. Luke never came back. Hunger pangs eventually convinced her to emerge from hiding. She got to the kitchen without encountering Luke, where she discovered a plate waiting on the stove, covered and still warm. She had to assume it was for her. If Luke was in the house, she couldn't hear him.

Jade sat down and wondered what would happen next. They couldn't avoid each other forever. Would he try to talk her into his bed? Seduce her with his voice, his hands, his mouth? Or come out of nowhere and grab her?

That last thought should have frightened her. Her appetite fled when she acknowledged just how much it didn't. She wanted to make love with Luke. Wanted to feel all those incredible sensations again. Wanted everything she'd talked herself out of just a few hours ago.

Don't do this. You can't fight a battle on two fronts.

She forced herself to eat, but the chicken and rice dish was tasteless. Every tiny noise made her flinch. In the end she scraped most of her dinner in the garbage, then sat brooding over a cup of herbal tea.

Three more weeks of this, before she could escape. Luke would probably go back to treating her like dirt under his shoes. She buried her face in her hands, but pride kept her from indulging in helpless tears.

She had to *do* something.

Jade washed her dishes and dried them, neatly

returning them to their places in the cabinet. The thought of returning to the emptiness of her bedroom was unappealing, and a show of cowardice as well.

She wasn't going to hide from him, she thought, and walked out to the deck.

The sky above the dense canopy was streaked with a dozen colors. Apricot, gold, and navy blue clouds trailed like so many rippling scarves over the matte violet sky. She was certain she'd never seen that kind of sunset before. She even went so far as to pick a banana for her dessert, taking care to stay away from the edge of the pool.

If she fell in again, this time Luke just might let her drown.

The subject of her thoughts appeared on the far side of the pool, wearing only a pair of denim shorts. It was becoming too dark to see his expression, but she doubted he was pleased to see her. The silence stretched out until she held up the banana in her hand for him to see.

"I just came out for some fruit. There's no sun now, so I thought it would be all right."

"Stay away from the pool," Luke said, then executed a flawless dive.

Jade sat down on one of the lounge chairs. He swam with long, clean strokes, making several laps around the perimeter before stopping to tread water directly in front of her.

He pushed the wet hair from his forehead and

propped his elbows on the edge of the deck. "Did you eat?"

She nodded. "It was delicious." It had tasted like cardboard. "Thank you."

To her relief he pushed off the edge and continued his swim for another half hour. He didn't say anything until he pulled himself up out of the pool.

Moonlight glistened on his wet skin, the light carving his features like smooth stone. His broad shoulders stretched above a perfectly proportioned chest, which tapered symmetrically to a slim waist. Curly amber hair pelted his long, well-developed legs and muscular arms, but his chest was smooth as polished wood.

What would it feel like under her hands? Her mouth? When he'd hauled her to the bed today, his passion and strength had kept her from finding out. Luke would be a dominating lover. It was part of the attraction. He'd indulge her desires, but only at his leisure.

What else would be at his whim?

She switched her attention to the vast night sky, afraid to keep staring, afraid he'd suspect what she was thinking, afraid of what would happen next. What Luke said then didn't frighten her.

It stunned her.

"You said you worked with computers. I've got another problem. Will you take a look at it?"

Was Luke actually asking for her help? He must be desperate. Or ill. "Of course."

"I'll get changed and meet you in the den," he said, then crossed the courtyard and disappeared into the house.

Jade sat staring after him. Big Bad Luke was just full of surprises.

She beat him to the den. The computer had been turned off, and she decided the safe bet was not to touch it until he showed up. *Let him tell me what to do. That seems to make him happy.*

There was a wall unit set off to one side, but all the doors were locked. Too big for a filing cabinet. What was in there? On either side of it were framed maps. In fact, there were maps all over the walls. Some were standard geographic maps of different global regions. The Mediterranean. The Persian Gulf. The Sea of Japan.

One yellowed, irregular-shaped chart was pressed beneath a glass frame on the wall. It was a world map, but the continents didn't look right. Jade stepped closer. The writing on it was too faded to decipher. Over the area between Asia and the Philippines, someone had scrawled "The Gates of Shuiba" on the glass. There were other names, too. "Fu-Chou." "Timor." "Ceylon." "Malaya."

What was a surveyor doing with a ratty old thing like this? Who or what was Shuiba?

Maybe Luke simply collected maps and books. Some of the stuff on the bookcases seemed positively ancient. There were even some tattered-looking scrolls tied together here and there. Afraid she'd be caught snooping, she moved toward his desk.

A stack of thick folders had been left out on top, held down by an unusual stone paperweight. She picked it up and discovered it was extremely heavy, and made from what appeared to be very old marble.

"—I will uphold this cause," she read the words chiseled into the worn surface out loud. "As though it were that of my own father, and will leave no stone unturned in my search . . ." Puzzled, she placed it back on top of the folders. "Who said that? Indiana Jones?"

"Sophocles, from *Oedipus Tyrannus*."

Luke stood in the doorway. The T-shirt and jeans he wore were faded but dry, his damp hair combed.

"Oedipus? The guy with the mommy complex?"

"Yeah. Sophocles liked to write about what happened when a powerful individual struggled against fate. They always suffered or died."

"That's pretty gruesome. Why this particular quote?"

"It's my personal motto. I'm a gruesome kind of guy. Let's get started."

Luke gestured to the chair in front of the computer. Once she was seated, he leaned over her.

"I start it up," he said, demonstrating by pressing the power switch. "And nothing happens."

He was right. Nothing happened. The monitor remained dark and blank. The power and drive indicator lights didn't come on, either. Probably a connection problem. She hoped. She doubted Luke wanted to hear his power supply components were fried.

"Did you spill something on the keyboard, or on top of the unit?"

"No."

"How about your generators? Any blips or interruptions from them?" He shook his head. She stood up and looked behind the tower, checking the cables where they connected to the various ports. Everything was in place, tightly fastened, and none of the cords appeared frayed or damaged. She put her nose next to the unit vents, but smelled nothing that would indicate an electrical short.

Had to be external.

She traced the power cord down to the floor, where it and several others were plugged into a multioutlet strip unit. A surge protector, she realized. The strip switch was off. She pressed it on, and heard the computer's hard drive hum as the system came on line.

Jade straightened, kept her face straight, and pointed to the culprit.

"The surge protector was off. You may have accidentally stepped on the switch."

"Figures." He thrust a hand through his hair then—incredibly—he laughed. "Last time I knocked the plug out of the wall. Took me an hour to figure it out."

The way he said it made her smile. "That's happened to me a few times, too."

As she said that, he looked at her mouth. Amusement faded from his face and became something much more elemental. That startled her. And fascinated her. And charmed her.

Time to go back to her room.

"It should be fine now," she said. His hand caught her wrist as she walked past him toward the door, and tugged her to a stop. She didn't try to resist.

"Can you type?"

It was such an anticlimax that Jade choked. She covered it with a fake cough and nodded.

Luke released her, and tapped the stack of bulging file folders with his fingers. "I need to get this data entered, and my hand is out of commission for a few days."

For the first time she realized he had been using his left hand to do everything. Luke was right-handed. She looked down—said right hand was neatly wrapped in a gauze bandage—then looked at his face. He wasn't going to beg her, that was pretty obvious.

"Show me what to do."

Luke took the top file from the stack and sat down in front of the computer. From the main menu, he accessed a database program labeled "Shuiba" and brought up a complicated spreadsheet. He explained how the handwritten columns of statistical data had to be transferred from each report into the program. The data was numeric, some with extended decimals, others with what appeared to be time and degrees.

By the time they switched places, she felt confident enough to begin. She examined the first report, then fed the figures into the computer with rapid, precise keystrokes. Luke observed her speed on the keyboard without comment, until she paused at the end of the report.

"Check it," she told him. He did, from the paper to the screen, slowly and thoroughly.

"Perfect," he said at last, startling her again with that quick, devastating smile. "Let me know if you have any questions." Luke pulled another chair to the opposite side of the desk, and took a rock out of one of the sample containers scattered around the den. He started scraping bits off it into a petri dish.

All of the reports were titled with the same word. "What does 'Shuiba' mean?" she asked.

He didn't look up from the notes he was reading. "The dam."

"The damn what?"

"The d-a-m."

"Oh." That was clear as mud, Jade thought. Mr. Congeniality was in no mood to elaborate, either. She went back to work.

There was no clue in the numbers themselves as to what they represented. Jade assumed the time and degrees had something to do with longitude and latitude, another column appeared to be depth

measurements. The rest were a mystery. Every report she worked from was labeled "Shuiba." Like
the writing on the glass. The Gates of Shuiba.

Whatever The Gates of the Dam were, they
meant a boatload of paperwork. And what was
this uneasy feeling she got, looking at the Chinese
words? It made her want to crumple up the papers and burn them. But why?

Despite the large number of reports in the file
he'd given her, Jade swiftly completed the data
entry. When she turned to tell Luke, he merely
handed her another file without comment. He
wasn't going to applaud, she could see that. She
smiled slightly as she went back to work. Even indifference was better than hostility and contempt.
Or punching out walls.

Hours later, when she'd finished entering the
entire stack, Jade yawned until her jaw cracked.
Luke heard her and looked at his watch.

"It's midnight," he said, and got up from his
chair to stretch his arms over his head. Jade neatly
restacked the last of the reports she'd entered before handing them back to him in the file.
"Thanks."

She gave him a small, drowsy smile. "You're
welcome."

"Will you give me a hand tomorrow?"

"Of course." She did owe Luke for rescuing and
taking care of her. Perhaps if she kept busy enough,
he'd forget about what had happened this morn-

ing. Then she met his eyes, and saw something besides fatigue darkening them.

He wasn't going to forget a blessed thing.

Jade managed to keep her expression blank as they left the room together. Luke didn't touch her, but shadowed her all the way to her bedroom. The tense silence got worse with every step.

At her door, she stopped and half turned away. Luke came closer. His breath stirred the hair at the side of her face. Jade waited, not sure what would happen next. She wanted, so badly, to turn to him, to touch him, to take what he offered. But it wasn't right. She had no memory of anyone else, but that didn't mean there wasn't someone.

She didn't move. "Good night, Luke."

He didn't say anything, and the moment seemed to stretch into eternity. At last he moved away and continued down the hall to his room.

Swiftly she slipped into her bedroom and shut the door, leaning back against it in relief. She waited and listened for a few minutes, until it became apparent he wasn't coming back.

How could she expect to keep Luke at a distance if her own body wasn't willing to cooperate?

You could be in his arms right now, that sly inner voice whispered.

"Don't even go there," she said, and went to brush her teeth.

*   *   *

By the time Yu-wei had arrived at his hotel in Miami, a stack of phone messages waited for him. Most were from his assistant back at Shandian's headquarters. General Sung's secretary had also left three messages over the last hour, using the standard alias.

Once inside his penthouse suite, Yu-wei ignored the hotel phone and used his personal cellular unit to place the call. He flicked a scrambler switch to insure no one would accidentally—or otherwise— gain access to the conversation, then dialed a private number.

"Biotechnical research, may I help you?"

"Mr. Sung, please," Yu-wei said. "This is Chang Yu-wei."

Since he'd given the correct code, the call was put through directly to the general's office. "Sung."

"General," Yu-wei greeted his superior in their native language without identifying himself. "I received several messages upon my arrival. Is there a problem?"

Sung got right to the point. "The chairman wishes to know the status on the project. Why are you in Miami?"

"The situation is under control," Yu-wei said.

"I am scheduled to appear before the chairman in an hour to discuss this situation. Now you will tell me exactly how I am to assure him of your control."

"Unfortunately, a minor problem has arisen, and details are not yet completely finalized," Yu-wei said. His manicured nails dug into the plastic phone case. "I assure you, it will be resolved shortly."

"Idiot. Your problems are not my concern. Nor do I desire assurances. I want the project completed *immediately*."

Yu-wei disliked being called an idiot almost as much as he disliked the blustering, greedy fool on the other end of the phone.

"I regret to inform you that is not possible, General. I am still in the process of acquisition."

"You do not have it yet?" The general's voice acquired a note of panic. "You will retrieve it at once, Chang, or—"

"Or what?" Yu-wei finally lost his reserve. "You will tell the chairman that the funds you appropriated were misplaced? Or wrongfully received by our Swiss banker?"

Sung said nothing. His breathing, however, indicated he was on the verge of a bronchial attack.

Yu-wei smiled. "I would suggest you assure the chairman that all will be resolved by the end of the month."

Before General Sung could respond, Yu-wei shut off the cellular's power switch and tossed the phone back in his briefcase. His superior would do as Yu-wei had advised; Sung had no other choice. A negative report would have sent the general to be questioned by the special investigators, and no one ever survived their interrogations.

Yu-wei wondered why the American computer

scientist had balked at the last minute. Walter Carter had sold his soul to Shandian for mere pennies, considering what the man had promised to steal for them. Yet Carter had seemed more than satisfied with his share.

After the project abstracts had been delivered, Yu-wei had gone directly to General Sung, who offered to appropriate the funding for "development" from Beijing. Yu-wei saw no reason to turn him down. Nor did he tell the general he was only one of Yu-wei's international circle of buyers.

Ambition was often born in the squalor of an Asian ghetto; Yu-wei was not the first to nurture and use it to escape the hopelessness of poverty. Sung was but another rung on the ladder of ascent to complete freedom and fortune. Yu-wei had carefully planned for this day, and when the general had proposed his scheme to embezzle the funding, he'd realized it had arrived.

Seventeen million American dollars had been deposited in a joint Swiss bank account, and six months later Carter had succeeded, far beyond Yu-wei's wildest expectations. Bidding overseas became spirited.

Had Walter Carter developed a conscience at the last moment? If he had, it had been a costly mistake—both for Carter and Yu-wei. However, now Carter was dead, and once more Yu-wei was within reach of his goal.

Nothing would stop him.

He ordered a meal from room service, but decided not to engage the services of one of the high-priced American call girls the concierge had discreetly recommended. In his present mood, Yu-wei might kill her before he was through.

He wanted to save his energy for Carter's partner.

Chapter Five

The first morning, Jade rapidly completed her first task and handed the paperwork back to him. "Done." At his surprised glance, she shrugged. "What can I say, I'm fast."

Luke handed her another stack. "Then let's see if you're consistent."

She'd show him how consistent she was. An hour later, she finished. "Here." She dropped the file on top of the map he was charting, and enjoyed his startled reaction. "So, do I get the rest of the day off, boss?"

"No." He pointed to another pile on the desk. "Start on those. Unless you're too tired?"

She'd type the skin off her fingertips before letting Luke exile her to that bedroom again. "I can handle it."

Over the next week, Jade spent most of each day at the computer. Luke dumped plenty of work on her but otherwise left her alone.

Things between them changed. She insisted that they eat their meals together, and he stopped arguing about it. Luke became so in tune with her habits that coffee, iced tea, or juice appeared at Jade's elbow before she thought to get them herself. A few times he noticed her stiffness, and would silently massage her neck and shoulders before they quit for the day.

Those were the most difficult moments for her. Probably for him, too, but he didn't say anything. When Luke touched her, even casually, Jade had to steel herself not to turn and melt into his arms. Keeping her hands to herself was as much of a challenge as the work itself. As a result she worked that much harder to avoid temptation.

Her determination paid off. Within a week Jade had efficiently completed the massive data entry the project required, and once he'd spot-checked it, Luke started her on the next phase.

The computer collated the enormous input, then extrapolated a long series of chart coordinates with corresponding depth measurements and what was labeled "site declarations." All the information had to be separated, sorted by value, and reentered onto yet another spreadsheet. Still puzzled as to the purpose of the calculations—Luke continued to display a distinct reluctance to explain much about them—Jade pressed on.

One night, after a particularly grueling session at the computer, Jade fell asleep as soon as her head touched her pillow. The extra sleep made her wake up earlier than usual the next morning.

Jade stretched, then rolled out of bed and slipped

into her clothes. Luke wouldn't think about breakfast for another hour or two. Since she was already up, she decided to make it herself.

She went into the kitchen, being careful not to make any noise. It would be fun to cook for him, for a change. As long as she didn't accidentally set the kitchen on fire.

She was flipping the last pancakes when she heard Luke's voice coming from the den. For once he wasn't cursing the computer. She could tell by the pitch.

Was he laughing? No, that wasn't it. It sounded like he was talking. How could he be *talking* to someone?

Excitement nearly made her drop a skillet on her foot. If someone had arrived on the island, a boat had come with them. That meant she could return to the mainland and go to the police. They'd have a missing person's report on her, wouldn't they?

She went to find out.

The doors to the den were closed—as usual. She lifted her hand to knock.

"How long before she gets here, over?" she heard Luke ask. Her hand halted in midair. There was a crackling, electrical sound coming from inside the den.

Radio static. Luke had a radio. A *working* radio.

"A week, old buddy, if we're lucky," a deep voice replied through a tinny speaker. "And she's Deanna now."

Jade couldn't move. She stood and stared without blinking at the door, as if expecting it to explain how this could be possible.

"What's the track look like?" Luke asked.

The gravelly voice grew serious. "Fast and jittery. The NHC is watching it like a hawk, over."

Luke cursed, then said, "I'll keep in touch, over."

He'd keep in touch, Jade thought as her hand dropped to her side. Of course he'd keep in touch. The radio was working perfectly.

"So, tell me, how's your new lady, over?"

"She can type eighty words a minute, over," Luke said without a trace of gratitude.

The deep voice laughed. "You're a lucky SOB, over."

"Yeah, she's not entirely useless, over."

New lady? Lucky SOB? Not *entirely* useless?

Jade went back to the kitchen. She set the table for breakfast, hardly aware of what she was doing.

Luke wasn't a lucky SOB. He was a *dead man*.

Her victim appeared in the doorway a few minutes later.

"You're up early." Luke didn't bother to look at her as he poured himself a cup of coffee and went to the table. "Been busy, I see."

Not as busy as he'd been. Jade glanced at the wooden knife rack hanging on the wall. She measured the sharp blades suspended from it with a discerning eye. It was almost worth it.

"Smells good," Luke said. "This is a surprise. I didn't know you could cook."

He had no idea of what she could do, Jade thought. But he was about to find out. She picked up the plate from the stove and carried it over to the table.

"Pancakes?" For the first time he smiled. "What are they, blueberry?"

She smiled back. "Uh-huh."

"Did you find the—"

Jade dumped the plate of pancakes on his head. He sat motionless, in stunned silence.

"Find what? The syrup?" She displayed the squeezable container. Before he could move, she squirted it on top of his head. When it was half empty, she dropped the bottle in his lap.

Still in shock, he caught it reflexively. "What—"

"Or did you want bananas?"

Jade went to the counter and grabbed the bunch. Swiftly and methodically she threw them at him, one by one. It took four direct thumps on his head and face before Luke batted the last one away and jumped to his feet.

"What the hell is wrong with you?"

"What's wrong with me?" She threw the rest of the bunch at his head. He ducked, and the heavy cluster hit the wall behind him with a smack. "What's wrong with *me*?"

"Yeah!"

Jade stalked to the door.

"What?" Luke managed to get one hand on her shoulder before she whipped around and knocked his arm away.

He looked ready to kill her. Good. In the state she was in, that would make it just about fair. She swung around and kept going.

"Jade." Luke followed her out to the front of the house. "Jade!" His footsteps thudded behind her. As she reached for the door to the beach, he exploded. "Damn it, answer me!"

"Let me guess." She turned on him. "You just got that radio fixed this morning, right? Found the parts you needed in a bottle, washed up on the sand?"

"Oh, shit. You heard me talking to Mike."

"Uh-huh. I sure did. You *jerk*."

"Jade—"

"Shut up! Don't *lie* to me anymore! You've been deliberately keeping me, the whole time!" She dropped her hands, straightened, and lifted her chin. "And for your information, you moron, I type *ninety* words a minute!"

Rage-blind, she yanked open the front door and strode out of the house. Sunlight poured over her. The sharp, salty smell of the sea hit her nose. Jade could have been walking straight into a blast-furnace for all she cared. Behind her, Luke called her name again.

But Jade wasn't her name. *He'd* given her that name. The way he would name some *stray*. Did he think of her like that? No, even a *dog* would have gotten better treatment. He'd worked her at his damn computer until she was ready to drop, every day.

Poor Luke. Stuck with a shipwrecked amnesiac. So put out, so put upon. How had he been able to tolerate so much inconvenience? All the accusations, and grumbling . . . and the whole time *poor Luke* was nothing but a two-faced fraud.

She kicked the sand, sending a spray into the air.

The radio didn't work, he'd said. *I can't get you out of here*, he'd said. *We're stuck with each other*, he'd said.

A hungry seagull swooped down to hover in front of her, screeching like a banshee. Jade looked at the tiny black eyes inspecting her, and the bird took off. Too bad she'd wasted those pancakes on Luke's head.

Luke had been lying to her from day one, and like a fool, she'd believed every word. He'd made her feel *guilty*, made her feel *obligated*. The worst of it all, he'd made her feel *grateful* to him, made her *work* for him, made her *care* about him—no. She didn't. She wouldn't. He was beyond a jerk.

Something else made her stop in midstep. If he'd lied about the radio, what else had he lied about?

Jade heard Luke behind her. The man definitely had a death wish. Could she kill someone with her bare hands? It was a real shame she couldn't remember.

Without turning, she yelled, "Stay away from me, you bastard!"

She ran toward the pier. Now she'd see if the boat situation was as true as the broken radio. Jade was almost there when Luke caught up to her. He grabbed her with one sticky hand, and jerked her around.

"Oh, you took the pancakes off your head. I'm hurt."

"Yeah, I did."

"Too bad I forgot to add those hot sausage drippings."

"Where do you think you're going?"

"Let go of me."

He shook her once. "Tell me."

"There." She pointed to the dock. "To find the boat. You know, like the working radio? The one you *don't* have?" She jerked away from him and marched on.

"I lied about the radio, but *there is no boat.* Jade? Did you hear me?"

She didn't miss a step. "I heard you. Get lost."

"I can explain this."

"I'm thrilled. Take a hike."

"Look, I'm sorry I lied to you."

"Sure you are. Drop dead."

"I know it was wrong."

"Congratulations. Leave me alone."

"Will you stop and listen to me? For one damn minute?"

"No. Go to hell."

"You don't know—"

"I don't know a lot," she said through teeth she was trying very hard not to grind together. She stopped, and so did Luke. She punctuated the rest of what she said with jabs of her finger on his syrup-splattered chest. "Like who I am. Who you are. Why you did this."

"I had my reasons."

"Reasons?" She laughed. "There's a reason you lied to me? A reason for deliberately keeping me here? For all the insults and complaints and bitching about your dumb project, your stupid island, and your pathetic privacy?"

"Yeah."

"*Why?*"

"I can't tell you."

Jade could only stare at him at this final insult. "You deceived me, kept me prisoner, made me feel like it was all my fault, and now you won't tell me *why*? You can't be serious. I want to know exactly what is going on. Right now. Start talking. And make it good."

"I can't. Listen—"

She hit him in his jaw with as much force as she could pack behind it. Pain slammed through her knuckles and shot up the length of her arm as Luke stumbled back a half step. Too bad she couldn't knock him on his butt. She could only hope she'd rung a few of his warped bells.

"Shit. Goddamn it." He grabbed his jaw. "What the hell did you do that for?"

"Stay away from me. Unless you don't *like* your teeth where they are."

Fury made her walk. Common sense sent her

away from Luke. She was stepping up onto the pier when he grabbed her around her waist.

"Hold it." Luke tried to pull her back down to the sand, and she kicked him. He held on, swore, then twisted her around and slung her over his shoulder.

"Let me go! Who do you think you are? God-damn it, I've had enough!" She was so mad she tried to bite his shoulder, but she was bouncing up and down too hard. She tried to slam her knees into his stomach, but he clamped his arm over the back of her legs. "If you think pancakes and syrup were bad, just wait!"

"Once we're back in the house, we're going to talk."

"You can't tell me anything more, remember?" She jerked one leg loose and kicked his thigh. He grunted. "Put me down *now*!"

"Shut up." Luke yanked the front door open and stepped into the house. The cool air hit Jade's face like a slap.

"Just what are you going to do to me now? As if I couldn't guess. This won't work," she said, and managed another kick. "You can't weasel your way out of this. Not this time. I'll get loose, and I'll get to the boat, and then I am out of here."

"Goddamn it, there's *no boat*." He walked back through the house, out to the porch, and kept going.

Jade realized where he was headed and strained

wildly. "So help me God, if you don't let go of me, I'll—"

Luke tightened his arms over her legs, then jumped into the pool.

Jade would have yelled, but she was too busy holding her breath. Luke surfaced, still holding her, and jerked her up against him. She held on to him, spitting water in his face.

"Are you insane?" she said as soon as she got enough air. "Yes, you probably are. I can't believe this. How did I manage to get marooned on the only island in the world occupied by a complete maniac?"

"You're a lucky girl." Luke held her against his chest. "Now, quit fighting me, or I'll let go."

Jade tried to smack him, and in the next moment had to grab his shirt.

"I warned you." Luke's hands slid around her waist once more. "You done?"

"I'm going to get you for this," she said, still holding on with a death grip. "If it's the last thing I do. You're going to regret you ever messed with me. I'm going to make you suffer for every second you've kept me on this stupid island."

"I'm sure you'll try," Luke said. "Now, you either listen to me, or drown. Your choice."

"Oh, now you're going to tell me you're—what? Doing classified work? Top secret stuff?" She needed time to think up creative ways to kill him slowly. "Sure, I'll listen."

"Good." Luke shook the wet hair back from his

brow. "I can't let anybody find out I'm here," he said. "Not the Coast Guard, not the police, no one."

"Fine. I'll be sure to dig a deep hole."

"I couldn't radio the mainland for help, because anyone who did come out here would recognize me." When Jade opened her mouth to find out why, he shook his head. "Don't ask me to explain. I can't."

"What about that guy? The one on the radio? *He* knows you're here."

"Mike is an old friend. I trust him. He won't tell anyone."

Meaning she wasn't trustworthy, and he didn't think she'd keep her mouth shut. She looked at him through wet lashes and let go of his shirt to wipe the water from her eyes. "So have your old friend Mike come and get me."

"He will," Luke said. "In two weeks."

"That's not good enough."

"It'll have to be. Look, here's the deal. You're going to listen to me, calm down, and work this out. Or I *will* tie you up."

"Go get the rope. I need some, too."

He didn't like that. "Settle down."

"When hell freezes over." His hold loosened, and she snatched at his shirt again. "Okay! Okay! Fine!"

"I knew you'd understand."

She really might have to kill him. And why was he breathing like that? His arms tightened around her, and she got her answer as she felt him against her. His erection was as hard as the coral rock pool deck.

Oh, no, you don't. Jade turned her face and stared at the side of the pool. "Get me out of here."

"Not yet." He cupped the back of her head and turned her face to him. "There's one more thing we have to settle."

His wet mouth was on hers before she could blink. At the same time, the only arm holding her let go, forcing Jade to hang on to his neck to keep from sinking.

God, he had some nerve. The jerk, the sexy jerk. She should bite him, really hard. But then he might let her drown.

Some things were worse than drowning, so she bit him.

"Damn it." He grabbed her jaw and applied pressure until she let go of his bottom lip. "Stop fighting me." Then he kissed her again, holding her face, forcing her.

She forgot about biting him. Soon nothing mattered but his mouth, and what he was doing to her with it.

Luke lifted his head. "Kiss me back," he said. Immediately she clamped her mouth shut.

"No, don't start that again. Open your mouth." Wet fingers coaxed her lips apart; one fingertip touched the tip of her tongue. "Give me this again."

She twisted her head away. "Cut it out."

"You want to, don't you?" The edge of his tongue delicately traced her ear. He pressed her

hips against him. "Why are you trembling, sweetheart?"

"I'm cold. Stop it."

"I can't stop." His words sounded vaguely
slurred as he brushed feathery kisses over her
mouth. "I can't stop thinking about it. The way
you taste. Your mouth is so soft. Sweet. Hot. It
burns into me. Burn me some more, baby."

His erotic demands were making her crazy. Her
skin felt acutely alive; her breasts swollen against
his chest. His lips slanted over hers again as he
probed, his tongue making those slow, gliding penetrations. The feel and the taste of his mouth were
drugging her, making her unable to resist the lure.
Before she knew it she was kissing him back, open-
mouthed, giving him everything he wanted.

Yes, she'd burn him. The fury over her discovery blended with ravenous need, and she let it go,
pouring the heat back into him. By the time they
were finished, the pool water would be steaming
around them.

Luke groaned, and the sound separated them
for a moment. Jade tasted something sweet, and
licked her lips. Strong arms hoisted her up. Luke's
mouth glided down her throat. She put a hand in
his hair, and felt a sticky residue on her fingers.

Sweet. Sticky. *Pancake syrup.*

"No!" Jade shoved him away from her, and sank
at once. Luke grabbed her and pulled her back up,
but now she fought him.

"Hey—hey!" He hauled her over to the side of

the pool. "What are you trying to do? Drown yourself?"

"*This* from the cretin who just threatened to do that very same thing?" She pushed at his chest.

"Christ." As he had once before, Luke pushed her up and onto the deck. This time Jade didn't wait for him to get out, she wasn't entirely stupid. She pushed herself to her feet and marched to the porch, pausing only once to look back at the pool.

Luke stood on the deck, completely soaked. "Where are you going?"

"To get dried off." She jerked on the handle. "And for your information, I'm *shutting* my door."

One light eyebrow arched. "It doesn't have a lock on it."

"I know. That's why I'm pushing the armoire against it." Jade let the door slam behind her.

The chartered boat circled around the island, which was only a quarter mile in length. The thick growth of trees and brush extended to the water's edge, making habitation, not to mention a landing, highly unlikely.

"Nothing over there, Agent Morris," one of the men called from the chartered boat's bridge. "You want to head back?"

Morris was hot, sweaty, and angry. This was the sixth day he'd spent looking for Carter's accomplice. A dozen more of his men had been scouting the islands for the last week as well, with the same lack of success. A waste of time. Yet he had no choice.

"Keep going," Morris shouted above the noise of the powerful engines. He pulled open the map and scratched through the coordinates for the corresponding location.

Thirty miles away, Laurie Anderson and her best friend, Jeff Carr, were headed for a different spot on Morris's map. Earlier that morning, she'd called Jeff and convinced him to meet her at Anderson Services' dock.

Jeff hadn't been happy about taking a day off work. "Why can't we do this over the weekend, Laurie?"

"I've got to go today, and Dad won't let me take the boat out by myself," Laurie replied. "C'mon, Jeff, it's really important."

Luckily Mike hadn't gotten suspicious about Laurie's restlessness, and had handed Jeff the keys to the skiff without hesitation. They'd often gone out fishing together, and he trusted his daughter's friend to keep her out of trouble.

"Be careful," her father called out from the pier as Laurie released the rope lines and Jeff expertly maneuvered the Grady-White out of dock. She smiled at her father and waved, not feeling the least bit guilty. After all, it was Mike's fault for keeping her in the dark about Paradise Island.

"Laurie, just who is supposed to be out here?" Jeff wanted to know once they had left the marina and headed out into open ocean.

She was secretly glad her father had turned the helm over to Jeff; he was a much better sailor than she was. The son of an affluent Caribbean real estate developer, Jeff had learned to handle boats practically before he could walk.

"I don't know," she admitted as she looked over his brown shoulder at the map. Laurie had plotted their course from the information she'd gleaned the night before at the library. "But we're going to find out."

Jeff regarded her with mild amusement. A head taller than Laurie, he was blessed with a handsome face, a perfect tan, and warm brown eyes. The female university population really liked him. The small gold hoop in his ear and mane of sun-streaked brown hair didn't hurt, either. "Can't stand not knowing what your old man is up to, can you?"

"I just want to take a look," she said. "Dad has been acting really weird lately. Shutting the door during his radio transmissions, meeting with that FBI agent, sending these shipments out. You know. Didn't I explain this?" Jeff rolled his eyes, and she gave him a disgusted look. "Where's your sense of adventure?"

Jeff laughed. "I must have left it back home with my Boy Scout uniform."

"I give up." Laurie plopped down on the bench beside him. "You're starting to sound like my mother."

Her best friend stretched out his long legs before he gave her a sideways glance. "What happened between the two of you, anyway?"

"The usual." She stared out at the waves. "She started lecturing me on how worthless I am. I got mouthy. So she kicked me out. Again."

"Blowing up half the chem lab didn't help, either." Jeff checked their position, adjusted their heading, then sat back down beside her. "What were you trying to do? Kill yourself? You could have really been hurt."

"I should be so lucky." She gave him a sad smile. "You know, you're the only one who really cares about me."

"Bull," Jeff said. "Who threw you a Surprise Birthday Beach Bash?"

"Dad only did that to get me out of his hair for the weekend." Laurie made a dismissive gesture and abruptly changed the subject. "Listen, don't forget to cut the engines when we get within range. My father will blow a fuse if he finds out we've been snooping around, and I'll have to move in with you."

Her best friend gave her a peculiar look. "Aye-aye, Captain."

An hour later, Jeff checked their position on the instrumentation and then scanned the horizon. "Heads up, Laurie." He pointed to a dark green mound in the distance. "There she blows. Paradise Island."

"Kill the engines," Laurie said, and climbed up on the bow. She raised her binoculars to her eyes

and surveyed the west side of Paradise Island. She
stopped when she spotted two people standing on
the beach.

"Well?" Jeff asked.

What was *Uncle Luke* doing over there? Laurie
didn't recognize the small, dark-haired woman
who appeared to be arguing with him. It didn't
make sense. Her father's best friend had avoided
women like the plague for the last year. Her fingers strayed to the gold cross dangling from the
chain around her throat.

Jeff's persistent voice broke into her thoughts.
"So? Who is it? *Madonna?*"

"No." Laurie had to muffle a gasp of shock as
she watched her godfather hoist the woman over
his shoulder and carry her, fighting every inch of
the way, back into the house.

What was *that* all about?

"Laurie?"

She dropped the binoculars and assumed a
bland expression for Jeff's benefit. "It's just a friend
of Dad's. And his wife." Laurie quickly stowed the
glasses in their case. She couldn't tell him Luke
Fleming was on the island. Jeff was a marine bi-
ology student at the University of Miami; he'd
jump at the chance to meet his idol.

Plus it didn't look like her godfather wanted to
be interrupted by *anyone* at the moment.

Wasn't he supposed to be in the Mediterranean
for the summer? Laurie recalled her father telling
her that. And why was that woman fighting him?

Females usually stuck to Uncle Luke like thirsty leeches. Could she be the one Agent Morris was looking for?

Laurie didn't know what to think.

She nudged her best friend toward the helm and tapped the panel. "We better head back."

"We're not going ashore?" Jeff fanned himself with the map she'd plotted. "I could use a cold drink."

"I've got some mineral water over there in the chest." Laurie gave him a wry look. "You don't want to interrupt a second honeymoon, do you?"

"I'm hungry, too," Jeff said even as he restarted the engines.

"You're always hungry." She gazed fondly at him. Good old Jeff, he was so uncomplicated, so reliable. As long as his bottomless stomach was fed at regular intervals, he was happy. "We'll have lunch at my house." She was going to find out why her dad was lying through his teeth about Paradise Island.

Two hours later Mike met them at the warehouse entrance. "I thought you guys would be out all day."

Laurie shrugged but didn't say anything. Mike looked at Jeff. "What's she gotten herself into now?"

"Dad!"

"Not a thing, Mr. Anderson," Jeff said, covering for her. "Just moody. Like always."

After a brief argument with Laurie over how

much cholesterol it took to clog an artery, Mike phoned in an order and treated them all to pizza. Jeff departed soon after they'd eaten, promising to get together with Mike for a fishing trip on the following weekend. Laurie kept quiet as she went back with her father to his office.

Why hadn't he told her about Uncle Luke? Was he in trouble? Who was that woman? Why were they on Paradise Island?

As Mike reviewed the orders, Laurie studied him with a curious intensity. Eventually he stopped shuffling through the stack and settled back in his wheelchair.

"What's on your mind, Laurie?"

"You." Laurie decided to take the direct approach. If he really loved her, he would tell her. "Are you in some kind of trouble?"

Mike stroked his chin thoughtfully. "Not that I know of."

"Would you tell me if you were?"

"Why?" Her father's eyes crinkled as he grinned. "Do you want to give me pointers?"

"Never mind." Hurt propelled Laurie to her feet. She tossed the folder she'd been working on at him. "I'm going to take the truck and go for a ride."

Mike looked perplexed. "I thought you wanted to order in some Chinese, and watch a movie with me tonight."

Laurie turned away before he could see the tears that burned in her eyes. "I just lost my appetite."

She stopped by the apartment long enough to change and call Jeff. He wasn't happy to hear from her.

"I was just there and you couldn't wait to get rid of me." He made a sound like the one Mike made whenever Laurie got on his nerves. "Make up your mind, will you?"

To her complete horror, the threatening tears suddenly burst free, and Laurie began to sob.

"Oh, hell." Jeff groaned. "I didn't mean it, Laurie. Don't cry."

"I don't know what to do."

As usual, Jeff calmed her down and proceeded to coax the whole story out of her. Laurie told him everything. When she was through, he was silent for a few moments.

"Well?"

Jeff cleared his throat. "Why didn't you tell me all this when we were out on the boat, Laurie?"

"Because I didn't know what to think. I still don't." She twisted the telephone cord around her fingers. "That FBI guy spooked me, Jeff. This woman could be the same person he's looking for."

"You don't know that for sure. The guy didn't say he was looking specifically for a short, brunette *woman*, did he?"

"No. But what about the way they were arguing? Uncle Luke actually had to pick her up and carry her back into the house."

He snorted. "I think I know how he feels."

"Very funny. Hey, what if I called in an anonymous tip to the Coast Guard?" She brightened at the thought. "They could go out to Paradise Island and check her out."

Jeff's voice grew cautious. "If your dad is hiding your Uncle Luke and this woman on that island, there has to be a good reason. I wouldn't do it."

"C'mon. If she's involved with international espionage, Dad could be charged with aiding and abetting a federal fugitive."

"Which is exactly what will happen if you send the Coast Guard out there." He sighed. "Laurie, this is serious. You need to talk about it with your dad, not me."

"He won't tell me the truth," she said, getting angry now. "Look, I'm getting out of here. You want to get together tonight, or not?"

"Yeah," Jeff said immediately. "I do. Stay there, I'll pick you up."

"No. My father will be back soon, and I don't want to deal with him. I might end up pushing his chair into the ocean. I'll be at your place in a few minutes." She hung up, and hurried out to the truck.

As soon as the apartment door had closed, Paul Morris hung up the extension in Mike's bedroom. Lucky for him he'd decided to search Anderson's apartment tonight, and had the foresight to pick up the phone and listen in as the daughter called her friend.

He thought about what the girl had said. So Anderson had been secretly ferrying supplies out to Paradise Island. Supplies intended for Luke Fleming, the celebrity scientist, and an unknown, dark-haired woman. Of particular interest was the teenager's description of seeing the big man arguing with the small woman, then carrying her off the beach.

Those details came together all at once. Of course. The location fit. So did the circumstances. His mistake had been assuming an outsider had stolen the prototype, instead of someone who had direct access to the project.

As he passed by the mirror over Anderson's dresser, Morris lifted his head to check his face. He smiled at his reflection.

Now that he had figured out who Carter's accomplice was, all he had to do was report in, then find Paradise Island.

For the next twenty-four hours, Luke saw no sign of Jade. He spent most of that day sitting in front of the computer, pecking at the keyboard with his one good hand. Swearing came in a close second. After hours of futility, he gave up and went to bed.

Luke alternated between staring at the ceiling and walking the floor for half the night. Since he couldn't sleep, he argued with himself.

Okay, so Jade knew about the radio, and was furious with him. Maybe she even had the right to be. He could live with that for the next two weeks. So could she. It wasn't as if he'd beaten her or locked her in a cage. Most women would have killed to spend a vacation in the islands. Especially with the added prospect of being stranded alone with Luke Fleming.

Why did he still feel guilty?

Maybe because she's been working like a slave for you.

She had helped him. Tremendously. There was no doubt in his mind that the success of the project would be in large part due to her work. Hell, no matter what he'd asked of her, she'd done it. Willingly.

And if she's lying?

Luke got up and paced around the room restlessly. There were too many inconsistencies. Her blank, confused expressions seemed instantaneous. She had frequent headaches, especially when she tried to remember something. Even an idiot knew those symptoms indicated a genuine traumatic injury.

Jade didn't fit the part of a femme fatale, either. A woman who wanted to earn one hundred grand in bed usually had some experience. Jade's response to him had been wild but definitely unsophisticated.

One final problem—if the woman meant to seduce him, then why had she backed out like that, both times? The whole point was to get *in* bed with him, not run away from it. Or was it simply some kind of elaborate tease? Luke frowned. One minute she was burning as hot and hungry as he'd been, the next she'd acted like a terrified virgin.

As a result, he'd walked around with a knot in his groin for most of the day. Even now, he felt like punching out another wall. The thought made him flex his sore hand. Not a good idea. He'd managed to control his needs before. But how much longer *would* he be able to keep his hands off her?

Now that he'd had a taste of her? A day or two, tops.

The next morning Jade breezed into the kitchen while Luke was making coffee. She was wearing his mother's lavender jumpsuit. Or trying to. He lifted a brow at the sanguine smile she gave him.

Wasn't she all poise and control today. Little Miss Confidence was cooking something else up again, Luke thought sourly. And he wasn't going to like the taste of it.

She pulled a mug from the cabinet. The scent of herbal shampoo drifted from her hair. "I want to talk to you," she said, and held out the mug.

"Uh-huh." He poured the coffee, then watched as she sat down at the kitchen table.

"You have no intention of telling me why you're hiding out here, right?" Jade's gaze was direct and serene. A sure indicator the woman planned to do something stupid. Luke stepped out of hot liquid range before he nodded. "How's the hand?"

He held it up for her to see. "Still useless."

"I thought so." She took a sip of coffee before continuing. "Okay. I'll make a deal with you. I'll continue to enter the data into the computer for you today."

"You will." His brow furrowed. "Today?"

"Today. In exchange for my assistance, you'll keep your hands to yourself until the Coast Guard arrives." She pursed her lips and tilted her head to one side. "Did I mention you're going to radio them?"

Luke couldn't help it. He choked a mouthful of coffee back into his mug, then laughed. "What?"

"You're going to radio the Coast Guard and tell them to come and get me."

"No way."

"Here's the deal. You do it, or you don't finish your project."

"What makes you think I'll go along with that?"

Jade placed her mug on the table and folded her hands neatly beside it. "Did you know, Luke, that you sleep very soundly? Especially when you've been up half the night, pacing the floor."

Her brisk, sympathetic smile made him go still.

"Then there's the problem with the doors around here. No locks on any of them." She made a tsking sound. "You really should install some. Especially in the den. Computer equipment can be so, well, *vulnerable*."

Luke sent a panicked look toward the den. "You didn't."

She gave him another of those smiles.

He ran. He came to a dead stop just inside the doorway of the den. The monitor on the other side of the room was on, and had seven words displayed on it.

NOT UNTIL YOU RADIO THE COAST GUARD.

"I thought it was cute," Jade said from behind him.

"Cute?" he said, still staring.

"Finding out that, like most novices, you'd used your own name as a password," she said. "Not much of an obstacle, though."

Luke spun around, reaching for her. "What did you do to it?"

Jade took a gliding step back and waggled her finger at him. "Ah-ah-ah. Remember, don't touch."

He dropped the hands but kept coming. "What?"

"I told you I design computers, Luke. Your system's security program is pretty pathetic." Jade calmly studied the condition of her fingernails. "By the way, the password isn't *Lucas* anymore."

"You changed the damned password?"

"Uh-huh. Now there are four codes that have to be entered before you can gain access."

"*Codes?*"

Jade tapped a finger against her cheek and pretended to think. "I'll give you a hint. They're ten-character, case-sensitive, completely random alpha-numeric sequences." Now she gave him a dazzling smile.

"You cold-blooded little bitch."

She shrugged. "As soon as you radio the Coast

Guard, I'll give you the codes. Otherwise"—she waved at the computer—"bye-bye, Luke's Project."

Angry as he was, Luke couldn't help admiring her tactics. "What's to keep me from beating them out of you?" he said, and started after her again.

Jade lifted her chin. "You won't."

He stopped. Damn, he hated her for knowing that. "You're right. I won't. But I won't radio the Coast Guard, either."

She pivoted back toward the kitchen. "Just bellow if you change your mind."

Luke thought for a moment. He had to hand it to her—the woman was as brilliant as she was beautiful. But she wasn't the only one with a brain. He'd better start using his. So she wanted him to radio the Coast Guard, did she? "Jade."

She hesitated.

"I'll make a deal with you."

She turned and waited with a visible lack of enthusiasm.

"Stay, help me with the project, and I'll keep my hands to myself."

Jade smirked and mocked his own words. "What makes you think I'll go along with that?"

Luke resorted to good old emotional blackmail. "I saved your life, remember?"

"You also lied to me," Jade said, ticking that reason off her finger, and each one that followed. "You bullied me, kept me here against my will, attacked me, threatened to drown me—" She stopped when she ran out of fingers. "No, I think you've used that one up, Luke. Try again."

Frustration and something deeper forced the words from him, words that had nothing to do with the computer and everything to do with him. "Damn it, I need you."

Her eyes widened at that. Moments slipped away unnoticed as they stared at each other. Luke saw her hesitate and nearly say something. Then Jade simply shook her head. "No. I can't."

He grabbed her arm. "If you don't cooperate, I'll permanently disable the radio transmitter."

Her lips got white. "You wouldn't."

He showed her some teeth. "Try me."

They stood staring at each other, until Jade made an exasperated sound. "I should have known somehow you'd turn this into a standoff."

"You started it," he said, refusing to budge.

She shook her head, then astounded him by saying, "All right. I'll stay and help."

"Good." Luke released her arm, too stunned by her sudden cooperation to say anything more.

She rubbed the place on her arm where he'd held her, and her expression became solemn. "Just remember your promise."

Chapter Six

Jeff Carr got on the telephone with his boss early that morning, and called in sick for the second day in a row. Then he convinced one of his friends to cover an important lecture for him. When he hung up the phone, he bent forward and gently banged his head into the kitchen wall a few times.

If this kept up, he might lose his job. Flunk out of school. Jump off the nearest bridge.

"What the hell am I going to do?" he asked the wall.

The wall didn't answer. No one else did, either. The only sound in the apartment came from the sofa in his living room, where Laurie Anderson was softly snoring.

She'd gotten so plastered the night before, Jeff had been forced to drag her out of the nightclub and carry her to the car. It hadn't taken much to do her in. Laurie had one of those odd metabolisms that reacted strongly to alcohol. Two shots of straight liquor had put her under the table.

Jeff silently walked back out to where his best

friend lay sleeping. She looked about six years old, curled up the way she was, her hair all in her face, one hand tucked under her cheek. Completely innocent. Utterly adorable. Absolutely oblivious.

When was she going to wake up?

They'd been friends since the third grade, when Jeff had defended her on the school playground. A group of older kids had ganged up on her, calling her names and pushing her around. Jeff had seen the tiny redhead in the center, bravely trying not to cry or back down. A minute later he'd waded in and started swinging. It had cost him a black eye, a bloody nose, and a note home to his parents, but little Laura Rose Anderson became his friend for life.

The only problem was, Jeff didn't want to be her friend anymore.

He sat down on the shabby armchair across from her, and tried to remember when his feelings had changed. In middle school, when Laurie had suddenly developed an interesting assortment of curves? The day her braces had come off, when she'd rushed over to his house to proudly show him her straight, pearly teeth? The time she'd broken up with her boyfriend, and Jeff had stepped in to escort her to the senior prom?

No, Jeff remembered exactly when it had happened. In the third grade, immediately after a teacher had broken up the fight on the playground. Laurie had walked with him to the principal's office, and told him her daddy had recently come home from the war in a wheelchair.

"My daddy is the bravest man in the world," little Laurie had said. Then she reached over and shyly pressed her lips against Jeff's bruised cheek. "You're the second bravest."

After that first kiss, Jeff was a goner.

There were so many things about Laurie that drove him crazy. She had so much energy she practically threw off sparks whenever she moved. That, added to her insatiable curiosity, made her seem more vibrant and alive than other girls.

She was also easy on the eyes. Laurie wasn't beautiful—the red curly hair and freckles on her nose made her too cute for that—but somehow she made blondes appear insipid and brunettes boring. The tiny, courageous little girl had grown into a tall, lean tigress who would have graced the cover of any fashion magazine. Only someone as unpretentious as Laurie could saunter around completely unaware of her looks, and their effect on the opposite sex.

Jeff was no exception. On the contrary.

He'd made sure Laurie never knew how he felt. Jeff had suffered in silence for years. Through every single one of her boyfriends, including that horrible summer when she became convinced she was in love with a dopey-looking guy in her drama class. He'd listened to her talk about them, complain about them, sigh over them. Sometimes he'd even held her in his arms when she'd wept over them.

Through it all, Jeff had been what she needed most: a friend.

The situation with her father worried him. Jeff admired Mike Anderson, and knew how much Laurie adored him. He didn't have much use for Laurie's mother, who seemed to do nothing but criticize her daughter, or abandon Laurie when she needed her most. Laurie's insecurities, and current dilemma with her father, sprang mainly from the hurt and rejection she'd suffered at Meredith's hands.

Jeff wanted to help her, but he also knew he couldn't go on like this. The feelings he'd buried in the back of his heart had grown weighty over the years. Lately they felt like a concrete block. He'd lived with the daily fear that she might go and do something really stupid, like elope with some guy she barely knew. Now he was getting mixed up with an FBI case, all for the sake of friendship.

Friendship. He hated that word. Yet Laurie thought he was nothing more than good old Jeff, her buddy, confidant, and number one pal. High time she found out otherwise.

The truth was, Laurie's best friend Jeff was head over heels in love with her.

In the spirit of their latest truce, Luke prepared and served breakfast, avoiding a repeat meal of pancakes and sausage. He hid the rest of the syrup, just in case.

"You said you design computers," he said as he turned off the stove. "What else can you do?"

Jade tasted the omelet he'd made, then added a sprinkle of pepper before giving him a deliberately bland look. "You mean besides piloting the space shuttle, smashing atoms, and curing cancer?"

"Maybe you were a comedienne."

"Or maybe I was a heart surgeon. Or a professional assassin. Or a serial killer. Can I borrow your knife for a minute?"

He handed it to her. "Be nice."

"Just some of the possibilities." She buttered the toast and handed him a slice. "How about you? What else can you do? In addition to hiding out on tropical islands, lying through your teeth, trying to seduce stray women, and disabling radio transmitters, I mean?"

"Honey, if you ever learn how to swim, sharks will jump *out* of the water."

"Professional courtesy. And don't call me honey."

She was hungry, and ate everything Luke put in front of her. After the meal, they cleaned up together.

"I'm going for a walk," Luke said when they were done. "Come with me."

"Why?" Jade put away the last of the clean dishes and folded the towel she'd used. "Afraid you'll get lost?"

"Why? Would you miss me?"

"Not at all. I'll figure out how to work the radio eventually."

Luke pulled something from his pocket. "See this?" He rolled the oblong component over in his palm. "Doesn't work without it." He replaced it in his pocket.

She acknowledged his cunning with a regal nod. "Smooth move."

"Come on. We've both been cooped up in here too long."

He was right. She'd been stuck in the house for so many days she felt like building a hut on the beach and moving out there, permanently. "Where are we going?"

"For a walk. You coming, or not?"

"I could use the fresh air, but—"

He was already heading for the door. "Then come on."

Before they left the house, he handed her a pair of too-large deck shoes and a straw hat. Jade slipped the shoes on and tied them good and tight. She tried on the hat. "This is too big. Who does it belong to? Bambi or Candy?"

"Who?"

"Your girlfriend. The one who fills this out." She plucked at the sleeve of her jumpsuit.

"I don't have a girlfriend."

She eyed him. "You like wearing lavender when no one's around?"

"That outfit belongs to my mother, and her name

is Deborah. What made you think I had another woman around here?"

"I didn't know what to think. You won't tell me anything, remember?"

"Don't be cute." He took the hat and tossed her a Marlins cap, which fit Jade perfectly. "Let's go."

They walked out into a solid wall of heat. Sweat sprang up all over Jade's skin. It was really hot.

"Wow." How had she missed this yesterday? Probably because she'd been blazing herself. "It feels like an oven out here."

"That's why they call Florida the Sunshine State, honey." Luke pointed to the beach. "Let's walk down there."

"Don't call me honey."

"Okay, vinegar."

It was slightly cooler down by the water. Her feet made a crunching sound. There were bleached shells everywhere, tons of them sweeping in wide arcs over the sand.

"See that?" Luke pointed to a dark shaded area halfway out in the cove.

She squinted. "What's that? Seaweed?"

"No, it's the coral reef where I found you." Luke went on to explain how important it was to local marine life. She was astonished at the amount of detail he related. Latin words tripped off his tongue with careless ease.

"Did they make you learn all that stuff at undersea topography school?" she asked when he ran down.

"Some of it." Luke's expression changed, then cleared. "I like to dive, too."

"You must dive a lot." Jade scanned the inlet as they walked on. "I wish I could. It sounds gorgeous down there."

"Can't swim, can't dive," Luke said. "I could teach you."

"To swim?" That made her shudder. "Thanks, but no thanks."

"Might come in handy." Luke casually folded his hand over hers. "Seeing how you keep ending up in the drink."

Dangerous things happened whenever the two of them got near water, she thought. Things that had nothing to do with drowning. "I'll stick to walking."

His fingers squeezed hers gently. "Don't you trust me?"

"Sure. Just not near a body of water."

He laughed.

At the end of the beach was a cluster of mangrove trees crowded in the sand there, growing extended root systems that reached out to the saltwater like so many hungry fingers.

Jade noticed the ground around the trees was heavily pitted. "What makes all these holes?"

"Land crabs. Hungry ones."

She glanced around her feet in alarm, then back up at Luke.

"Better keep an eye on your feet. They like to snap off toes."

He sounded absolutely serious. Spotting a rapid blur of movement out of the corner of her eye, she yelled and grabbed his arm. Then she saw his face and hit him on the shoulder with her fist.

"That's *not* funny!"

He laughed. "Don't worry. Keep moving and they won't pester you."

"I can't believe I thought they were cute." Cute didn't come in hordes.

At last they cleared the cratered ground. Through a row of squat, thick plants with fanlike leaves, Jade saw a cleared area where a single, enormous tree grew. She was surprised to see ropes hanging down from the branches. Up in the branches she saw what appeared to be a small box.

"A tree house?"

"Fort Fleming," Luke said. "I killed a lot of Spanish conquistadors from that old fichus tree."

Jade tried again to imagine him as a boy. Hard to think of him as anything except Big Bad Luke. "And buried them all in unmarked graves, I presume?"

"When I wasn't hiding the gold doubloons I'd stolen from their ships. Would have been nice to have someone help me draw the maps."

"No equally bloodthirsty brothers?"

"No brothers. Just an older sister. But she was more interested in rescuing the dolls I'd captured."

"Were you lonely?"

"Sometimes," he said. "Old Jake made up for it. My grandfather," Luke added before she could ask.

He reached up for something. Jade watched as he plucked a couple of large, oval-shaped fruits from a low-lying branch. He showed one to her before he put them in his pocket. "Fresh mango. For dinner tonight."

Jade glanced back at the grove. "Gee, I was really hoping for some steamed crab."

"Yell at them the way you did at me this morning. That'll get them steamed."

Further along the bank were a bunch of green sticks stuck in the ground. "That's a bamboo hedge, isn't it?" She walked over to inspect them, touching one smooth cane. "I thought this stuff only grew in the Orient."

"There's a lot of exotics on the island. My grandmother was crazy about plants. This stuff loves Florida's climate. It even grows on the southern portion of the mainland." He reached out and tested the circumference of a particularly large stalk. "Bamboo is a grass, by the way, not a hedge."

"Grass?" Jade looked up at the tops of the canes. "When was the last time you mowed that lawn? During the Reagan administration?"

He just shook his head at her. "Your mouth never shuts down, does it?"

"Nope."

She was surprised by the many different varieties of flowers growing wild. A florist would fall in love with this place, Jade thought as she discovered a particularly gorgeous orchid with spotted yellow petals and a ruffled crimson throat. Fall in love, then mow everything down and make a fortune.

"This is beautiful," she said, caressing the bloom with her fingers. "I wonder what it's called?"

"That's a cattleya domiana, from the Philippines."

Most men would have just called it a flower. "Your grandmother imported this one, too?"

"No. I did." Luke plucked the orchid and handed it to her. "I got it on the big island, near Manila."

"So that's your big secret? Trafficking in Asian orchids?" She pulled off the ball cap and tucked the bloom above her ear.

"Only when I'm not smuggling stolen gems, illegal aliens, or counterfeit money." He reached over, adjusted the orchid, then smoothed her hair around the stem.

"What were you doing in the Philippines?"

"Why don't you want to learn how to swim?" Luke asked.

"Because I nearly drowned the last time." Memories flooded over her, she could see him as clear as day.

"Scared of a little water." Gareth had laughed at her. "It won't hurt you."

"No, Gareth! Leave me alone!"

"All you have to do is get in and start kicking. Come on!"

She could hear her own screams when he'd thrown her in. Lake water filled her mouth and nose, darkness

*closed over her head as she began to sink. If Gareth
hadn't dived in after her, she could have easily—*

"Jade." Luke was there, holding her upright.
"Breathe. Come on, breathe, will you?"

"Gareth." She clutched his upper arms. Her
voice sounded strange, even to her own ears. She
couldn't seem to blink. "Gareth pushed me in."

"Gareth?"

"I swallowed so much water I threw up. I
couldn't stop crying. We had to go back home
early."

"Who's Gareth, Jade?"

"He was—he's—" The memory dissolved into
overwhelming nausea. "I don't know." She pressed
her cheek against his shoulder. "Can't remember."

"Okay, baby. It's okay." Luke's hand caressed
the back of her head. "Don't push it."

"Don't call me baby."

He smiled. "Then don't stop breathing on me
like that."

She let herself relax against him, let him support her. The panic faded, leaving behind doubt,
frustration, and confusion. She rubbed her cheek
against his chest and sighed. It didn't matter. Luke
would keep her safe. Nothing would hurt her, as
long as—

Jade stiffened. Why was he comforting her?
Luke didn't believe a word she'd said about los-
ing her memory.

"It'll come back to you," he said.

"Maybe it won't." She pulled away. "What if I never remember?"

"Calm down, sweetheart." He reached for her.

"Don't call me sweetheart. Why are you doing this?"

He smiled at her whimsically. "I didn't think you minded, sweetheart. Why am I doing what?"

Jade's hand swept out in a half circle. "You brought me out here, held my hand, showed me the island. Why?"

His grin vanished. "I just wanted to take a walk with you."

"Really? So we could get to know each other better? Become friends? Maybe lovers? Or did you want to talk me into clearing the codes off your computer?"

"Christ." Luke gave her a startled look. "This has nothing to do with all that. Wait a minute. What was the third thing on your list?"

He was laughing at her. That felt good. She took the flower from her hair and fingered the soft petals. "I know. You're planning to abandon me here with all the buried treasure."

"Stranded computer designers tell no tales."

The heat combined with the new memories, and made Jade feel wrung out. She pressed the back of her hand to her sweaty forehead. "Unless they're bribed with a cold drink."

Luke studied her face for a moment, then put her cap back on her head. "You're getting over-heated. We'd better head back."

Back at the house, Jade drank a large glass of water and went to her bedroom.

"Take a nap," Luke said. "I'll wake you up in an hour."

She washed her face, then gratefully sank back on the bed. She hadn't slept at all the night before. Slowly she closed her eyes.

Luke didn't come for her, but the past did.

She was working in the Clean Room, during the final phase of the project. The quasicrystal processor performed like a dream. No bugs to work out, not this time.

"It's incredible," the man beside her said. They stood side by side and watched the levels on the main terminal edge past the target range. "This will knock off so many socks the whole country will be walking around barefoot."

"Don't get cocky," Jade heard herself say. She lifted a gloved hand to the screen as the loop of data ran faster and faster. High-speed flashes of light emitted dazzling patterns from the open drive unit. "We still have to perform about a million tests before we can present it at the fall TechExpo."

"So I won't start chilling the champagne bottles— yet."

She heard herself laugh. "Well, maybe we can pop open a couple of beers."

"Why don't we celebrate in style?" The man sounded eager. "You're flying down to Miami for that meeting, right?" She nodded. "I'm taking my vacation that week—"

His blurred, smiling face melted into a chalky, blood-streaked mask of terror.

Jade squeezed her eyes shut, blocking out the sight of Walt.

"I don't have it," he kept saying, over and over. "I don't have it I don't have it I—"

The dream melted into confined, airless darkness. Jade could smell acrid sweat, coppery blood. Walt was whispering, afraid the others would hear, and come for them both.

"Don't make a sound." He tried to smile, and she saw broken teeth. God, what had they done to him? "I'll keep them busy."

She clutched at his hands, trying to drag him with her. "I can't leave you like this!"

"This is my fault. I'll handle it now. Promise me—"

"Jade." Something was shaking her. "Wake up."

Where is it? Where is it? Where is it?

"I have it," the woman who wasn't Jade whispered.

"It's not here! I don't have it!" Walt shouted from a distance. Then he screamed. Over and over and over—

She had to tell them this time. "Please, don't hurt him anymore. It's me, I've got it."

"Jade."

"I have it—I'll give it to you!"

"Come on, sweetheart." Hard hands were shaking her now. "Wake up."

She opened her eyes, and shrieked.

"It's me." Luke's pale face was above her. His

fingers were wiping the tears from her cheeks. "Don't cry. What happened, bad dream?"

She shuddered. "Yeah, a real nightmare."

"Guy with the knife?"

"It was a man named Walter. I know him. He tried . . . at the last minute, he—" Pain slammed the door shut.

Luke brushed the hair back from her face. "Walter was the man with the knife? The one you dreamed hurt you before?"

"No. I don't think so. I'm not sure who Walter is, except that I know him." She pressed a hand to her forehead. "My head hurts."

"Want something for it?"

"No. I don't want pills. I want to remember." The steady, careful stroking of Luke's hand seemed to ease the pain. She wiped away a stray tear. "Did I say anything else?"

His hand slipped down from her forehead to slide under her neck, where he massaged the taut muscles. "You kept shouting for someone to stop. That it wasn't here. Then you said you had it. What were they after? What did you have?"

"I don't know." She sat up, then scooted herself away from him. "The dream—it's gone."

"All right." Luke got to his feet, and propped his hands on the canopy. "Still willing to help me?"

She suspected she was getting to the point where she'd be willing to do anything he'd ask. *Anything.*

"Of course." Jade slid off the bed and straightened her clothes. "What do you want me to do?"

"Come on. I'll show you."

Back in the den, Luke sorted through another stack of reports. Jade sat in front of the computer and quickly input the access codes while he wasn't looking. As soon as he heard the keys being tapped he swung around, but she was already finished.

"You're too damn fast." When she didn't say anything, he thumped a stack of data next to her. "Here. This should keep you busy."

She was halfway through the pile when she heard the radio crackle to life behind her. Jade glanced over her shoulder and saw Luke doing something with the receiver. "Calling your friend Mike?"

"Yeah."

"Ask him if he'll be in the neighborhood anytime soon."

"Keep inputting, and stay out of this," he said, then spoke into the microphone. "WID714 to Marathon WAX237, over."

A minute later Jade heard the deep voice of Luke's friend reply, "Twice in one day? You getting lonely out there, old buddy, over?"

"Forgot to get the latest on Deanna, over," Luke said.

This Deanna again. "Another woman?" She wanted to smack him. "What are you trying for? A *harem*?"

"Quiet," Luke said to her.

Mike said a moment later, "Sorry, what was that last part, over?"

"Never mind, Mike. Did you get an advisory yet, over?"

"Just got them in." Mike read a series of numbers to Luke, then added, "The NHC just went on the air a half hour ago. It's official, Luke, over."

Luke swore, then said, "Track still holding steady, over?"

"Straight as the Seven Mile Bridge, over."

"Okay, Mike, thanks. I'll contact you tonight, over."

"You're in the pocket, old buddy. WAX237, out."

Jade glanced over her shoulder at him. "What is that, some kind of guy club?"

Luke switched off the radio. He didn't look happy. "Huh?"

"The NHC—what's that stand for? The Nasty Hermits Club?"

"No Helping Castaways," he said, and closed the cabinet. "You're going to get me kicked out."

"Me, or this Deanna?"

"You."

"So, who's Deanna?"

"She's not a woman. She's a storm." He went to the wall chart. "Are you going to input, or talk?"

"Yes, sir." Jade turned back to the computer. She didn't see Luke make a new circle on the map above his radio, or the worried look on his face.

As soon as Jade finished one stack, she reached back for another, and knocked off a folder on the edge of the desk. With a sigh she reached down to pick it up, and it fell half open in her hands.

The papers inside were written in Chinese, and a series of English words had been marked at various points in the margins.

"Last expedition 1433 AD." "Admiral Chêng Ho." "Emperor Yung Lo." "Ming Dynasty."

The sight of the Chinese characters made her feel angry. Shuiba . . . no, that wasn't it. But something close . . .

"Let me have that." Luke took the folder out of her hands.

"I can't read Chinese. Even if I could, who am I going to tell?"

He tossed the file aside. "If anyone could find a way, it would be you, sweetheart."

"Don't call—oh, never mind. What's the big deal with the Chinese?"

"Too much MSG in their takeout."

"Very funny. What, there's a big demand for inside information on the Ming Dynasty? Who's this Chêng Ho? Wasn't he the one who invented chopsticks?"

"Jade"—he gave her a frustrated look—"you aren't going to give up, are you?"

"Nope. Not until I remember something, or you start talking. It's not fair. You know plenty about me," she had to point out. "I don't even know your last name."

He gazed at her for a moment, as if deciding something. "It's Fleming," he said.

"That's better. Luke—" Jade took a skittering

step backward, and dropped on her chair, stunned. "Luke *Fleming*?"

The shaggy blond head nodded.

He was Luke Fleming. *Dr.* Luke Fleming, the famous marine archaeologist. Darling of the National Geographic Society and scores of other scientific and archaeological organizations.

"Unbelievable," she said. An incredulous smile spread across her face. "You're really Luke Fleming? *The* Luke Fleming?"

"Yeah." Luke watched her closely. "That's me."

"No wonder you looked so familiar to me. Now I recognize you—God, who wouldn't? But what is a major celebrity like you doing on a deserted island?"

"Vacationing."

"This is incredible. You're one of the most respected scientists in the world. I've even seen you on television."

He gave her a big shrug.

"You're also news. Big news. Hot, en vogue, and absolutely scandalous. The trash press really loves you. Considering how many times you've been in the tabloids, you must be one of the most recognized men in the *world*. So what are you doing stuck on an island out here?"

"I had to get away. Things have been crazy, ever since I found the *H.M.S. Falconhurst* in the South Pacific."

"I remember seeing a documentary about that. Everyone was so excited about the find, and the public just fell in love with you. How crazy has it been?"

"It wasn't that bad at first. Then I started getting bags of mail from all over the world. People hounding me in the street for autographs. Fan clubs in thirty countries. And the photographers, Jesus, they never sleep."

"You made *Hollywood Weekly*'s Top Ten Hunks List," she said. "I remember seeing that on television."

"Yeah." Luke looked down at his chest. "They liked my pecs."

"And there was that article in *People* magazine, too."

"Please." He looked pained. "I agreed to that, hoping it would get them off my back. It only made things worse."

"I seem to remember a full-page photo of you on some boat. You were half-naked in that one."

"I was working on deck, hauling one of the remote cams back on board. That idiot reporter caught me without a shirt on."

That idiot reporter's candid photo had gone on to become one of the hottest-selling posters that year, she remembered. "What about all the rumors that Harrison Ford is going to play you in the movies?"

"My life story." He snorted. "Yeah, some studio called. I told them where to stick their offer."

She grinned. "You're about as popular as Prince William these days, aren't you?"

"You have no idea. The paparazzi has my apartment in Miami staked out. I tried moving during the middle of the night one time. They found my new place in less than a day."

"They aren't the only ones who stalk you. What about all those women? I've seen the way they swarm around you. I heard they've broken into your house and your car and your office building and didn't some teenager stow away on your ship during one of your expeditions?"

"Not for long. We found her puking over the railing about an hour after we left dock."

"The tabloids loved all that stuff. God, they've practically declared open season on you. Didn't one of them come up with that title? What was it—The World's Most Elusive Sex Symbol, right? Didn't that same sleazy rag offer a lot of money for any woman who could prove she'd spent a night with you?"

He nodded, watching her.

"Oh my God." Jade's jaw sagged. "You thought I was a fan? You thought I came here for that?"

He shrugged.

"Well, I'm not!" She shot out of the chair and started to pace around the desk. "I've only seen you on PBS. Why would I chase after someone I don't even know?"

"I can think of a hundred thousand reasons."

"I don't dare kill you. You're too famous to murder. Damn it, I wouldn't do something like this for a hundred grand. Not for ten *times* that kind of money."

"Most of my fans would."

"I'm not one of them." She wasn't so sure about that, considering how many documentaries she now remembered watching. Still, he didn't need to know that. "So that's the reason you've kept me here?"

"Part of it." Luke's expression grew bleak. "In less than two weeks I'm appearing before the United Nations." He paused to take another folder from a drawer in his desk. "A group of archaeologists will be presenting evidence about shipwrecks discovered in the South China Sea. I can't let the press find me until after I testify."

"That's it?" She made an incredulous sound. "What do a bunch of shipwrecks have to do with me?"

"Nothing. But you'd tell people where *I* am."

"Okay, I promise not to say a word." She pointed to the radio. "Call the Coast Guard."

"All it takes is one slip. Then I'd be up to my neck in reporters and fans. I'd never finish in time."

"All this, just to get some paperwork done? Go somewhere else."

"It's not that simple. The press has people in every major city, watching the airports and hotels. Even my colleagues and family are under constant surveillance."

"Buy a fake beard and a moustache. Take a bus."

"I tried that. I look good in a beard. You can see the photos in the May issue of *The Investigator*."

She was nearly laughing even as she said, "Hire a bodyguard."

"I have," he said, nodding, all serious. "Three, as a matter of fact. They all quit. The last one suggested that if I wanted privacy I'd better move to Tibet."

She rubbed a hand over the back of her neck. "I think you took a wrong turn at Albuquerque."

"Look, Jade, neither of us is going anywhere. The minute I step off this island, they'll know. And they'll start swarming again. Live with it."

"All right, so where do we go from here?"

"I'm not going to radio the Coast Guard."

"No, that's not what I meant." Jade sat back down at the computer. She wondered how well-stocked his supply of aspirin was. "I'll remove the security codes. What do we have to do to get this project of yours finished on time?"

Silence. When she swung around, she saw Luke standing there, stunned. He hadn't expected her to cooperate, Jade realized. For once, *she* had gotten the better of him, and it felt pretty good. In fact, the entire situation seemed rather ridiculous. Of all the men in the world to be marooned with— she had to pick the hottest bachelor in the western hemisphere.

"You're laughing at me," Luke said.

"Of course I am. Do you have any idea how

silly you look right now, Mr. National Geographic?"

"I bet Jacques Cousteau never had this problem." Luke started toward her.

"On second thought . . ." Jade stumbled out of her chair, holding out one hand to ward him off as she tried to stop laughing. "You look much more dignified in person." Her hip knocked a book off the desk. Luke only stepped over it. "I mean compared to that magazine photograph—"

"I know." Luke kept coming. "Calvin Klein offered me a modeling contract."

"Underwear?"

"Yeah—stretch boxers."

She kept backing up. "I don't suppose Julia Roberts really asked you to marry her?"

"No. Neither did Cindy Crawford, much to my personal disappointment."

"What a shame." She laughed as she edged around the desk. "So who *are* you seeing these days? Pamela Anderson, or Britney Spears?"

"Not my type." He looked like a man with a mission. "I prefer short brunettes."

Jade turned and ran, her laughter loud and sweet. It was no use; Luke tackled her before she'd taken half a dozen steps. They both went down on the carpet. Luke flipped her over, straddled her, and pinned her arms above her head.

"Still think it's funny, huh?"

"Oh, no, it's not funny at all," she said, before bursting into more laughter.

Luke watched. "Somehow I pictured you having a different reaction."

That only made her laugh harder. "Sorry—to disappoint—you."

He pushed her hair out of her eyes. "Beats the hell out of pancake syrup."

Jade stopped laughing when he bent down and kissed her. "I should slap you," she said very seriously. "Or at the very least, give *The Investigator* an exclusive."

"They pay five thousand per story, but you have to name three sources."

"Do crabs count?"

"I'll check. Later."

Luke slid his arms under her, lifted her up against him, and kissed her again. Jade's lips parted under his on another laugh, then she didn't want to laugh anymore.

He didn't kiss like an international celebrity, or a Calvin Klein model. He kissed her like Big Bad Luke. Cindy Crawford had no idea what she was missing.

It didn't take long before she was kissing him back, pressing closer, moving under him, aching with need. Being on the floor didn't help. She was pinned flat. Her hair got caught between her shoulder blades and his arm, making her wince.

Forget the pain. It was worth it.

Luke pushed himself off her and dragged her to her feet. The momentary interruption cleared her head. She needed to get away from him, now, before this got completely out of hand. When he bent to kiss her again, she moved back. "We can't and you know it."

"We will. In about two minutes."

"What about your promise? What about trust? What about who I was before I got smacked on the head? We can't forget it, Luke."

He straightened and took a step back. "Right. My promise. Trust. Who you are. Damn it." He swore.

Jade retreated slowly. "I'll make us some more coffee."

He stomped off into the den, while she headed for the kitchen. Once there, she reached blindly for one of the chairs, sat down at the table, and groaned.

Oh, God, I can't hold him off for two more days, much less weeks. Despite what I might have been before I landed on this island.

She should be furious over what he'd done. Yet none of that seemed to matter anymore. A strange calm fell over her when Jade realized why.

She *wanted* to stay on the island. She didn't want to leave him. Her hands trembled as she buried her face in them.

She didn't want to leave Luke because she was in love with him.

"Oh, no."

Jade had fallen in love with Luke the Hermit, not Dr. Luke Fleming, the renowned scientist, scandalous celebrity, and poster boy on half the bedroom walls in America.

She pictured the infamous photograph, the one where Luke was standing on the deck of a ship, hauling something out of the ocean. His arms had been stretched over his head, and he'd been straining to pull the rope. Every muscle had been clearly detailed. Sun-bleached hair had fallen in his eyes as he turned to look at the camera.

All that wonderfully grim, sweaty determination had sold lots of posters. No wonder half the women in the world were in love with him.

The press loved him, groupies regularly mobbed him, and super models wanted to go out with him.

How could she hope to compete with all that?

Love me, Luke. I can type ninety words a minute.

No. She couldn't tell him. Not now. Maybe not ever.

Jade went to the sink and washed her hot face with cold water. That helped clear her head. She prepared two mugs of coffee and walked back to the den.

Luke looked up, wary.

"Don't worry," she said. "I've almost forgiven you."

He looked at the coffee dubiously. "You know, I think I'm really in the mood for tea."

"I couldn't find any poison. Have you got any aspirin out here?" She rubbed her temples. "I've still got the mother of all headaches."

After he'd given her a pill from the bottle in his

desk, they went back to work. Jade tried to keep her mind on the project data.

"Can I ask you a question?" she asked. Now that she knew more about what he was working on, the names seemed even more interesting than ever.

Luke looked up from his chart. "Yeah?"

"This Shuiba project of yours, what does it have to do with the Ming Dynasty? I thought all they did was make pretty vases."

"I've been gathering evidence about overseas exploration during that period in Chinese history. It was a unique point in time."

Luke the Hermit grumbled, but Dr. Luke Fleming lectured. The contrast made her suppress a smile. "What made it so unique?"

"Early in the fifteenth century, a court eunuch named Chêng Ho was appointed to command a number of massive expeditions to explore and annex outlying areas."

"A court *eunuch*?" Jade's brows rose.

Luke nodded. "It's true. Emperor Yung Lo gave the admiral complete control of the operation, and his faith in him was justified. Chêng Ho was a genius, who used the voyages as a means of establishing imperial suzerainty and trade bases. His fleet went as far as Madagascar, off the east coast of Africa."

Jade glanced at the old map on the wall. "Did they go to Fu-Chou, and Timor, too?"

"Fu-Chou was where Chêng Ho raised his fleet

and manned it. Some seventy ships, and more than seventy thousand men, in all," Luke said. "Timor was one of the islands the Chinese visited in the Malay Archipelago."

The strange words sounded so exotic. For a moment, she wished she knew more about his field of study. "So these shipwrecks you're testifying about belonged to Chêng Ho's fleet?"

Luke looked down at his chart, but not before she saw the change in his eyes. "Twenty-six of the shipwrecks have been linked to seven major expeditions conducted by Admiral Chêng Ho, yes."

He was still holding something back. Jade could tell from his body language. "So the *Mao*, the *Haixing*, and the *Sha Chengbao* are the names of ships?"

He frowned at her. "What? More top secret stuff?"

"You're from Georgia," Luke said, "or you lived there when you were a kid."

"What?" That threw her completely off balance. "Why Georgia?"

"Your accent and speech patterns. One of my regular crew is a native of Atlanta, and you sound just like him." Luke drank the last of his coffee. "Atlanta is one of the largest corporate centers in the country. It would make sense to work there, given your knowledge of computers."

"I don't think—" Jade concentrated for a moment, then sighed in defeat. "Nothing. I don't know. It sounds familiar, but I can't bring up a single memory of living there."

"What did you do last month, on the fifteenth?" Luke asked.

"I gave a seminar at Duke on drive design." She blinked, realized what she'd said, then laughed. "Lord, where did that come from?"

"You weren't *trying* to remember." He grinned. "I thought that might work."

Excitement made her lean forward eagerly. "Do it again."

"Won't work. You're thinking about it now."

"Damn." She tapped a finger against her chin. "Why would I remember that, and not my name?"

"You remember skills, facts, generalities, but almost nothing of your identity or personal history. It could be due to an emotional trauma, as well as the head injury."

That definitely described the gaps in her memory. "How do you know that?"

"I took a few basic psych courses back in college." He rubbed a hand over the back of his neck. "Do you know someone named Paul Morris?"

"No. Should I?" He shook his head. "This is so frustrating." She pressed her fingers against her temples. Thankfully the pain was nearly gone. "I know I've been to college, I design software, and I teach sometimes. I've been on a boat, I can't swim, I've seen dolphins recently, and then I showed up here in my underwear and a robe. That's it."

Luke narrowed his eyes. "Dolphins? You mean you've seen dolphins from a boat?"

"I dreamed of them, that first day."

"From the port or the starboard?"

Once again, Luke's trick worked. Jade's voice took on a trancelike quality. "We saw them off the starboard. I wasn't seasick, but I'd never been out that far. There was something else—" She closed her eyes and made a harsh sound in her throat.

"You said *we*." Luke came to her and put his hands on her shoulders. "Who was with you? Was it Gareth?"

"I don't know." Jade opened her eyes. "It's as if I'm almost there, and then . . ." She shuddered. "It's gone. It's just gone."

On the east side of Paradise Island, the incoming tide swirled around the stolen charter boat. He had dropped anchor an hour ago, but had waited before launching for shore. No one had emerged from the thick foliage, so everything was going according to plan. Once on the beach, the launch had to be hauled from the water and pulled up beyond the tide line.

Making a path through the tangle of brush took time, but patience was something he had in ample supply. Especially now, so close to his goal.

At last the undergrowth thinned, and the back of the house appeared. He silently advanced to stop below an open side window. There was the sound of a man's voice.

"What did you do last month, on the fifteenth?"

Then a woman spoke. "I gave a seminar at Duke on drive design."

He listened intently. This was an unexpected bonus. It also meant adjusting his strategy. Chang had been specific about how to handle these two, especially when he'd learned who Carter's accomplice was. He was supposed to wait until they were asleep before breaking in and getting what he came for.

Now he could play it the way he wanted to.

He remembered how much he enjoyed working on Carter. It was a shame he'd have to restrain himself this time. Once this was taken care of, however, he'd pay Mike Anderson a visit. The screwed-up daughter alone made the trip worth it. Anderson, being stuck in that wheelchair, wouldn't be able to do anything but watch. After he had some fun with the little redhead, he'd pop them both.

Silently he moved away from the house, and walked back into the brush.

Laurie woke up and found a three-foot-high purple gorilla staring down at her. With a small scream she bolted upright, and clutched the soft quilt to her chest.

"Morning, sunshine," Jeff called from the kitchen.

She looked around, groaned, and sagged back on the sofa. She'd won the gorilla for him at last year's Monroe County fair. She was at Jeff's apartment. Why and how she got there was still muddled. Her best friend appeared a moment later, carrying a large glass of orange juice and a bottle of ibuprofen. He was wearing only a pair of sweat pants, which showed off his lean chest, nice muscles, and impeccable tan.

"Here." He set the glass down, shook out two pills, and handed them to her. "This will help."

"No it won't." Laurie swallowed the medicine, grimaced, and chased it down with a sip of the juice before handing the glass back to him. She glanced at the stuffed gorilla sitting next to her. Apparently she'd used it as a pillow during the night. "What did I do?"

"Before you drank two straight shots of tequila, or after?"

"Never mind." Ignoring her throbbing head, Laurie rose to her feet and staggered toward the kitchen table. It didn't take long. Jeff's apartment, like most of the ones occupied by U of M students, was small enough to pass as a closet.

He followed her and set the juice down in front of her. "Drink the rest of this. It'll make you feel better."

Tousled red hair hung in her face as Laurie propped her brow on her fists. "Two straight shots? Why didn't you stop me?"

"I tried," he said. "Next time I'll club you over the head and drag you out by your hair."

Jeff lazily scratched his chest. He must have been working out, Laurie decided after a sideways glance. She'd never noticed all those muscles before.

"Stop smiling at me," she said. Why was he standing around half naked, when he should have been at work? She made a shooing gesture with one hand. "Don't hover, either. I'll survive. Go on, I know you have to get out of here. I'll lock up."

"I'm not leaving you by yourself. We need to talk."

If Laurie remembered correctly, that was the reason she'd gone with him to that crowded yuppie bar last night. She wrinkled her nose. What had she been thinking, dragging Jeff to a meat market? Or had he dragged her? She wouldn't put it past him to get her sloshed so she'd stay out of trouble.

"No, thanks. I think I'll just go back to bed."

"Laurie." Jeff sat down next to her, and curled his long arm around her shoulders. "You can't hide out here forever."

He smelled good. He must have taken a shower, his hair was damp. So was his skin.

"Watch me."

Jeff's warm brown eyes turned cold. "You need to go back home and talk to Mike. Today."

Home? She had no home. "If you don't want me to hang around, just say so." She shrugged his arm away and drank the rest of the juice. It did make her feel better, but she wasn't going to tell him that. "I'll find another place to stay."

"No one else will have you."

"Gee, thanks." Some friend he was. Furious, she shoved the chair back and got to her feet. "Where's my purse? I'm outta here." Jeff's long fingers latched around her upper arm. "Let go of me."

"No." He sounded odd. "No, I'm through doing that."

Jeff pulled her against his chest, caught her chin and pushed it up. A second later his mouth was on hers, his tongue forcing her lips apart, his hands molding her long body to his.

He was kissing her. *Jeff* was *kissing* her!

Her nerves crackled to life as his kiss deepened. His hands clenched on her hips. Laurie's eyes squeezed shut as she felt him against her stomach. Jeff kissed her the way a starving man would go at a banquet, without restraint or finesse. His fingers stroked her sides, her breasts, her throat. Everywhere he touched her, answering need exploded into life. He wanted her and oh God, she wanted him.

This couldn't be happening. Jeff was her best friend. He was like a brother to her. Wanting him was almost as bad as incest.

Wasn't it?

Jeff tore his mouth from hers, saw her expression, and groaned.

"Jesus, Laurie, don't look at me like that." His hands released her, and Laurie stumbled several steps back. "I didn't mean to scare you. It's just"—he made a frustrated gesture—"I've been waiting for you to wake up. For years."

"Your timing stinks."

"Honey—"

Soul-shaking fear made her bolt. "I can't do this now." She spotted her purse, grabbed it, and headed for the door. "I'll talk to you later." No, she wouldn't.

"Where are you going?"

She didn't look back at him as she jerked open the door. "I haven't the faintest idea."

Then Laurie simply ran.

Chapter Seven

Jade finished working on the computer sometime around midnight, and left Luke to stagger off to bed. The emotional overload and hours of data entry had taken their toll, but it was a good one. She slept soundly without dreaming.

Morning brought sunlight streaming through Jade's bedroom window, but that wasn't what finally woke her up. It was the sound that came with it—a faint, low, droning sound. Bees, she thought, and rolled over. But the sound grew steadily louder, until it made her lift her head from the pillow.

No, it sounded like an engine. A second later she shot upright.

"An engine?" She listened for a moment. "A boat!"

Jade slid off the bed and swiped at her borrowed clothes as she hurried over to the window. The bright daylight prevented her from seeing for a moment, then her eyes cleared and widened.

It *was* a boat.

Jade's heart pounded wildly. A way to leave the island. She could go back to the mainland, learn what had happened to her. But what about staying and helping Luke?

It wouldn't take that long. Once she knew, she could come back and tell Luke everything. Her name. Her past. Her life. More importantly, that she loved him, that she was *free* to love him.

I don't want to go.

She wasn't leaving Luke. Not really. She'd come back, right away. Just as soon as she had all the facts. Without them, there was no possibility of a future with Luke in it.

She quickly dressed, never turning from the window. The large cabin cruiser came to a stop in the center of the cove. Jade heard the sound of the engines die while she fumbled with her buttons. She watched as a man lowered a spade-shaped weight from the bow. Another man stood watching him. Both were too far away for her to make out their features, but it didn't matter.

The boat appeared to be staying, at least, for the moment. It was too bad she didn't know how to swim. All she could do was go out on the beach and try to get their attention. Surely after she explained the circumstances, they would help her get back to the mainland, unless—

"Luke."

Luke would try to stop her. That was a given. If the sound had woken her up, he'd have heard it, too. Unless he was working. Maybe, if the door was closed and he was buried in his research, as usual—

Jade couldn't let him stop her. It was too important. She might have a minute, two at the most, to get out of the house and wave them down. She hurried away from the window and yanked open her bedroom door, ready to run.

Luke stood just outside the threshold, leaning against the wall, waiting.

Busted.

She smiled at him. "Hello."

"Hi." He surveyed her from crown to ground. "Going somewhere?"

"Maybe." She faked a lunge toward his right. Before he grabbed her, she dodged around to the left of him and ran.

"Jade!"

She didn't look back as she headed for the front door, only to see he'd locked and bolted it.

Luke's arms clamped around her waist. "Don't even think about it."

She tried to yell, but he covered her mouth with his hand and hauled her up under one arm. Jade fought him, but it would have been easier to get out of a straitjacket. He hauled her back to her bedroom.

"Meh me oh!" she yelled against his palm.

"Quit wiggling."

Luke carried her over to the bed. On the way, he grabbed the shirt he'd given her to wear yesterday.

Jade found herself flat on her back with Luke straddling her. She'd fantasized being in this position a few times. Just not quite like this. His legs kept her pinned, so she tried to bite the hand still covering her mouth. Luke snatched it away, then tore one sleeve from the shirt.

"Let me up," she said. "Come on, we're pals now, remember? I won't tell them who you are."

He twisted the ends of the sleeve around both hands, and gagged her.

"Now, we can do this the hard way, or"—Luke grunted as she hit him—"the hard way it is."

He tore the other sleeve from the shirt. With a loop and a jerk he tied one of her wrists to the headboard.

"I knew I'd end up tying you to a bed," he said as he tightened the knot. "Stop struggling." Luke eased back and studied the bed frame for a moment. "Your arms are too damn short."

Jade looked up from one corner to the other. It was true; her arms weren't long enough to span the length of the headboard. The gag didn't do much to muffle her acid laugh.

"Stephen King never has problems like this." Luke tore a strip from the remains of the shirt. "We'll just have to improvise."

He improvised by tying one wrist to the other. The awkward position had her head jammed between her upper arms. She arched her back and turned her face to one side, then suggested he do something anatomically impossible with one of King's books.

Despite the gag, he understood every word. "I don't think Stephen would appreciate that." He tested the knots around her wrists. "There. Almost as good as handcuffs."

She kicked him.

"Got to do something with your feet, though."

Jade's expression told him exactly what she planned to do with one of them.

"You can try that later." With the last of the shirt, Luke bound her ankles together. One big hand patted her on the head. "Now stay put. I know what you were trying to do—you want to find out who you are, how you got here. But listen to me, Jade. I just can't take the chance of letting you go now. There's too much at stake. Please, trust me."

Her expression softened.

He grinned. "And once I get rid of this joker, we'll find out if you're into bondage."

The gag didn't allow her to bite him, but she tried anyway.

"Hold that thought. I'll be right back."

The moron had dropped his anchor on the reef, Luke saw as he walked down to the beach. That would tear the coral all to hell. Had to be tourists. No islander would have done something that stupid.

He waited as a smaller launch was lowered into the water off the stern. A few minutes later it came buzzing across the inlet toward the island. There were two men in it, one dressed in, of all things, a business suit.

"Probably needs a battery for his damned cell phone."

The second man wore a wide-brimmed straw hat pulled down low over his face. Charter skipper, from the look of his tan and sun-bleached clothes.

Luke made no move to help the launch make shore. The legs of the stranger's suit trousers got soaked as he climbed out into the shallows. The one with the hat stayed in the launch and started fiddling with the small outboard.

"Good morning." The suit trudged up the wet sand and held out ID. "Agent Paul Morris, Federal Bureau of Investigation. And you are . . . ?"

Luke deliberately folded his arms. "Not interested. Shove off."

"Excuse me?" Morris didn't like that. "What did you say?"

"You're trespassing, pal."

"This is official government business," Morris said. "I'm investigating a highly sensitive case of international espionage."

"Your boat is anchored on a coral reef." Luke kept his tone bland. "You're destroying my highly sensitive property."

Morris glanced back at the bigger boat, then shrugged. "I'm looking for Kathryn Anne Tremayne."

"Don't know her."

"According to my information, a woman matching her description was seen here on the island yesterday. I don't know what she's told you"—he eyed the house—"but she's in a great deal of trouble. Concealing the whereabouts of a federal fugitive won't help you, either."

They'd both been out on the beach yesterday. Twice. "Who spotted her?"

Morris removed a notepad from a jacket pocket and consulted it. "A Laurie Anderson in Marathon reported the sighting. Apparently her father has been bringing supplies to your island, and she became curious. She and a friend of hers brought their boat out here yesterday."

That sounded like Laurie. So Jade was a fugitive, wanted by the FBI. It wasn't entirely unbelievable. The woman knew a hell of a lot about computers. She'd showed up alone, injured, frightened. At the same time, she didn't seem like the criminal type. Luke needed to find out more.

"What did she do? Rob a bank?"

Morris glanced at the house again. "Why don't we talk inside?"

"Got a warrant?" Luke asked. The agent shook his head. "Then we don't go inside."

"Here, take a look at"—Morris fished a wallet-sized photo out of his breast pocket—"this."

Luke took the photograph and glanced at it. The woman he knew as Jade was standing next to a heavy-set, balding man with a cheerful grin. The man had his arm around her. Both wore casual clothes, and suitcases were piled on the deck beside them. A large marina served as the backdrop.

Who was the guy in the picture?

"Well?" Morris asked.

"I've seen her before. She showed up on a boat yesterday, with a different guy." Luke gave Morris a nasty grin while he deliberately rubbed his bandaged hand with the other. "They didn't stay long."

"Did they say where they were going?"

"Didn't ask." Luke resisted the urge to crumple the photo.

"Very well. What I'm about to tell you has to remain confidential," Morris said. "This case is extremely sensitive."

"I'll keep my mouth shut. What is she, some kind of spy?"

"No, though she might think she is." Agent Morris rolled his eyes. "She's the wife of a prominent businessman, Gareth Tremayne."

So she was married.

Morris didn't notice how pissed off Luke was getting. "The husband's computer design firm—Tremayne Systems—is a major government contractor. Evidently he found out she was having an affair, and confronted her. She denied everything. The next day Tremayne woke up and she was gone. Turns out the wife cleaned out their accounts, then went to his plant and stole a valuable prototype. There's some indication she made a deal to sell it to the Chinese government. After that, she took off with her boyfriend for the islands."

"A real calculating little thief, huh?" Luke's teeth clenched. He made himself look at the picture again. There was no mistake. It was definitely Jade. Same hair. Same eyes. Same ring.

"The husband thinks she's had a mental break-down," Morris said. "According to him, she suffers from paranoid delusions—always thinking she's in danger, and that someone wants to kill her. She has blackouts, too. He's had her in therapy for years."

"Is that right."

"Yeah. She's a real nut."

"Wish I could help you." Luke wanted to hit him. "But like I said, I haven't seen her since she took off with this other guy yesterday."

Morris looked irritated. "If she does show up here again, call me at the number on the back of the photo."

Luke wasn't going to point out there were no phones on the island. He wanted the fed gone. "Sure."

"Thanks."

He watched the man climb gingerly back into the launch, where he consulted briefly with the charter skipper. Neither man looked back at him. A minute later they were both on their way back to the bigger boat. Luke stood sentinel until the cabin cruiser weighed anchor, started its engines, and headed back out to sea, before he returned to the house.

"Look, lady, all I want to do is leave a message for Agent Paul Morris. He's working on a case down here," Laurie said. She pressed her fingers against her other ear, to block out the noise from the cars driving past the pay phone. "Can't you just write this down?"

"I'm sorry, ma'am." The receptionist at the FBI's Regional Headquarters was polite, but firm. "As I told you before—"

"Oh, just forget it!" She slammed the phone back on its hook, and stalked off to the truck. Once she'd climbed up into the cab, she sat staring blindly through the windshield at a colorful billboard across the road. It depicted a gorgeous woman in a microscopic bikini, accepting a piña colada from a tall, muscular man in a spotless white suit. Why were the women always nearly naked and the guys fully dressed?

THE FLORIDA KEYS—WHERE TO GO TO GET AWAY FROM THE WORLD.

The sign had it wrong. Paradise Island was more like it.

Laurie didn't know what to do. Her mother certainly didn't want her around. If she went back to her father's place, she'd only end up in a shouting match with him. And after what had happened with Jeff? No way was she going back there.

How could he do this to me?

He'd kissed her. Exactly the way he would have kissed one of his girlfriends. No, from the way he'd touched her, more like one of his lovers. Even worse, she'd liked it. Just thinking about it made her ache, deep down. No boy she'd ever dated had ever kissed her like that. Not even that heartthrob in her drama class who she'd thought she was in love with.

How long had Jeff been hiding the way he felt from her? Was she that stupid, that she'd never noticed? All the times they'd spent together, had he been just pretending to go along for the ride? All the while thinking of what he really wanted to do instead?

Now that she knew Jeff's real feelings, it changed everything. Laurie recalled countless situations when he'd touched her in the past. Jeff always seemed to be putting his hands on her one way or another. Hugging her. Slinging an arm around her shoulders. Rubbing her back. She'd never suspected it to be anything more than simple, uncomplicated affection. It was humiliating to think he'd done it because he had the hots for her.

How could she have been so blind?

She knew she'd never be able to look at her best friend again without remembering. The way he'd yanked her up against him. The feel of his mouth. The way he tasted. Even the smell of the soap he'd showered with. She'd enjoyed it, until she remembered it was *Jeff* who was kissing her, *Jeff's* hands that were touching her, *Jeff*'s chest she was digging her nails into.

When had it happened? More importantly, why? Not that it mattered. Their friendship was over.

The phone call to the FBI hadn't worked. How could she track down the fed, if his office wouldn't even take a telephone message for him? It wasn't as if she could drive up to Miami and leave a note for him at his office. No, she had to find Agent Morris, and convince him to tell her the whole story. But how? He hadn't left a number with the answering service. He'd talked to her father, and then . . .

The sound of Mike's deep voice echoed in her thoughts.

Leave a number where I can reach you, and I'll see what I can find out.

Through the window outside her father's office, Laurie had seen the fed hand Mike something. A business card? That had to be it. For his office was in Miami? No, he wouldn't give Mike that as a contact number. He was working in the Keys; he'd never commuted back and forth. Like most people, Morris was probably staying at a local hotel.

She snapped her fingers. That was it.

Morris gave her father the card for the hotel he was staying at. Out of habit, Mike stuck all the cards he received in a black index box on his desk. All Laurie had to do now was go back to the office, wait until her father went out with an order, go in, and get it.

Laurie grinned, started the truck, and threw it into drive. She'd show her father just how lame Nancy Drew really was. She hit the accelerator, and never noticed the car that pulled out to follow her.

As he drove toward Marathon, Chang Yu-wei noted the large number of cars traveling north on U.S. 1 from the Florida Keys. He could not understand why Americans, like the Japanese, chose to live in regions with such unpredictable and dangerous climates. Surely the preservation of one's life was more important than the charm of one's view.

The one small hole in the shack he'd been born in had looked out on a filth-strewn alley. It had let in the rain and the wind. The stench of the gutter. On rare occasions it had even let in a shaft of gray light to dispel the gloom. No one cared. The men who came to use his mother's body were not interested in looking at her.

Yu-wei recalled staring through that ragged-edged portal, watching the huddled figures who stumbled by. Often he'd watched robberies as they occurred, and had studied the mostly inept methods employed by thieves as they plied their trade. Once he'd witnessed two young men engage in a vicious knife fight, and the subsequent murder of one when the other cut his throat.

Young Chang Yu-wei had made that view into his first and only classroom, and learned from it well.

A horn blared beside the Mercedes, catching his attention. The snarled traffic made him briefly wish he'd brought his driver with him from Atlanta. Yu-wei preferred the calm luxury in the back of his limousine to the exasperating demands found behind the wheel in the driver's seat. Yet it was vital, now more than ever, that he perform these last tasks himself.

His man in the Keys had provided a wealth of information when he'd called the day before. The American claimed Carter's partner was living on a remote island, and had no apparent means to leave it. Even more interesting was the revelation of who Carter's partner was.

When Shandian had made the initial offer for the prototype to develop it, Yu-wei himself had gone to personally present the contract. The reception he'd received had been less than enthusiastic. Laws were mentioned, questions were asked. He'd been forced to withdraw from the meeting far sooner than he'd preferred.

In less than six hours, he would make one final bid for the project data. If his offer was refused again, he'd allow another talented hireling to exercise his considerable powers of persuasion. Once the prototype was secured, all Yu-wei had to deal with was his incompetent subordinate.

From the beginning, Yu-wei had suspected the American intended to retrieve the project and sell it himself. It would explain why his subordinate had killed Carter and the invention of the mysterious partner. Now this latest development, in which that partner had turned out to be—most conveniently—the only other person with access to the project data. All excellent ploys to keep Yu-wei at a distance.

A master of duplicity had no difficulty recognizing the capacity for betrayal in others. Remarkable how the American was trying to do the very same thing Yu-wei had arranged to do himself.

It would be most interesting to hear what the American had to say on this subject, when he returned to his hotel room and found the president of Shandian waiting for him. If Yu-wei gave him the opportunity, of course, to say anything at all.

Jade was still having no luck with the knots when Luke returned.

The bedroom door banged into the wall as Luke shoved it open.

"Miss me, honey?" He had something in his hand. "No use pulling on them. Those are slip knots. They just get tighter."

Jade had already figured that out, from the numbness of her hands. She tried to squirm away as he sat down beside her.

"You never give up, do you, Jade?" His voice was low, lethal. "Or is it Kathy?"

Jade went rigid.

Kathy. Her name was Kathy.

"Coming back to you now?"

How had he found out her name?

"Your name is Kathryn Anne Tremayne." He bent closer. "Pretty, isn't it?"

What was wrong? What had happened?

He reached out, making her flinch. But Luke only stroked her hair. "You're in trouble, Kathy. The FBI is looking for you."

She closed her eyes.

With a few deft motions, Luke unknotted and removed the bonds from her mouth and wrists. "Open your eyes, baby. No, don't look at me like that. Want to hear the rest?"

"Tell me."

He told her. What he said made her feel sick, especially when he added, "You forgot to tell me you were married."

She stopped rubbing her wrists. "Luke, I didn't forget. *I don't remember.*"

"I think I can jog your memory." He handed her a photograph. The picture showed Jade standing next to an unfamiliar man. From the location and the way they were dressed, it was obviously a vacation shot.

"Who's this?"

"According to the FBI, Mr. and Mrs. Gareth Tremayne."

Her stomach lurched. No, she was almost positive she wasn't married to the man in the photograph. But how could she use that feeling as a defense, when she had no other explanation? She said slowly, "No, that can't be right."

"Then who is he?"

It hit her then. "His name isn't Gareth. It's Walt. Remember, when I had that nightmare?" She handed the photo back to him and shook her head. "I'm not sure, but I think he's dead."

Callused palms held her face still as he looked at her. "Are you lying to me?"

"No."

"It doesn't matter. I don't care who the guy in the photo is. You belong to me."

She wanted to tell him she loved him. But what if she had come here, trying to escape the authorities, hiding from a husband she couldn't remember? "Let me leave the island. I'll turn myself in."

One long finger slowly traced the wet path of a tear that had spilled down her cheek. Suddenly Luke thrust himself up off the bed. A moment later, her legs were free. Then he walked out of the room.

Jade followed after a minute. She had to convince him to let her go back to the mainland, to find out if what the agent said was true.

"Luke?"

He was standing at the porch door, looking at the pool. "Forget it, Jade. You're not going anywhere."

"On the contrary," a calm voice said as the front door of the house opened. A blond-haired man in a suit stood there, looking determined. "She's under arrest."

A half hour later, once Agent Morris finished

reading her her rights and questioning her, Jade
was still trying to grasp it all.

"Tell me something, Agent Morris." Luke had
been pacing around the room while the other man
had interrogated Jade. Now he stood in front of
them, his expression pure stone. "Why didn't the
boyfriend come after her?"

"In his statement, he indicated both of them had
been drinking heavily, and had a fight over the
money," the agent said. "She split the cash, took
the component with her, and headed for this island. He was angry, and drunk, so the boyfriend
took off. When our people picked him up in Key
West, he couldn't remember exactly where Kathryn
had gotten off the boat." Morris shrugged, dis-
missing the unknown lover. "He was smart enough
to confess and make a deal. You should do the
same, Mrs. Tremayne."

"What about my husband?" Jade asked.

"He's cooperated fully with the Bureau." The
fed patted her shoulder. "Just tell me where you've
hidden the prototype, Mrs. Tremayne, and I should
be able to reduce the charges against you and
Gareth."

"You're charging the husband, too?" Luke asked.

"Unless Mrs. Tremayne makes a statement on
his behalf, clearing him of any involvement, he
faces the same conspiracy charges." Morris turned
his attention to Jade. "What do you say, Mrs.
Tremayne?"

"I'm still not sure what happened." Until she

knew more, she wasn't going to tell him about Walt, or her nightmares. "I recognize my name, and the name Gareth. I know the man in this photograph." She rubbed her temples with the tips of her fingers. "I don't remember what or where this prototype is."

"What about the boyfriend?" Luke asked. "What if he came after her, and took it from her?"

"We've searched him, and the boat. He doesn't have it. You know, when that clown told me you took off wearing a bathrobe and hardly anything else—" Morris chuckled. "You two must have really put the booze away."

That seemed to confirm it all. How else could the agent have known what she'd been wearing? Could she have done all that? Stolen from her husband, run off with another man, gotten so drunk she'd nearly killed herself? What kind of a woman was she? What had made her do this stuff? Greed? Boredom? And how was she going to make up for it? What was she going to say to her husband?

Jade's head pounded. "What happens now?"

"I'm going to take you and this man back to Miami. You'll have to undergo a psychiatric evaluation, Mrs. Tremayne. Once we've established your mental condition, you'll be transported to our field office in Atlanta for the arraignment. If you've already sold the prototype to the Chinese government, you'll do some federal time."

It was all true. She was really going to jail.

"I still haven't seen an arrest warrant," Luke said.

"There wasn't time to get one." Agent Morris showed the first signs of impatience. "I can go back to the mainland and get it, of course. However, that won't help her case. Or your involvement in it."

"Luke had nothing to do with this."

"We'll assume that, for now." Morris put one hand on her back. "It's time to go."

Jade glanced at Luke, saw his expression. "All right. May I have a moment to wash up first?"

Morris nodded, and she left the room. Once inside her bedroom, she closed the door and leaned back against it. Slowly she slid down until she sat on the floor, cradling her knees with her arms.

The FBI agent's voice kept ringing in her ears.

She'd had a husband . . . an affair . . . stolen government property . . . run away with her lover . . . *you must have really put the booze away.*

"Why can't I remember it?" If it was true, her life was ruined.

Wearily she pushed herself up from the floor and went into the bathroom to wash her face. This time she didn't bother to look at the woman in the mirror. Whoever she was, Jade didn't want to know her.

Yet why, *why* did it feel so wrong when she thought of herself as a married woman, adulteress, and thief? How could she have done all those terrible things? Had she hated Gareth that much?

No, her heart answered. I loved Gareth. I loved him. I'll go back, and deal with the mess I've made of my life.

It wasn't much comfort, but at least she could begin repairing the damage she'd done. She owed her husband that much. She owed Luke even more. Maybe someday she could come back here, and face him again.

If she ever got out of prison.

"So this is the life, huh?" Morris said to Luke as he looked out through the front windows at the inlet. "How's the fishing?"

Luke was in no mood for small talk. "I don't fish."

"Nice pool." Morris had strayed toward the back of the house, and stood looking out at the deck. "Bet that set you back a good chunk of change."

"Yeah." Luke didn't trust the man. Morris came on just a little too strong. Then there was his story. Even with the identifications and photograph, there were too many holes. Backgrounds could be checked. ID forged. Photos retouched.

He didn't know much about Jade, but he knew she couldn't have done what Morris had claimed. But how could he prove that? She couldn't remember what she *had* done.

"Use it a lot?"

Luke's opportunity appeared like a gift-wrapped present. "I can't keep Jade—Kathryn—out of it." The other man was unable to see his slow, menacing smile. "Guess she's used to that, what with that big pool she had back home in Atlanta."

"Yeah, Tremayne put it in especially for her. Said she used it every day." Morris shook his head sadly. "Guys like that spoil their women."

"Every day, huh?"

Morris must have picked up on something in Luke's voice, for he glanced back at him cautiously. "Far as I know."

"That's interesting." Luke smiled. "Because *Mrs. Tremayne* nearly drowned when she fell in mine."

Morris tried to cover his mistake. "Well, naturally—I mean—she could have—"

"You screwed up, pal. She doesn't know how to swim." Luke advanced on Morris, not bothering to hide his fury now. "Next time, do the research. Who sent you after me? Was it the Chinese? Or was it OPEC? Start talking."

"Back off," a new voice said, and Luke's head whipped around. The charter skipper walked out of the kitchen, the gun in his hand pointed directly at Luke's chest.

"About time!" Morris said as he pulled out his own weapon and trained it on Luke. "He knows, Carlos."

"What gave it away?" Carlos wanted to know.

"Chang never told me the broad couldn't swim," Morris said. "She's back in the bedroom—go get her."

Chang—that meant the Chinese were involved.

"Why do you need her?" Luke asked. "You've got me. Leave her here."

Morris smiled. "Why would we want you, Fleming? *She's* the one we came for."

So it *was* about Jade. "You're not taking her anywhere."

Morris moved forward with confidence. "Feel free to try and stop me. Please."

Carlos went around them and disappeared down the hallway.

"Who is she?" Luke asked, trying to stall. "Why do you want her?"

"She's nothing but an interfering bitch." Morris's smile turned sinister. "Tell me, is she any good in the sack?"

"She's not back here," Carlos called from the bedroom. "Where—" His voice was cut off by a huge crash, then a heavy thud.

That distracted Morris, just long enough. Luke tackled him. Morris's gun dropped from his hand and slid across the floor. As it bounced into a baseboard, the weapon fired.

"Luke!" Jade screamed.

"Get out of here!" he yelled back as he wrestled Morris. Morris's heavy fists slammed into the sides of Luke's head, but he held on.

Out of the corner of his eye, Luke saw Jade coming toward them, a porcelain bowl in her hands. She must have used the pitcher on Carlos. Resourceful woman. He was going to strangle her, just as soon as he pounded Morris to a pulp.

Morris smashed an elbow into Luke's face, twisted free, and went after Jade. She threw the bowl, but Morris ducked just in time. The porcelain smashed on the floor behind him. Luke struggled to his feet.

"Bitch." Morris backhanded her with his closed fist, sending Jade to her knees.

"Get away from her." Luke swiped the gun from the floor. Morris ran for the front door and disappeared outside. "Jade, stay here!"

Outside Luke caught up with Morris just as he was getting ready to push the launch into the water. He jerked him around, and punched him in the face. Flailing wildly, Morris fell back into the water.

Luke wasn't finished. With a feral laugh he lifted him up by the front of his suit and hit him again. He grinned at the sound of Morris's nose breaking, and pulled back his fist to do some more rearrangement.

"Luke!" Jade was there, splashing through the knee-high waves, tugging at his arm frantically.

Couldn't the damn woman do what he said for once? "Get back inside!"

She didn't. "That's enough!"

He let go of Morris, who fell to his knees.

"Jesus, look at your hand. Don't hit him again, you might break it this time."

He examined the damage. His hand was throbbing, the knuckles split open again, and it never felt better. Nothing like seawater and pounding the hell out of someone for an old wound. He saw the launch drifting into deeper water and went after it.

"Oh my God," Jade said. Then she screamed, "Luke!"

He spun around just in time to watch Carlos raise his gun and fire it. Something fast and powerful slammed into him. Luke reeled back against the waist-high waves, then slid under the water.

When she arrived at the office, Laurie discovered her father was already out picking up orders around town. Getting the card from the box on her father's desk took only a minute. She called the hotel at once, got the room number, and even learned Morris was expected to be out for the day.

Quickly Laurie wrote a note for Mike, telling him she'd decided to spend the afternoon shopping. From there she took the warehouse truck and drove to the other side of Marathon to Agent Morris's hotel.

Getting into the room was even easier. Laurie watched from one end of the building as the cleaning crews worked their way down the long rows of rooms. When the cart stopped in front of Morris's room, she walked down to the door and breezed inside.

"Hi," Laurie said to the woman making the bed, startling her. Deliberately she dropped her purse and keys on the bedside table. "Don't worry about tidying up now. I'd really like to take a nap."

The cleaning woman smiled and offered her extra towels before she left. Laurie thanked her and took two.

As soon as the door closed, Laurie let out a huge sigh of relief. It had worked. Now all she had to do was wait for him to show up. In the meantime, maybe she could snoop around, find out what Agent Morris was up to.

Laurie methodically went through the drawers and closet, but found little more than clothes and personal grooming supplies. From the collection of bottles in the bathroom, the guy was really obsessed with his hair.

That was when someone knocked on the door, and she froze.

"Laurie?" a low voice said. "Open the door. Now."

With stiff, jerky steps she strode across the room and yanked open the door. "What are you doing here?"

Jeff stepped inside and closed the door behind him at once. He scanned the room, then spotted the suits in the closet. He pushed past her and went immediately into the bathroom. When he came back out, he looked ready to choke her.

"Who is he?"

"What are you talking about?"

His dark brown eyes were flat with rage. "The guy you're going to meet here. Who is he?"

"I'm not meeting *anyone*."

"Those suits aren't your size, Laurie. Plus you don't use aftershave. Who is he?"

"This *room* belongs to that FBI agent, Morris."

"You *are* insane." Jeff made a disgusted sound. "What are you trying to do? Get yourself sent to a penitentiary?"

"I want to know what kind of trouble my father is in!" she said, and gave him a push. "I don't need your help, either. So get lost, will you?"

"Laurie, if you think—"

They both froze as someone else knocked on the door. Laurie lifted a finger to her lips and pointed to the closet. "In there," she mouthed the words.

Jeff gave her a furious look, and shook his head.

"Do it, or so help me God, I'll start screaming." When he didn't move, she took a deep breath. At last Jeff pushed past her impatiently and ducked into the cramped closet.

"Don't open the door," he said.

"Shut up." Laurie closed the door in his face. She turned in time to see the room door swing open.

An Oriental man with silver hair stepped inside. He was tucking something in the pocket of his immaculate gray suit when he spotted Laurie standing on the other side of the room.

"Who are you?" he asked, his black eyes surveying her thoroughly. "What are you doing here?"

"I'm Laurie Morris. This is my room," she said, then rushed to add, "My husband stepped out for a minute, but he'll be right back."

"Will he?" The man seemed slightly amused.

"You have the wrong room, mister." Quickly she went around the bed and picked up the telephone. "Why don't I call the front desk and get the right room number for you?"

"That's not necessary."

"No, really, I don't mind." Laurie looked down at the telephone for the dialing instructions, then found the man standing over her. She gave him a bright, helpful smile. "Who are you looking for?"

"Your husband."

Yu-wei gently took the phone out of her hand.

Chapter Eight

Jade woke up on the deck of a boat. Her head was pounding, her stomach roiling. Instinctively she turned on her side as bile filled her mouth.

Someone swore. "Paul? Paul! She's throwing up! What do I do?"

Another voice said, "Carlos, you've got to go back and search the house."

The other man muttered something in Spanish. "You didn't hear what I said. The girl's puking!"

Morris swore this time. "Get her below, will you?"

Someone grabbed her arms and dragged her across the deck into a dark cabin.

"You gotta throw up again?" she heard Carlos ask. She shook her head. "Okay. Stay put."

For several minutes Jade lay on the floor, unable to sort out what had happened. Disjointed images and voices filled her head. The boat. Luke tying her up. Morris.

Don't move.

The echo of Luke's low, harsh voice made her press a trembling hand to her head.

I like how your hair feels.

Where was he?

I'll take care of you. I'll give you what you need.

She covered her face with her hands. Why did her head hurt so much? Her clothes were still damp from seawater.

Luke yelling at her. *What are you trying to do? Drown yourself?*

Surely this wasn't her fault. She'd run after Luke and Morris . . .

He had used his fists on Morris. *Get back inside!* A shuffling sound behind her. Turning. Seeing the other man holding something . . .

Her own scream. "Luke!"

The dark, undulating stain billowing beneath the waves. She'd stared at it, unable to believe her eyes. Then the terrible blow at the back of her head, the way she'd fallen into the water. She'd wanted to die. Had been ready to die.

Now she remembered why.

Morris's partner, Carlos, had been holding a gun.

He'd shot Luke.

Oh, God.

Luke was dead.

Jade pulled herself up and stumbled through the dark cabin until she found the head. Just in time. She vomited until she could only heave. Then she slid to the floor and pulled her knees up against her chest.

They'd killed him. He was dead.

"No. He can't be." But she'd seen the blood on the water, watched his body disappear. "No, not Luke, not like this, please God please."

Nothing banished the memories. They remained, bright and fresh as a new wound. Her mind raced in an endless loop. Her fault. The man she loved was dead. Killed by the men who had come for her. Her fault.

A strange coldness fell over her. It didn't dull the excruciating pain, but promised an end to it. She'd witnessed a murder. No matter what they wanted, they couldn't afford to let her live.

These men were going to kill her.

That was fine with her. Luke was gone. Her life would soon be over. She really didn't want to live any longer. Not in a world without Luke. Not knowing she was responsible for his death.

No, an alien voice sneered inside her. *Still trying to hide from all of it, aren't you? Coward.*

"Luke." She couldn't move. Couldn't weep. "I'm sorry. I'm so sorry."

The small light in the head suddenly snapped on. Jade didn't move. Didn't care if they shot her right there. It was only what she deserved.

Someone bent down over her. "So this is where you're hiding."

A hand tangled in her hair and dragged her out from the small bathroom. Instinctively she fought at first, clawing at his hand and arm, until he kicked her. Wrenching pain drove the air from her lungs.

"Hello, Kathy," Morris said as he dragged her to her feet. He gave her a hard shove and she fell back on a bench seat by the wall. The interior cabin light snapped on. He was holding a gun. "Good to meet you at last."

Jade stared at him with dull eyes, clutched her aching ribs, and said nothing.

"Aren't you happy to see me?" Morris stuck the gun in the back of his trousers, then pulled up a chair and sat down in front of her. "We'll have to get to know each other better now. I already know one thing." He touched his badly swollen nose. "Your taste in men sucks."

Luke must have broken it, Jade thought, then stared at the wall behind Morris's head. She could smell blood, liquor, and rank sweat on him.

"A shame they keep ending up dead," Morris went on. "I thought Walter was too stupid to try anything. He must have slipped it to you before he got you off the boat." His pale eyes glittered as he laughed and produced a sharp-looking knife. "You missed the best part."

Why did the sight of the knife make her sick, when the gun had barely made an impression?

The tip of the knife lightly traced down the length of her nose, then over her cheek and down the side of her neck. "Took some time to track you down, too."

Tired of listening to his pleasant killer's voice, Jade met his gaze. "What do you want?"

"You know, Kathy."

She looked blankly at him.

"So the amnesia wasn't an act, huh?" Morris whistled and edged the chair a little closer. "Do you want me to tell you the story of your life? It isn't very interesting."

"I want you to die," Jade said. "Badly."

"Funny. That's what I was thinking about you." He got to his feet and went to the door. She heard the sound of the lock turning. "Now, let's talk."

She had nothing more to say.

"Carter gave you the SOAR prototype." Morris positioned the knife an inch from her right eye. "Where is it now?"

The name sent another shaft of pain through her chest. Still, nothing he did would force her to help him. Even if she knew what he was talking about.

He jerked her head back and made her look at him. "Tell me what you did with it. Now."

Kill me, she thought, and remained mute.

Her continued silence earned her a hard back-handed slap. Jade would have been thrown to the floor if Morris hadn't held on to her hair. Tears of pain streamed from her eyes as her cheek began to swell.

"I don't want to hurt you." Morris gently caressed her bruised face with the sharp blade. She could hear it scraping over her skin. "Talk to me, Kathryn."

After a few seconds, he slapped her again. This time her teeth cut into the side of her cheek, and she felt blood trickle from the corner of her mouth.

"Did you hide it somewhere on the island? Or is it in Fleming's house?"

He waited a full minute, then hit her with his fist. Pain exploded just beneath Jade's right eye. A veil dappled with bursts of light and patches of darkness blocked her vision, and she sagged beneath his hand. Her ribs ached in dull harmony with her face. If he punched her one more time, she'd probably lose consciousness.

That was fine with her.

Morris's eyes came to her level as he kicked the chair out of the way and knelt down before her. He grabbed her chin to study her face. The feel of his fingers on her skin made her want to vomit again. Luke had been killed, just so Morris could get to her, to do this. He'd murdered the only man she'd ever loved.

Scalding rage slowly boiled up inside her. She wasn't going to die. Not right away. Not without avenging Luke. Life and purpose poured into her. Made her stare up at Morris.

Morris misread her expression and grinned. "Scared? You should be. Where is it?"

"The prototype?" If he spread his legs just a little farther apart, she might be able to kick him in the groin. "I don't know."

"I can do this all day, Kathryn," he said. A warm

glow lit his close-set eyes. "In fact, I'm looking forward to it."

"You're going to kill me," she said, preparing to ram her leg into his crotch. "Why should I tell you anything?"

"You're very delicate." He nodded toward the locked cabin door. "Carlos will be done searching the house soon. He'll want to take his turn. But he'll have to wait." Morris ran his tongue over his lips and studied the opening of her jumpsuit. "It'll be a while before I'm finished with you."

Luke crawled up from the edge of the water, rolled on his back, and stared at the mangrove canopy above him. With a groan he pushed himself up, and checked the position of the boat. Still there, right over the reef.

Jade. The men had taken her.

After Morris's partner had shot him, he'd allowed himself to sink out of sight. Once below the surface, Luke swam silently along the bottom until he was far enough away to risk coming up for air. Morris and Carlos must have assumed he was dead, for they'd never seen Luke as he'd briefly surfaced to fill his lungs.

Conscious that he could still be spotted, Luke crawled on his belly over the carpet of knobby roots and into the brush. Only then did he lurch to his feet and look out at the cove.

Morris and Carlos were already speeding on the launch toward the anchored boat. When they reached it, he saw Morris climb on board, then lean over the side. He watched Carlos lift Jade up onto the boat, then climb up himself.

He would have gone after them, but by then Carlos returned to the launch and headed back to shore. Probably to search the house. That would buy him some time. He had to get to the storage shed.

He felt blood running down his arm, and checked the gunshot wound. The bullet had gone clean through his bicep. He flexed it, grimaced, and watched the blood pulse out of the wound. He'd have to deal with it before he went after them.

Carefully Luke crouched over and worked his way through the mangroves, keeping out of sight. Once he was clear, he broke into a flat run. Alone, Jade didn't stand a chance against Morris. Every second Luke delayed getting to the boat gave Morris more time to work on her.

He'd get her back. And if Morris so much as breathed on her the wrong way, Luke would rip him to pieces.

He circled around the back of the house to the aluminum shed, ducked inside, and got his gun. He heard scuffling and thumping sounds across the yard as he came back out. From the direction, it appeared Carlos was in Jade's bedroom, tearing it apart.

Soundlessly Luke entered the house through the porch, and made his way toward Carlos. Once there, Luke kicked the door in, aimed the barrel at the astonished man's heart, and fired. The only sound that came from the gun was a soft, short hiss.

With a grunt, Carlos crumpled to the floor.

Luke spun on his heel and went from there to the den. The radio crackled to life under his hand as he made the call to Marathon. Mike Anderson responded at once. Luke changed frequencies several times while he explained the situation in terse sentences.

"I can be there in two hours." Mike's deep voice lost its usual inflection of humor. "What do you want to do with these guys, over?"

Luke told him. That took more frequency changes.

"Christ Almighty." Mike was silent for a few seconds. "All right, Luke, I'll do it. You going after her now, over?"

"Yeah." Luke paused. "If this doesn't work, don't waste any time here. Find her, Mike. Whatever it takes, over."

"Count on me, over. Anderson out."

Luke turned off the radio and went to the kitchen for the first-aid kit. He cleaned out the bullet hole with peroxide, then bandaged it. Blood in the water would attract sharks; they could smell it from half a mile away. To prevent that, Luke used an old diver's trick. He doused the gauze around his arm with vinegar, sucking in his breath at the burn. Then he bound the saturated bandage with plastic wrap. Finally he sealed the edges with duct tape.

A quick trip back to his storage shed provided the rest of what Luke needed. He changed, belted what he could to his waist and dumped the rest in a waterproof bag. Once he'd checked his equipment, he headed back to the mangroves.

Morris's knife sliced into the neckline. Fabric parted as he cut it open to Jade's waist.

He was breathing hard now. "I didn't have this much fun with your friend Carter," Morris said. A strand of hair fell into his eyes, and he carefully patted it back into place. "Remember old Walt now?"

In that instant, she did remember. Everything came back to her: Gareth. Morris. Walt. The *prototype*. She had done her best to keep it from falling into the wrong hands. Walter Carter had died for the same reason.

Maybe it was best that Morris kill her now, Kathryn Anne Tremayne thought wearily.

"Do you like this?" Morris grabbed her breast. "Or should we cut to the chase, Kathy?" He pulled her down on the deck, and ripped the tear to the crotch.

She wasn't Kathy, she thought. Not anymore. She'd become Jade. For these last minutes of life. That was who she'd be. For Luke. All she had to do was go back to that quiet abyss. The place that had kept her from remembering the horror.

Something heavy thudded against the cabin door. Morris's hands stilled.

"I'm not done yet, Carlos," he yelled, then went back to working the ruined jumpsuit over Jade's hips.

The cabin door burst open, and a man came in. He was wearing a wet suit. Seaweed hung off his mask and shoulders. In his hand he carried a large gun, which he stuck in the wide utility belt around his waist.

"You are now," a distorted voice from behind the mask said.

Morris thrust Jade to one side, his battered face set in ugly lines as he went after the other man with his knife. A moment later he staggered across the cabin, collapsing against a bench with a hand pressed to one eye. With a roar he thrust himself up and lunged again.

Why were they fighting over her? Jade pulled her clothes back on and crawled awkwardly out of the way.

The two men fought, grappling for control of the knife. At last Morris pushed the other man off and slashed at him, forcing him back through the door and onto the deck.

She had to get up. This might be her only chance.

She got to her feet and stumbled out to the deck. The two men were wrestling against the side of the boat. Morris was pushing the other man backward over the railing. The knife in his hand gleamed as it came down.

Let them kill each other, the cold voice inside her head said. *Do it now. You'll have a better death than Walt had, than Luke had.*

She went to the other side of the boat, and stared down at the water. God forgive her for doing this, but she had to. She wanted to be with Luke—wherever he was. Ignoring the groans and choked breaths behind her, she planted her hands on the railing.

"Scared of a little water."

They'd been camping out in the Blue Ridge mountains, and stopped at a beautiful lake for the weekend. Gareth had laughed at her for being afraid. "It won't hurt you."

Her parents had gone on a hike, and left them alone at the campsite. It had been Gareth's idea to go swimming. Now facing the huge expanse of the water, ten-year-old Kathy had balked at the last minute.

Gareth had picked her up in his arms and carried her to the edge. The closer she got, the more frantic Kathy had become.

"No, Gareth! Leave me alone!"

"All you have to do is get in and start kicking." He waded in until the water reached his hips. "Come on!"

She could hear her own screams of terror when he'd dropped her in. The lake water filled her mouth and nose, the darkness closed over her head as she began to sink.

Who is Gareth, Jade?

We were children. Only children. Gareth didn't

know how much he'd frightened her. And later, he'd even tried to make up for it.

I can do this, she thought. For Gareth. For Walt. For Luke.

There was a splash, and a shout. Someone yanked Jade away from the side.

"Oh no, you don't." Morris held the knife to her throat and pulled her over to the helm with him. "You're not going anywhere."

Pinning her against the corner of the helm controls, Morris vented the motor compartment, then punched the ignition. The engines roared into life. He opened the throttle up, and the boat jerked wildly.

"Frigging anchor." He cursed as he dragged Jade back to the stern with him. Once there, he hoisted the anchor with one hand, and in the process lost his grip on Jade. She immediately jumped toward the side.

"No!" Morris shouted, and jerked her back.

He clipped her across the face with his fist, and knocked her to the deck. Before she could get up, Morris stowed the anchor and hauled her back to the helm again. This time the boat moved across the waves as the powerful engines propelled it away from the island. The choppy surface of the sea made the cruiser bounce up and down.

Morris held on to her with one arm as he piloted the helm. "Ungrateful little bitch. Don't try that again."

Jade's eyes widened as she saw a groping hand

come up, seemingly out of the ocean, and curl around the railing. There he was, she thought. An arm, and a leg followed. Finally the entire body. Carlos was coming back for another shot at Morris.

She made no sound as the man in the wet suit slipped onto the deck. The sound of the engines covered the small noises he made. Jade simply watched him.

He didn't try to sneak up on them. One moment he was steadying himself on the wet deck, the next he came at Morris's back, hands outstretched. At the last minute Jade realized he was reaching for her, not Morris, and let herself sag against Morris's arm.

"Gonna faint on me—"

Morris swung around in time to get a black-gloved fist in his face. Jade went to her knees and rolled away as the fight renewed. The boat crashed into the crests, making the hull bounce up into the air. The wheel spun wildly, and the boat made a sudden turn, throwing both men to the deck. A compartment on the starboard console popped open, and a pistol fell out.

Have to get it before one of them do, Jade thought, and inched away from the thrashing bodies.

The bloody-faced man slumped over on the deck. Pity it had only taken three solid blows to knock Morris out. He could have cheerfully pounded on him for another hour or two. He shoved the unconscious man aside, went to the helm, and shut down the engines.

Where was she? Then he spotted her, on the deck beside the starboard console. He scooped her up in his arms and carried her into the cabin. Jade pulled away and backed into a corner.

What was the matter with her? "Jade?"

"Stay back." She raised and pointed a pistol at him. "Or I swear to God I'll shoot you."

Of course. He still had his gear on—she couldn't see his face. He reached up and tore off the dive mask and rubber hood covering his hair, and stripped out of his wet suit.

She lowered the gun. "Luke?"

"Yeah, it's me."

At the sight of his grin, Jade dropped the gun and slid down the wall to the deck. She pressed both hands over her face.

Luke bent down to get to her. "Jade? Honey, talk to me."

Her fingers slid down to her mouth. "You're alive," she whispered.

She was in shock, Luke realized. He kept his voice low and gentle. "I'm alive, sweetheart."

Now he saw the bruises on her face. The scratches on both breasts. The torn strips of jumpsuit around her waist. She'd been beaten. Mauled. Violated.

Those thoughts roared in Luke's head as a dispassionate tranquility settled over him. Morris had done this to her. He jerked a knife from the belt on his waist and fingered the blade as he swung back toward the cabin door. He was going to do the world a favor, and gut that miserable bastard. Maybe he'd wake him up first.

"Don't. I'm all right."

Jade's voice stopped Luke when little else could have. He'd take care of her now. Then he'd come back and cut the worm's throat. He sheathed the knife and went back to her. As he reached for her, Luke hesitated. After what she'd been through, maybe she wouldn't want him to touch her.

"You sure you're okay?" Luke asked.

Jade nodded, and held out one of her hands toward him. Despite what she'd been through, she was reaching for him. Luke swore as he helped her up, then pulled her into his arms.

Mine, he thought. My woman. Or she would be, the very second after he took care of this mess.

Jade ran her hands over him, as though she couldn't quite believe he was real. She pressed her face against his neck and muttered something, over and over.

She was repeating the same two words. "I'm sorry. I'm sorry."

"No," Luke said, and rubbed his cheek against the top of her head. "This wasn't your fault."

"Oh, God." She'd discovered his wounded arm, and made a choked sound as she touched the duct-taped plastic wrap. "You're shot. You're hurt."

"Just a scratch. I'll live."

She lifted her face just as he went to kiss the

top of her head. Luke tightened his hold as he kissed her mouth instead, and tasted blood and heat.

"Luke." She held on to him with tight hands. "I wanted to die."

"Because of what he did to you?" Luke kissed her bruised cheeks. The cut on her lip. Everything he could get his mouth on. When she didn't answer, his hands framed her face. "Baby, did he rape you?"

"No." She shook her head as he nuzzled the tears from her face. He barely heard the rest of what she said. "I was going to drown myself. I didn't want to live without you."

Did she have any idea what she was doing to him? Probably not. She was hurt and traumatized. They'd knocked her out to get her on the boat, she might have a concussion. Luke carefully set her on her feet and checked her eyes again. But she wasn't looking at him. She was staring out at the deck, at Morris.

"Jade. Tell me what he did."

Jade swallowed once. "He hit me. Kicked me once. He was going to rape me. But then you got here."

Not soon enough, Luke thought. "It's over, honey. He won't ever touch you again. I know, don't call you honey."

She tried to laugh, but it came out with a sob. "You can call me anything you want."

He held her until her legs steadied, then steered

her out of the cabin. "Come on. We're getting off this bucket."

Once they were back on deck, Luke pulled the gun from his belt, and calmly shot Morris. A large red cartridge dart hit Morris's chest. Then he pulled her over to a bench seat and sat her down. "Stay here."

Jade watched as Luke dragged Morris back to the motor compartment hatch. He released him long enough to yank the small door open, then shoved the unconscious man down into the compartment.

"What did you shoot him with?"

"Same thing I shot the other one with. Tranquilizer gun. It's a shame, but that's all I've got." He locked down the hatch, then unlashed the spare inflatable from its rigging and lowered it into the water. "Come on."

He helped her down into the raft and piloted it quickly back to the island. Once there, he carried her into the house.

"Luke, your arm."

"I'll live," he told her.

Luke carried her back into his bedroom, and set her down carefully in the center of his bed.

"We keep doing this."

The way she said that made him frown. "Honey, listen to me." He sat down beside her and took her hand. "I've got to go get Carlos and take him back to the boat."

"No." She clutched at him. "Don't leave. I have to talk to you—I have to tell you—"

"Shhh." He stroked a hand over her hair. "Mike's on the way. We're going to get them out of here. I'll be back before you know it, sweetheart." She nodded reluctantly. "Then I'll let you hit me a few times for not believing you the first time you opened your beautiful, sunburned mouth, okay?"

"Where do I get to hit you?"

"Anywhere but the arm."

That made her cry, and he held her and rubbed her back. After a few minutes he eased her back on the pillows. "Okay now?"

"No."

"Stay put." He kissed her forehead, because touching her anywhere else would have finished him off. He drew the covers up over her before he left.

Once he'd dragged Carlos outside to the beach, Luke checked the boat through his binoculars. No movement. It took a minute to remove the tranquilizer dart and load Carlos into the launch. Then Luke went back to the boat.

Mike Anderson's Grady-White skiff appeared just beyond the curve of the island. From the deck of Morris's stolen charter, Luke waved.

The two unconscious men were now tied up on the deck. Mike came alongside, and Luke stepped from one boat to the other. Juan, a swarthy Cuban-

American, quickly secured the lines that would keep both boats from floating apart.

"Juan, you know Luke," Mike said as he propelled his custom-designed boat chair from the helm to the stern. "Now forget you ever saw him."

Juan's white teeth flashed in his dark face. "*Sí, jefe.*"

Luke filled Mike in on the details he'd been unable to transmit over the radio. Anderson's fists bulged as he gripped his chair's wheels, but he was silent until Luke was finished.

"Ought to drag them in a trawl net all the way to Key West," Mike said, then ran a hand over his graying hair. "I checked with a cop friend of mine who has a connection at the Bureau. You were right; there is no Agent Paul Morris. You sure you want to do this?"

"Yeah." Luke glanced at the other vessel. "Mike, if it's the boat—"

"Get real," Mike said. "You think I give a shit about the boat? Problem is, garbage like this generally work for someone. When they don't show with the woman, the head scum will send more trash out to find her."

"I'll deal with that when it happens." Luke eyed his friend. "You get the stuff?"

"Yeah." Mike made a disgusted sound. "There's always plenty floating around town. Makes me sick."

"I owe you." Luke held out his hand. "Big time."

"Yeah, you do." Mike snorted, then took it. "I better never hear another word about the Roselli twins for the rest of my life."

The silver-haired man pulled out a gun and trained it on Laurie. "Tell me what you're doing here. At once."

Laurie had never been so frightened in her life. She couldn't stop looking at the cold, black hole in the gun barrel.

"I came here to see Agent Morris. I wanted to know if my dad is involved in the case he's investigating." Jeff was in danger; she had to somehow warn him the man had a gun. She said, really loud, "Please, don't shoot me. I know I shouldn't have been poking around in here. Arrest me, if you have to."

"I don't think that will be necessary." The man calmly shoved Laurie toward the door. "Walk."

Please, Jeff, stay where you are. As soon as she stepped outside, she tried to bolt.

"No, Miss Anderson." He hauled her back against him, and she felt the gun press into the small of her back. The soft murmur by her ear made her flinch. "You will do exactly as I say."

Maybe she could catch someone's attention. Unfortunately the open hallway and half-empty parking lot were completely deserted. The man guided her toward a long black car, and pushed her in the back. Then something hit the back of her head, and knocked her out.

When she woke up, Laurie had no idea how long she'd been unconscious. The smell of stagnant water made her stomach heave. She realized she was gagged, and swallowed hard. She couldn't throw up like this, she'd choke to death.

Wherever she was, it was dim and cool. Her arms were stretched behind her, pinned on either side of what felt like a tree trunk. Water lapped around her ankles. Not a tree trunk, then.

She craned her head, trying to get a better look around. Irregular blocks of coral rock, stained brownish green at the waterline. A roof of boards above her head stretched out into the sea. Weathered pilings, still bearing traces of their original tar coating.

She was under a pier. But where? Why?

"I see you're awake, Miss Anderson." The silver-haired man stepped behind her, and she felt him checking the tight loops of rope around her wrists. "You have caused me a great deal of inconvenience."

He'd hit her on the back of the head, as soon as they had reached his car in the hotel parking lot. She'd gone with him because she'd been afraid for . . . Jeff.

"You are worried about your father, are you not?" the man said as he stepped back around to face her. She nodded frantically. "I have not been to see him yet."

He hadn't found Jeff. Instant relief flooded Laurie, and she barely flinched when she felt cold fingers brush over her throat. The man yanked the gold cross and chain from her neck, then dangled it in front of her eyes.

"I'm afraid I must borrow this. It will encourage your father to help me retrieve my property." He put the necklace in his pocket.

Behind the gag, Laurie's mouth went dry. What did he mean about her father? What property?

"I am certain he will cooperate." The man smiled. It was an ugly thing to see. "Naturally I cannot give him your actual location. By the time he realizes that, the storm will be here, and it will be too late."

The hurricane. Laurie's eyes widened as she looked back out at the ocean. This close, with the storm surge that had been predicted he would never make it. If Dad was out searching in the storm—

"Good-bye, Miss Anderson."

Laurie watched him slog through the water back up to the beach. She could have killed him herself. But she wouldn't think about him now. Surviving was the only thing that mattered.

As soon as the man was out of sight, Laurie began twisting her wrists against the tight ropes. Barnacles growing on the wood scraped her arms. Maybe their sharp edges would help her get the ropes off. She began to rub the knots against the piling.

She had to get free. If she didn't, Laurie knew that one of the two men she loved would die.

*   *   *

Jade watched from the window as Luke and an-other man transferred Morris and Carlos from one boat to another. The man who helped Luke jumped on Morris's boat, loaded the launch back on board, then sped away from the cove. A few minutes later, Luke jumped into the water, and the second boat left as well.

He was alive.

They hadn't killed him.

Somehow, she'd gotten a second chance.

She wasn't going to waste this one.

Jade was waiting at the front door with a towel when he came in, and handed it to him. Luke stripped out of his wet suit, dried himself, then frowned at her. "You should be in bed."

She shook her head, then looked at the window facing the cove. "Is your friend coming back?"

"No." He lifted the towel to dry his face, and winced.

"Your arm." Jade saw fresh blood staining the gauze beneath the plastic. "Let me take a look at that."

Luke gave her an odd look. "Not going to yell at me for letting Mike leave?"

"Thanks for reminding me, but I'll yell at you tomorrow. Come into the kitchen."

Luke had left the first-aid kit on the kitchen table. After she washed her hands, Jade used a pair of scissors from it to cut the duct tape, plas-tic, and vinegar-soaked gauze from his arm. The swollen edges of the wound looked painfully raw and still oozed blood. Then she found the exit wound.

"Good, it went straight through."

"Yeah. It looks worse than it is." He picked up a packet of iodine swabs. "Let me do it."

"No." She snatched the packet from his fingers and tore it open. "I can handle this, you know."

"I know you can." Luke's breath became ragged as she cleaned the wound out thoroughly. He eyed the tweezers she took from the kit. "Whoa. I thought you said you weren't mad."

"I'm not. There's some lint stuck in there." She picked several bloody shreds from his wound. "Okay." Carefully she wrapped his arm with clean gauze and taped it securely.

When she was done, Luke flexed his arm. "Nice job. Maybe you were a nurse."

"I was a candy striper." Jade cleaned up the mess on the table and threw the old dressing away. It kept her from flinging herself at him and covering his face with kisses. "Every summer in high school."

"You remembered that?"

"Yes." Jade sat down next to him and resisted the need to touch him again. "I remember everything."

"*Everything?*"

"Morris didn't lie about one thing. My name *is* Kathryn Anne Tremayne."

Luke reached over and took her hand in his. "Go on, honey."

That simple contact made it easier to tell him. "You were right, I grew up and live in Atlanta. I'm not married. I didn't steal anything from a computer design firm. I *own* one. It's called Tremayne Systems." Her throat tightened. "Gareth wasn't my husband. He was my older brother."

For a moment, Jade actually wished she could forget everything all over again. Gareth. As big and hardheaded in his own way as Luke was. Instinctively she knew the two men would have liked each other. Knowing they would never meet tore a new wound on top of the old one.

He scooped her out of her chair and onto his lap. Jade settled back against his uninjured side. He gave her a minute, then said, "Tell me about him."

"Gareth worked as a geologist for a mining company. He got caught in an avalanche at the site." She remembered the phone call, and closed her eyes for a moment. "They never found his body. That was three months ago."

Luke didn't say anything, but his hand began stroking her back.

"Gareth was all the family I had left. Our parents died in a car accident while I was in college."

He kissed the top of her head. "Is he the guy in the photo?"

"No. That's Walt Carter, my assistant." She took a deep breath. "This all started two years ago. One of my customers said it would be great if we could develop a computer that never ran out of memory. I remember how excited I was when that little remark gave me an idea. I went into my lab and didn't come out for days. At the time, I had been researching quasicrystal synthetics, and his comment gave me an idea. Quasicrystals have a nonperiodic atomic structure, and some don't generate heat or magnetic fields."

"I've read about them," Luke said. "They've opened a whole new range of scientific applications."

"Exactly. I experimented with several quasicrystal compounds until I created one that suited my needs. Walt and I used it to build a prototype storage/processor unit. By injecting certain additives into the unit's bioliquid encasement, the quasicrystal core actually grew, allowing for greater capacity storage."

Luke stopped rubbing her back and turned her face toward his. "Are you telling me you invented a computer that can expand its own memory?"

She nodded. "We called it Storage, Operations, Access and Retrieval—SOAR, for short."

"That's unbelievable."

"A Chinese corporation called Shandian somehow found out about it. I was contacted by their president, a man named Chang Yu-wei, who offered to buy the technology and the prototype outright. I refused, mainly because I wanted to make the technology available to everyone. For security reasons, I transferred all the hard data onto the prototype processor and destroyed the originals."

Luke whistled. "No wonder they came after you."

"Walt knew I always took the prototype with me when I traveled." Jade slid off his lap and walked to the window. "I came to Miami for a business meeting a few weeks ago. Walt was already here on vacation. He invited me to go out on his boat. He must have made a deal with Shandian."

"Taking you out to meet his buyers," Luke said, "the slimy little bastard."

"No. It wasn't like that. Walt had changed his mind, and was trying to get me off the mainland. But everything went wrong. Once we were at sea, the engines failed. I'd just gotten out of the shower when I heard Walt arguing with Morris.

"Morris never knew I was there. He threw Walt in the cabin with me while he and his men searched the rest of the boat. Walt told me everything, then smuggled me through an access hatch onto a raft tied to the bow. I didn't want to leave without him. Walt hit me over the head and knocked me out. He must have set me adrift in the raft. When I came to, I was only a few feet away from the boat."

She pressed her forehead against the windowpane. Luke came up behind her, and his hands settled on her shoulders.

His deep voice stirred her hair. "Don't, sweetheart."

"I'm all right." Jade had to tell him everything. "I came to, and saw Walt on the boat, shouting at Morris. He probably did it to create a diversion so I could get away. Morris had two of his men hold Walt, and then he started hitting him. Walt begged him to stop. He didn't. He beat Walt to death." She choked. "Then I had to watch them as they . . . they dismembered Walt's body . . . and threw it in the sea."

"Jesus."

"I should have tried to stop them." She finally broke down and wept. "Oh, God, I was so scared. I knew if they found me, they'd do the same thing to me."

Luke held her in his arms, saying nothing, providing the comfort she needed. Gradually she pulled herself together, and dried her face with a napkin.

"I remember rowing away from the boat. It was dark, and they never saw me. Then I found out there was no gas in the outboard." The memory of those desperate hours made her shudder. "I lost one of the oars when a wave knocked it out of my hand. I didn't have any supplies. I never saw land. The next thing I remember is waking up here, with you."

"That's enough," Luke said. "The head trauma, then witnessing Carter's murder caused your amnesia."

"Maybe I wanted to forget that I did nothing to save him."

"There was nothing you could have done."

His hands slid down her arms, pulling her back against him. Jade wanted to turn around and take more than the comfort he offered. She didn't move.

She had to make him understand.

"Luke, if I stay here, you'll be in danger. Morris has to be working for Shandian. They'll send more men after me." She stepped out of his arms.

"So you don't want to be found, either," Luke said, and smiled.

"Don't joke about this." She was angry. "This isn't about some moldy old shipwrecks. I've got to get out of here, or they'll kill you, too."

His smile never wavered.

"What do you think Morris is going to do when that tranquilizer wears off? Even murderers are entitled to a phone call!"

"With where he's headed, he'll have a problem getting connected."

"Why?" Jade went still. "Luke, you didn't kill him, did you?"

"Morris is alive. He just picked the wrong part of the world to be running drugs."

"Running drugs?" She frowned. "What do you mean? Drugs have nothing to do with this."

"Now if the Monroe County sheriff had caught him, I'd say you were right about the phone call. But Morris and his pal are headed a bit further south." Luke rubbed his jaw. "I wonder if he speaks Spanish?"

"Luke!" Jade pounded a fist on the counter. "What are you talking about?"

"A boat set on autopilot only has to go ninety miles from Key West before it smacks into Cuban territorial waters." Luke appeared suddenly, savagely satisfied. "When that tranquilizer wears off, Morris will have to explain to some very upset officials in Havana how they came to be there. In a boat Mike reported stolen from Marathon an hour ago. With traces of cocaine belowdecks."

"How?"

"Mike Anderson took care of it. He'll see that the stolen charter is returned to its owner, too. I owe him a new boat, and whatever it cost him to buy enough street coke to salt the hold and make it look good."

Jade cleared her throat. "Is it too late to apologize for every rotten thing I've ever done to you?"

"There's just one thing I want to know," Luke said. "Where's the prototype?"

"I've had it with me all along."

"Have you? Do I get to frisk you for it?"

An exciting thought. "You don't have to." She showed him her right hand.

"The ring." Luke lifted it to examine the square-cut stone. "Not a jade?"

"No. It's the quasicrystal processor." She took off the ring and rolled it between her fingers. "Walt died because of this. I should toss it in the ocean."

"Don't." Luke took the ring and slipped it back on her finger. "It's too important, Jade."

"I guess. Speaking of important stuff, shouldn't we get back to work?"

"You'll stay?"

"I'm staying."

"Good." Luke took her hand and tugged it. "My turn. Come on."

Jade wondered why Luke suddenly stopped at the threshold of the ransacked room, until she looked around him.

The computer equipment had been knocked to the floor.

"I didn't see this when I radioed Mike," Luke said as he knelt beside it. "Old Carlos must have been in here, searching for your prototype."

More destruction, because of her. Jade closed her eyes. When would it end?

Several shelves were cleared, books thrown to the floor, maps torn. The floor was carpeted with papers. Luke's desk drawers were wrenched out and emptied, too.

The computer monitor was intact, but the drive tower was dented. Jade went to that first, and pulled it upright to remove the case. She could smell the faint odor of burnt electrical wiring.

She unplugged the power supply and removed the program boards. She probed until she located a small square component board, then looked up at Luke.

"How bad?" he asked.

"The power supply is shorted." Suddenly she knew what she had to do. It was so simple, really. "If you've got some wire cutters and a soldering iron, I can fix this."

"How long will it take?"

"A couple of hours." She straightened and stepped away from the computer. "I'll do it in the morning."

"Right. You must be tired."

"No. Tonight I want to make love with you."

Chapter Nine

Luke's reaction was immediate and violent. He grabbed Jade and spun her around. "What did you say?"

"You heard me." It wasn't so easy this time, facing him. "I want to make love with you."

His gaze scoured her features without mercy. "Why now?"

"I thought I lost you today," Jade said, and moved closer. His breath warmed her brow as she pressed her body to his. One brave hand slid up his chest to rest over his heart. The heavy beat beneath Jade's palm began to accelerate. "It terrified me. Because . . ."

He splayed his hands over her back, urging her closer. "Because?"

Jade felt the way he was tensed and ready. Knew it would only take another moment to demolish his self-control. Boldly her arms curled up around his neck. "Because I thought you'd never know how much I wanted you."

"Good enough." Without another word, Luke

swung her up against his chest and carried her out of the den. When he got to his bedroom, he shouldered the door open and put her down.

"Are you sure?" he asked, his voice strained.

Jade reached over and snapped on the lights. "It's all I've thought about for the last two weeks."

"All right." His hands cupped the curves of her shoulders, and tested the fragile bones there. She felt so small next to him. "You're *mine.* And I'm going to take you. All of you."

Her eyelids drifted down as she felt her entire body throb with sensual hunger.

"Jade."

She lifted her face, opened her eyes. She didn't try to hide the quiver that ran through her limbs.

His voice deepened. "Tell me again. Tell me you've wanted this as badly as I have."

"Yes. I want you. I love you, Luke."

Something made his face darken, then fill with self-disgust. "Shit." Unexpectedly he released her and backed away. "I can't do this." He began to walk back out of the room.

"Luke," she cried out. "Don't go—*don't.*"

"Too much happened today." He halted but didn't turn around. "You're on emotional overload. I won't take advantage of that."

Fury exploded inside her. "I tell you I love you and you think it's because I've had a bad day?"

"Yeah." He still wouldn't look at her. "I do."

"Well, you're wrong." She came after him, and

hit his back with her fist. "Damn it, Luke, don't you walk out on me!"

"I don't think I can." He swung around, and before she touched him, Luke held up one hand. "Be sure." She could almost see the wildness snarling inside him, close to breaking free. "Once I touch you, I'm not letting you go."

Her anger melted away, and she recalled what he'd said to her. *Good enough.*

Luke examined her face as if every feature were new to him. "Nothing matters but this. Right here, right now."

Her heart pounded as she reached up for him. "Nothing else matters but you."

Luke pressed a kiss in the palm of her hand, his tongue moving in a slow, erotic circle against the wet skin. It intensified the aching throb between her thighs, filling her with needs that ran the gauntlet from wanting to kiss him to needing to wrap herself around him. He lifted his mouth from her hand, his breath quickened, his eyes a firestorm in evergreen.

She stood on her toes to press her mouth to his briefly. It had been so long . . . years . . . and then she groaned. "Oh, no." Jade silently cursed her new wealth of memory. "Luke, I'm not using any birth control."

"I had a physical before my last expedition." He nuzzled her hair. "I haven't been with a woman since then. I'm healthy."

"I don't mean that. I trust you," she said, then

raised troubled eyes to his. "Luke, what if I get pregnant?"

"Pregnant." He tried out the word, then gave her a slow smile. "I'd like to get you pregnant." He tossed her on to his bed. "Now."

"Luke!" She propped herself up. "I'm serious."

"So am I." He climbed up over her and used his weight to pin her beneath him. His big hands stroked down her body. "Now kiss me."

Everything blurred as Luke took her mouth with his.

No man had ever kissed her like this, Jade thought wildly as the hot, wet thrust of his tongue met hers. Abandoning the last of her doubts, she met the probing, plundering strokes eagerly. His fingers slanted her face to deepen his possession.

"Jade," he said against her lips.

His heart hammered into hers with the rush and swell of each quick breath. The smell of his skin became the air she breathed. The feel of him became the world. Jade clutched at him, needing more, demanding more.

"Oh, God." Luke tore his mouth from hers, his breath hot and fast against her skin. "I've got to have you." Soft, compelling sounds colored the air and Jade realized dimly they were coming from her. "You don't know how much..." He let the words trail away as he ran his palms from her hips up to the sides of her breasts. Brazenly she changed the angle of her thighs, rubbing against the rigid length of him, luring him on.

With a savage jerk, his hands tore the front of her blouse apart, sending buttons bouncing around them all over the bed. Jade groaned as he filled his palms with her breasts, kneading and massaging the weight there.

"Luke!"

"I'm here, sweetheart." His head dipped as he found one nipple and sucked it between his teeth. At the same time, his hands peeled the blouse from her, moving down to the loose waistband of her slacks. He raised himself long enough to strip them away, leaving her pale body naked and trembling beneath him.

He frowned while his fingers gently trailed over her breasts. "Damn. I'm sorry, sweetheart, I forgot. I'm being too rough."

Jade looked down and saw he was tracing the marks Morris had left on her. "No. Forget about them." She pressed her hands over his. "Make *me* forget about them."

A slightly menacing smile appeared. "I can do that."

Luke rolled over long enough to remove his trunks and toss them over the side of the bed. Jade's eyes traced the length of his form, pausing to admire the proud, erect shaft of his penis as it rose from the amber hair between his thighs. Tenderly she reached out to caress him. The hard heat enticed her fingers to curl and stroke.

"Not a good idea." He caught her wrist and

eased her hand away. "Unless you want this to be over fast."

"Let me touch you," she said, pleading now.

"Tomorrow." Luke pushed her on her back with barely suppressed savagery. "You can touch me tomorrow."

He edged off the mattress to kneel beside it and pulled her toward him. Jade's legs slid over his shoulders, until he had her balanced at the very edge of the mattress. Calloused fingers slid up between her thighs, gently insistent. He raked them over the soft triangle there, moving down to explore the damp, swollen flesh it fleeced.

She arched up, biting her lip to keep from crying out.

"No, honey. Don't hold back on me. Let it out." Luke parted her folds to expose the small, hard nub they protected. Jade gasped as she felt one fingertip circle and stroke it. "That's it. Oh, yeah . . ."

Her hands tangled in his hair, tugging to urge him up. He only lowered his head to her, until his mouth and tongue replaced his fingers.

"Luke!"

As he held her hips down, his slow, slick nuzzling tormented her. Jade was imprisoned, made helpless beneath his clever tongue. She clutched the sheets beneath her convulsively. As he gently used his teeth, it became too much. Intense pleasure smashed over her, sweeping her up to the wild extreme of release.

*   *   *

Jeff had never been so afraid in his life.

Laurie and the man who'd abducted her had disappeared from the hotel parking lot. Crouched in
the closet, Jeff had been unable to get a look at the
man. He hadn't tried to open the bifold door, fear-
ing the man would shoot Laurie or him before Jeff
could say a word.

He'd listened to their conversation, and as soon
as the room door had opened and closed, he'd
pushed himself out of the closet. Knowing the man
had to be holding Laurie at gunpoint, he'd looked
first through the peephole, then opened the door.

The parking lot was empty of everything except
parked cars.

Jeff knew he should go to the police, but he had
to find Mike and tell him first. In a cold sweat he
ran to his car, jumped in, and roared off.

On the way to Anderson Services, he replayed
everything he'd heard in his head. If only he'd gotten a look at the guy, he could have given the police a description.

Please, don't shoot me. Whoever had come in had
pulled a gun on Laurie. *Arrest me, if you have to.*
She'd thought the man was working with Morris.

I don't think that will be necessary, the man with
the gun had said.

What was it about that voice? Jeff wondered. It
bugged him, it wasn't right. No accent, but it had
been too perfect. That last word. He hadn't said it
right, either. He'd slurred the "r," the way Jeff's old
roommate had.

His old roommate had been Chinese-American.

He broke every speed limit in Marathon, getting to Mike's place, only to be told that Mike and his warehouse manager were out on a special run to the islands. Jeff had spent enough time fishing with Mike to know he never went out without a radio, so he went to Mike's office and tried to raise him on the shortwave.

Half an hour went by, and Jeff's voice grew hoarse from repeating the call signs. There was no response. At last, something came in.

"KDA559 to WAX237, over?"

Jeff checked the call sign list. The transmitter was one of Mike's HAM radio club friends. "This is Jeff Carr for WAX237, KDA559, over."

"Hi, Jeff. This is Stu, with ARO Disaster Support. We've been waiting to check in with Mike, too, over."

Jeff frowned, trying to think straight. "I can take a message for him, Stu, over."

"No, nothing like that, son. We're manning our stations for Hurricane Deanna. She's headed on a direct path at the middle Keys. Strike Zone probability puts her coming straight through downtown Marathon, over."

After talking with Stu for a minute, Jeff ended the transmission and sat helplessly in front of the radio array.

How was he going to tell Mike about Laurie if he couldn't find him? He had to call the police. Now.

The desk sergeant at the Monroe County Sheriff's Department answered, and listened patiently to Jeff's story.

"We'll put out an advisory. To be honest, son, I don't know what good that will do. We've started evacuating the Upper and Lower Keys. Everyone has to be out in twelve hours, so we'll have our hands full. I'll send a unit out to take your statement."

"This guy had a gun," Jeff said, wrapping the phone cord around one tight fist. "He's holding her hostage."

"We'll do what we can. Stay put."

Jeff slammed down the phone. Stay put. It sounded too much like *Let her die.*

For several dark moments, all Jade knew was the pleasure Luke had given her. Shuddering, spiraling back down, she opened her eyes to see him watching her intently. His mouth was wet from loving her. She could feel his heartbeat beating in his throat, against her thigh. Primitive masculine satisfaction blazed in his narrow eyes.

"Mine," he said. The possessive growl made her quiver, even as she smiled down at him. Luke slowly rose to his feet, looming over her.

Jade held out her arms. "Yours."

The long, hard length of his body descended on hers. Their bare flesh clashed, his taut, hers electrified by heightened awareness. She instinctively hugged his hips with her thighs, taking him in the oldest of embraces. He held her like that for a long moment, searching her flushed face for some sign.

"Please, Luke." Her hips undulated against his, excitement and need fueling each movement. "I can't wait."

"Amen," he muttered, and slid one hand under her hips. Her thighs tensed as his thick penis worked between her tight folds. "Easy, honey. Don't be afraid. I won't hurt you."

"I know," she whispered, still shocked by the way he filled her. The throbbing emptiness was gone, but what replaced it was almost as tormenting.

"Jade." Luke must have felt it, for when he had penetrated her completely, he stopped moving. "Look at me, sweetheart." Her eyes locked with his. "How long?"

"A long time." She moved under him, trying to adjust to the invading pressure. "Six years."

"You've been working too hard." He smiled as he brushed strands of hair from her hot face. "Don't worry. We'll take it slow."

Jade nodded, and felt him begin to move inside her, testing their fit with small, shallow motions. Gradually her tension dissipated, along with the constricted sensation between her thighs. The cautious probing became stronger, more intense.

"You're burning me up," he muttered before he took her mouth again. His tongue repeated the pattern of his movements, deepening as his thrusts did, until the simultaneous penetrations made her writhe out of control.

"Luke!"

He lifted his mouth. "That's what I want." His voice was low and urgent. "Come to me, baby."

He held her shaking body tightly as her climax came, driving into her fast and hard. Dimly she heard his grunt of satisfaction, felt his body strain, his muscles clench. She opened her eyes in dazed wonder. The moment he came, Luke groaned and buried his face in her hair. The warmth of his seed flooded into her.

"Mine," Jade whispered against his ear.

He rested over her for a long time, supporting himself on his elbows until she pulled his body down to hers.

"You can't breathe." Luke's hand skimmed over her face, his long fingers tracing each rosy feature.

"I don't want to," she said, and slid her arms around his waist when he would have lifted away from her. "No, please. Not yet."

"Did I hurt you?"

"No," Jade said. She didn't want to think about her one and only lover in college. The truth was, she could barely remember him now. "Was everything okay?" she asked, feeling awkward, but needing to know.

His smile disappeared while a confident knowledge gleamed in his eyes. "Okay doesn't quite cover it, sweetheart."

"You weren't so bad yourself."

"Glad to hear it." He explored her body leisurely, his touch seeking out the hidden, sensitive areas of her skin, bringing back to life the nerves that had just been so thoroughly satisfied.

Jade's eyes widened in surprise as she felt him growing hard inside her. Even more shocking, her own body flowered around him with its own warm, eager response.

"Surprised?" he said, and pushed a little deeper inside her. "I've wanted you since the first time I touched you."

"I didn't think you could—I mean, so soon—"

Luke released a low laugh as he rocked his hips slowly. "Do you want me again, Jade?"

She nodded.

"What do you want?" Luke cupped her face and forced her to look at him. "Tell me. Hearing you say it turns me on."

"I want—" She forgot shyness as she abandoned herself to his sensual demands. "I want you to touch me. Touch me with your hands. Kiss me."

"Show me," he said.

She took his hand and placed it on her breast, covering it with her own. With her other hand, she guided his head to the other aching peak, pressing his lips there.

"How tired are you?" His mouth nipped and tugged at her.

Sleep was the furthest thing from her mind. "I'm fine."

"Good." Luke laved her nipple with lazy thoroughness. "This feels like an all-nighter." He sucked at the hard bead for a moment. "Maybe an all-weeker."

The rediscovered muscles inside her contracted involuntarily at the thought of spending a week in bed with him. Jade saw his expression change, the acutely intimate grip apparently startling him. "Do you like that?"

He groaned as she did it again, this time deliberately. "You're going to kill me."

"Now you tell me, what do you want?"

He looked down where their bodies were joined, before returning his gaze to her face. "I want you. Under me. Permanently. Whimpering for me to do this. To make you come for me."

"I can do that." Jade nibbled at the side of his neck. When he tried to push her away, she licked the spaces between his long fingers. At the same time, she ran her fingernails down the flexing, smooth length of his back.

Luke finally lost control. He cursed under his breath, then hammered into her. Jade took what he gave her, and gave him back exactly what he liked.

General Sung had spent hours attempting to contact Chang in the United States. Every hour he felt the rope his former protegé had put around his neck grow a little tighter. At last the call went through, and Sung delivered his final ultimatum.

"Either you deliver the prototype to me within twenty-four hours," the general told Chang, "or I will expose you to the chairman as a thief and traitor."

"I would advise you to consider your own position, General. Not only have you aided me in defrauding the party, but you are implicated in the murder of an American citizen."

"Murder?"

Chang described how Morris had killed Walter Carter in exquisite detail.

Sung's blood turned to ice. "I never sanctioned such action to be taken!"

"Naturally you can surrender yourself to the Department of Special Investigations. They may believe your story. Then again, perhaps not." Chang did not sound optimistic.

Desperate now, Sung groped for a method to cover his involvement. "It is best we return the money to the party treasury, until delivery is made." Then he could claim ignorance, vindicate himself, and condemn Chang for the entire matter.

"I regret to tell you that is not possible. The funds have already been transferred to another account. One that only I have access to."

The old man's face turned a mottled color. "You intended to betray me from the first, did you not?" Sung shouted. "Son of an alley dog!"

"Yes, General. I did. I am. Good-bye."

Sung spent a few minutes listening to the empty dial tone. His intercom light flashed, and he stared at it blindly. At last he pressed the button.

"General? The head of Industrial Development wishes to speak with you."

The very man in charge of the appropriations for the project. "Tell him I must return his call."

"I did, sir. He says it's urgent that he speak to you immediately."

Sung swore violently. "Very well, put him through." He sat back down and cleared his throat before punching the button on his telephone. "Forgive me for making you wait. How may I be of service to you?"

"Sung, there are rumors that have come to my attention—"

His office door swung open unexpectedly, and the general looked at the two men who strode in.

"I beg your indulgence for another moment." He stabbed the hold button, then looked at the pair angrily. "What is the meaning of this?"

"General Sung." One of the men produced identification while the other shut the door and locked it. "The chairman would like to know why the developmental funding you appropriated has been deposited in Switzerland."

"I don't know what you're talking about," Sung said.

The two men removed their coats. One of them rolled up his sleeves, then opened a large black case filled with gleaming instruments. The other took out a miniature tape recorder and set it on the desk.

Sung knew what he had to do, and covered his face with one hand. With the other, he opened a small drawer in his desk and pulled out the gun he kept there.

"You will answer our questions, General," the investigator said, and pressed the record button down. His companion rubbed his hands together briskly, and flexed his arms to loosen his muscles.

"Chang has the money," the general said. "All I have left is this."

Before either man could stop him, Sung placed the barrel of the gun under his sagging jowls and pulled the trigger.

Since Morris had not checked in on schedule, Yu-wei had to assume he was either dead or in police custody. A hurricane warning had been declared, according to the radio, and all residents of Monroe County were ordered to begin evacuating the Upper and Lower Keys at noon.

Another man might be intimidated by these problems, but not Yu-wei. He saw it all as raw material to be turned to his advantage. In a few hours he'd be out of South Florida, the prototype in his hands, and on his way to one of the many secure locations he had set up for himself around the globe.

A half hour later, he arrived at Anderson Services, where he saw a sheriff's car parked outside the main office. He kept driving through the parking lot to the opposite side of the complex, where he could park and observe the front of the building unseen.

A young American man walked out with the uniformed officer, his tanned face earnest as he spoke in low tones. The officer shook his head, climbed back into his car, and drove off. The American stood watching him go, his rage and frustration only too evident.

An interesting development, Yu-wei thought, and went over his options. He used his car phone to dial the office number for Anderson Services, and watched the young man dart back into the office to answer the call.

"Hello?"

"Mike Anderson, please," Yu-wei said.

"He's not here." The American sounded angry.

"When is he expected?"

"I wish I knew, mister. Can I take a message?"

"Yes. Tell him that if he wants to see his daughter alive again, he should return to his office. Within the hour."

The American's tone changed at once. "You bastard, what did you do to her? Where is she?"

"Give Mike Anderson my message."

Yu-wei disconnected the call, put the phone aside, and settled back to wait and watch.

On the other end of the Keys, Mike Anderson watched from the bridge of Morris's charter as his favorite boat started the trip south to Havana. He'd rigged the boat to run on autopilot for the full ninety-mile crossing. If the two unconscious men happened to wake up before they reached Cuban waters, the specialized work Juan had performed on the engines and helm controls would prevent them from turning around. The only way off would be to jump in the ocean and let the boat keep on going.

"Juan, let's get the hell out of here," he said, and secured his chair to the helm. Laurie had been gone for more than a day now, and he was starting to get worried. The call he'd made earlier to Meredith hadn't helped at all.

"Did you know she tried to blow up an entire wing of the Science Building?" his ex-wife demanded over the telephone.

"I know Laurie didn't do it on purpose," Mike said. "Look, Meredith, she's been acting strange ever since she showed up on my doorstep. Are you sure she hasn't left a message on your machine?"

"I checked it already, Mike." Meredith sounded impatient. "She hasn't called. She wouldn't call me anyway, not if she got herself in trouble again."

Mike could understand why. "Thanks for the help, Meredith. Try not to worry about her, will you?"

His sarcasm earned him an eardrum-shattering crash from the receiver, then a dial tone.

Juan's voice interrupted his thoughts. "*Jefe*, you should check on *la tormenta*."

"The storm!" He'd completely forgotten about the damn hurricane. With a curse Mike tuned on the marine weather on Morris's radio. After a few minutes the local emergency marine broadcast gave the latest track. He heaved a sigh after he checked the latest coordinates against one of his maps. "They'll make it. She's still too far out. Looks like she might miss Cuba entirely."

Juan looked over his shoulder. "What about your friend?"

Mike stared at the coordinates, and drew an imaginary line with his finger. "Oh, hell. She's headed straight toward Paradise Island."

He turned on the remote transmitter, intent on warning Luke, then heard a familiar voice. He picked up the microphone and clicked in.

"WAX237 Marathon, this is WAX237 remote. Jeff, is that you, over?"

"Mike, thank God!" It was Jeff. "Where are you?"

"Down by Key West. What's the matter? My daughter ticked off at me again?"

"No, Mike." Jeff's voice went hollow. "Laurie's been kidnapped."

"Hey." Jade finally managed to lift her head. "Hungry? I could eat a horse. Tail, hooves, and all."

He didn't want to, but he got himself up and out of bed. "I'll make breakfast."

"Make a lot," she called after him.

As she left the bedroom, she smelled something delicious coming from the kitchen. But when she got there, it was empty. Puzzled, she followed the smell.

Jade found Luke on the deck. He was standing by a large gas grill in the classic male cookout stance: tongs in one hand, basting brush in the other, frowning down at his handiwork with unwavering diligence.

They were still stranded on an island, Luke trying to preserve history from being destroyed while she was being chased by hit men, and the man was grilling steak. She choked back a laugh.

He looked at her sideways, one eyebrow raised. "What's so funny?"

"Scrambled eggs would have been fine, you know."

"I need some real protein." Luke scowled at her. "I got shot, remember?"

His abrupt show of temper hurt. "Well, don't look at me. I didn't shoot you." He prodded the steaks, but said nothing. Jade took a deep breath and tried again. "Is something wrong?"

Luke snorted. "Other than the U.N. deadline, a wrecked computer, three years of work down the drain, the nuts trying to kill you, and a hurricane bearing down on us? Not a damn thing."

"Sorry." She backed away a few steps. "I'll go get the computer up and running."

"Later." He flipped the meat over. "You need to eat first."

"I'm not very hungry." That much was true.

Luke swiveled around and glared at her. "You're eating breakfast."

Jade's shoulders squared. "I said, I'm not hungry." She had to escape, before she did something ridiculous. Like breaking down and begging him to tell her he loved her.

But Luke had never said he loved her.

"Hold it." Luke put down his utensils and grabbed her by the waist before Jade could get to the porch door. "Don't turn your back on me."

She pushed at his chest. "Let go of me."

"When I'm good and ready." His hard, furious mouth collided with hers, and Jade twisted her head to one side as she struggled to free herself. "What's the matter? You were more than willing a few hours ago."

Jade managed to pull an arm free, and slapped Luke as hard as she could. For a heartbeat he stared at her, then thrust her away from him.

"Go. Work on the computer."

"Luke, I—"

"Go!" he shouted.

Jade accomplished a few blind, tottering steps before he caught her.

"Stop." Luke's hard hands held her in place as his low voice proceeded to demolish her soul. "It's not your fault I screwed up. I didn't mean to take it out on you."

He regretted last night. Her love. What they'd shared. It was over—that fast. Jade closed her eyes for a moment, and endured the beginning of what she suspected would be lifelong, unbearable pain. "I'm sure you didn't." She held herself very still. "I'd like to go fix the computer now. Okay?"

"Yeah." He let her go. "Sure."

*   *   *

Luke ended up throwing away most of the steak. His appetite, like his self-respect, had completely disappeared. He couldn't blame anyone but himself for this disaster, he thought as he stared at the darkening sky.

He was an idiot. A selfish, blind idiot.

It hadn't hit him until that morning, when he'd started cooking breakfast. He'd stood at the grill, grinning like an ape as he'd thought about Jade. Making love with her had been everything he'd wanted—and then some. He couldn't stop replaying every touch in his head, relishing the memories over and over. He'd even started thinking of what he'd like to do to her next time. Naturally it would be better, Jade wouldn't be as upset and irrational as she'd been last night—

Like when she'd said she loved him.

Luke rubbed a hand over his face. She'd been half out of her mind, and who could have blamed her? Witnessing what she'd thought was his murder. Morris's goon knocking her out. That would have been enough, but then Morris had gone from there and worked her over.

The image of Jade's white face came back to him. Terrorized and in shock, she'd clung to him. Cried in his arms. Later, when Luke had returned, she'd seemed calm. He'd been wired, but thought he had enough control to keep from touching her. Until she'd offered herself to him and called it love.

It wasn't love. More like relief and gratitude.

Luke knew that. He'd known it last night. As soon as she'd said it, he'd even tried to walk.

But you didn't walk, did you?

Guilt ground in Luke's belly. He'd taken her at her word, when he should have put her aside and left her alone.

All right, I won't touch her again. No matter what she says. Not until I know she's thinking with a clear head.

Yet the damage was done. *Luke, what if I get pregnant?*

Last night he'd liked the idea. Too much. The thought of putting his child inside Jade's small, slim body had aroused him as much as touching her. They'd make a good-looking kid together, he'd thought, then had thrown her on his bed.

Whether Jade was pregnant or not, whether she loved him or not, he had a responsibility to her now. Not a problem. He'd take her back to the mainland to meet his family, then they'd get a license. Be a hell of a challenge, trying to explain how they'd met, why Jade had been stuck on the island with him. His mother would probably want a big wedding.

That would work. Unless she said no. But Jade wouldn't say no. They were great together. Not just in bed. She wouldn't say no. Jade needed him. Jade—

Only she wasn't Jade.

She was Kathryn Anne Tremayne, company owner, computer designer, and he suspected, authentic genius. She'd devoted her life to building her career. Hadn't even bothered to take a lover in six years. She didn't need a husband. Especially one who barely knew how to turn a computer on without blowing the damn thing up.

Kathryn Anne Tremayne didn't need him. He'd already stranded her on the island. Lied to her. Refused to believe a word she'd said. Even when Morris had shown up, Luke had believed a total stranger over Jade. As a result? She'd nearly gotten raped, and killed. Why the hell would she want to love much less marry the man responsible for the whole mess?

He'd been brooding over that when she'd come out on to the deck, and laughed at him for cooking the steak. Doubt snarled into suspicion. Would she laugh when he asked her to be his wife? Fear over that had made him surly, and he'd snapped at her.

Is something wrong?

He'd made some asinine reply, all the while thinking, *Yeah, I just figured out how much I need you, and how little you need me.* Then Jade had apologized, and argued with him, and that had been the last straw. He'd exploded, like an idiot, seizing on the excuse to vent some of his temper.

"Good work, Fleming." Luke massaged the back of his neck. "She won't be able to keep her hands off you now."

The wounded look she'd given him, before her pretty face had gone blank. That had hacked into him like a blunt boning knife. He'd tried to explain, but suspected he'd only made things worse.

It's not your fault I screwed up. I didn't mean to take it out on you.

Luke swore and headed for the den. And nearly ran into Jade on the way.

She didn't look at his face, but he could see she'd been crying. "I need some tools and things." He opened his mouth to apologize, thought better of it as he saw her tense, and nodded. Briefly she described what she needed, then turned around and retreated to the den.

Jade had pulled the drive tower completely apart and had it spread around her on the puncheon floor by the time he returned with what she'd asked for.

"Here." He set the toolbox and some parts he'd scavenged together beside her. "How's it look?"

"I can fix it."

He reached for a screwdriver. "I'll help."

"Ever rebuild a power supply board?" He shook his head. "I didn't think so. Why don't you start cleaning up?"

As they worked, Jade noticed the growing stacks of papers and folders. "How long did you say it took you to gather all this information on Admiral Chêng Ho's expeditions?"

"Three years."

"Now that you've discovered the wrecks, you'll probably be even more famous." She sounded depressed. "Like Ballard was, after he discovered the *Titanic*."

She still didn't know, Luke thought. He hadn't even trusted her with the whole truth.

"Not likely." He rolled a map up and secured it with a rubber band. "At least, not in the eyes of the Chinese government."

"Why not?" Now she was confused. "I thought you said you were presenting evidence about Chinese shipwrecks."

"I am. I'm going to prove the shipwrecks don't exist."

"What?" She set down the pliers she was using and gaped at him. "You mean it's not true?"

"I'm sure there are plenty of wrecks out there. Just not where the Chinese say they are." He shuffled a folder to one side and pulled out a map. "Look at this. They claim the *Sha Chengbao* sank here, during a typhoon in 1421. The ship's navigational records indicate it sailed on four of the emperor's seven major expeditions, one of which occurred in 1432."

"So they're lying."

"They claimed the same thing with the *Mao* and the *Haixing*." Luke regarded her steadily. "The wrecks are a smokescreen they're using to gain control over the South China Sea. They've even seeded the sites with trace evidence. I can prove the ships they're claiming to have found never sank in the first place."

Jade tapped the monitor's casing. "All the calculations I've been entering?"

"Extrapolated from expedition records on seventy ships spanning twenty-eight years during the Ming Dynasty. They were discovered by a colleague of mine during a dig in Shanghai. He made copies of them before turning them over to the Chinese government."

"But why would they make up a story like that?"

"That was what I wanted to know. So I spent twelve months surveying each spot in the South China Sea, and took samples from the ocean floor. I didn't discover a single wreck. What I did find was evidence of huge reservoirs of crude oil, waiting to be tapped."

"So the Chinese want to drill for the oil."

"That's the short-term goal. The long-term is even more ambitious." Luke unfolded a map and showed her dozens of lines crossing the South China Sea. "These are major commerce navigational routes. Fifty percent of the world's shipping traffic uses lanes that pass directly through disputed waters. The Chinese call the project Shuiba—the dam—meaning to stop the flow."

"They're planning to stop the ships from sailing through the South China Sea?"

"Knowing the factions involved, yes, unless the shipping companies want to pay for the privilege," Luke said. "The State Department came to me to debunk the sites. They've scheduled me to appear at the same time the Chinese planned to make their first bid for control."

"If the media gets hold of your research," Jade said, "the Chinese would be forewarned."

"Exactly." He tapped a finger on the end of her nose. "And they'd simply rechart the sites a few degrees away, and dump some more ancient timber at each spot."

An hour later she had the system reassembled, and queued up the program. Luckily the data had remained intact. Luke crouched next to her as she tested the system's drive and memory.

"Looks good." She completed the standard checks and turned to him. "I can't guarantee the jerry-rigged board will hold indefinitely. How much more data do you have to input?"

He pointed to a towering stack of reports. "I figure another week."

"If that board burns again, I won't be able to repair it." Jade gnawed at the side of her thumb, then glanced at the system. "Tell me something. Did the firm that designed this give you a scanner?"

"Yeah. It came with it." Luke pointed to a box under the credenza. "I've never used one, so I didn't hook it up."

"Perfect. That's all we need." She bent down and grabbed the carton.

"What's so great about a scanner?"

"What if I told you we could turn two weeks' worth of work into two days?"

"Marathon WAX237 to WID714, over," Mike's voice interrupted them.

"Hold that thought." Luke went to the radio. "WID714, over."

"I've got to pick you two up, old buddy." Mike's

voice came across unusually terse and rough. "Pack your bags, over."

"Problem with Fidel's package, over?"

"No, package is on its way. Luke, somebody's snatched Laurie. One up, over."

Luke switched frequencies as Mike related Jeff's story. Jade moved to stand beside him and listen. No matter what Luke said, Mike wouldn't contact the local authorities.

"All right," Luke conceded at last. "In that case, don't worry about us now. Go take care of finding Laurie, over."

"No can do, old buddy. Deanna's a category three now, and headed straight for you, over."

Luke swore softly. "How long before she gets here, over?"

"Twenty-four hours, maybe less. Monroe County is starting standard evacuation procedures. Pack it up, old buddy. I'm coming to get you, over."

Luke looked up at Jade. "This scanner thing. Can it finish the input by tomorrow morning, if we both work on it?"

"If we start now, and don't stop . . ." Jade nodded.

"Mike, I've got a proposition for you," Luke said. "It'll be the last favor I ever ask of you, I swear, over."

Chapter Ten

Yu-wei waited patiently outside Anderson Services, until he saw a sports utility truck hauling a boat pull up to the main office door. A small dark man got out, removed a wheelchair, and pushed it around to the driver's side. A big man lowered himself into the chair as the young American appeared, and began speaking urgently to the other two.

Mike Anderson had arrived.

He watched the younger man climb into a sports car, and drive off, while the other two entered the building. He waited until the car had disappeared before he got out and approached the building himself.

Through the reception area window, Yu-wei saw the man in the wheelchair in an office, positioned in front of a radio array behind the desk. The smaller man was nowhere in sight. Quietly he opened the door to the office and walked in.

"Mr. Anderson?"

The big man didn't look back at Yu-wei. "Have a seat."

Yu-wei listened as Anderson broadcast the current marine weather conditions, noting the man's obvious familiarity with storm warnings. At last the wheelchair spun away from the radio console.

The American's expression became hostile. "What do you want?"

"A boat," Yu-wei replied. "Supplies, and a charted route to Paradise Island."

"No way. There's a category three hurricane bearing down on this area. You're not taking my daughter into the storm."

"I see you already know who I am, Mr. Anderson." Yu-wei inclined his head.

"Where is she?"

"Your daughter—Laurie, is it not?—is a beautiful girl." Yu-wei smiled, and removed something from his pocket. It was a thin gold chain, with a small golden cross on it.

The color drained from Mike's face. "I gave that to her for her sixteenth birthday," he said. If he'd had a gun, Yu-wei would be lying on the floor, bleeding. "Where have you got her?"

"At this moment, she is tied to a piling under a pier, waiting for the storm to arrive."

"Where?"

"I will give you that information, as soon as you give me what I want."

"What do you want me to do?"

"Turn off your radio, Mr. Anderson." Yu-wei rose to his feet. "You won't be needing it anymore."

Jade didn't waste any time. As Luke gathered the last of the reports together, she hooked up the scanner and created the simple data transfer program necessary to speed up the input.

"Now watch." She demonstrated the process for Luke by placing one of the reports in the scanner unit, and activating it. The image of the report appeared on the computer screen. She pressed a series of keys, and data that would have taken her fifteen minutes to enter by hand was added to the existing program in as many seconds.

"I'm impressed. Show me how to do it."

Luke was quick to catch on, and soon was able to operate the program on his own. For the rest of the day they worked to get the data into the system. Jade left the den only long enough to fix them both sandwiches and keep the coffeemaker going.

Even with the help of the scanner, it was a slow, repetitive process. Jade found herself yawning more than once, and shrugged when Luke noticed.

"Sorry. I'm a little tired."

"Ditto." He yawned back at her. "So tell me more about Kathryn Anne Tremayne."

She placed a new report in the scanner. "Not much to tell. Since college, I've been busy establishing my company. I hardly had time to do much more than work. You already know about my family."

"What's your favorite color?" he asked.

"Blue."

"Mine, too. Ice cream?"

"Coffee."

"Food?"

"Anything Italian." She eyed him. "Why are you asking me all this?"

"I'm going back to Atlanta with you, so you can pack your stuff. Then you're moving to my house in Miami."

"I don't remember agreeing to do that."

"I'm not asking for your permission," Luke told her. "You're living with me. Or I'm living with you. I don't care where. But I'm not letting you go."

As he reached for her, she ducked out of range. "We'll talk about this later." She permitted herself to feel a cautious surge of joy. "We've still got work to do."

The last of the data went into the computer just after midnight. Jade sat rubbing her eyes as she completed the transfer.

Luke took over the keyboard and entered a single string command. Then he took her hand and pulled her away from the system. "Let's go to bed, sweetheart."

Jade was so tired that when she stood, she swayed. "How long will it take to calculate the final report?"

"A couple of hours. Come on."

With Luke's arm supporting her, they walked back to his bedroom. He began stripping off her clothes, then picked her up and lowered her on the cool sheets. Jade fell asleep in his arms.

Luke woke up in an eerie silence. The sky was still dark, but he sensed something was wrong. There were no sounds coming in through the open window. The air held a waiting quality he'd only experienced a few times in his life. Calm before the storm.

The hurricane was getting close.

He eased Jade to one side and got out of bed to pull on his clothes. He watched her sleep for a moment, tempted to get back into bed with her. He'd never slept so deeply, or so peacefully, than when he'd held her.

He hoped it was the same for her, because he definitely wasn't letting her go.

Luke went to prepare what he needed to take with him when Mike arrived. Two and a half hours later, he went to the den and switched on the radio.

"WID714 to Marathon WAX237, over. Mike, are you out there, over?"

Luke repeated the transmission for fifteen minutes without a response. At last, a high-pitched voice answered on the same frequency.

"KDY338 to WID714, over."

Luke hesitated, then responded. "This is WID714, go ahead, over."

"Caught your signal for WAX237. Mike hasn't been broadcasting since last night. It's really weird, since he always covers the storms, over."

"KDY338, can you give him a call over a land-line for me, over?" Luke gave the boy Anderson's phone number.

"Stand by, WID714." There was a period of silence, then the young man's voice transmitted again. "WID714, all I get is the answering machine, over."

"Thanks, KDY338. Can you give me the latest on Deanna, over?"

"Absolutely, man, over." The young boy rattled them off, and Luke wrote down the coordinates.

The hurricane had swelled in strength and was now a category four. It had also picked up speed, Luke saw, from the advanced position of the storm center. The outlying weather bands would be reaching Paradise Island within the hour.

"Hey, are you okay out there, WID714? Do you require assistance of any kind, over?"

"Appreciate the offer, KDY338. Will keep you advised. WID714, out."

Luke switched off the radio, and ran a hand through his hair. That was when he saw Jade standing in the doorway with two mugs of coffee. Her dark hair was rumpled, and she'd pulled on one of his T-shirts. The hem skimmed her knees, and Luke suspected she had nothing on beneath it. Then he saw her expression, and guessed she'd heard some of the transmission.

"Morning, sweetheart." He held out his hand. "We've got a little problem."

She came over, set the coffee aside. "What problem?"

"Mike was supposed to be here two hours ago. I can't raise him on the radio, and he's shut down the office."

"Maybe he's on his way here."

"No. He'd have contacted me first. And he never shuts down his transmitter during storm warnings." Luke took her hand and walked with her to the front of the house. She noticed the changes the moment they stepped outside. The air was very still now, and clouds were rapidly approaching from the east.

"The storm will be here soon, won't it?"

"Yeah. I should have sent you back with Mike yesterday." Luke scanned the horizon. "It looks like we're stranded here for the duration."

"Is that a bad thing?" she asked, and put her hand on his arm. He slipped it around her and pulled her to his side.

"No, not if we take precautions. Come on. We've got work to do."

Jade admitted she had never been through a hurricane, and found some of the preparations a bit odd.

"Why fill the bathtubs with water?" she asked as Luke closed the drains in all three tubs and sealed them with caulking. They had already filled ten large storage containers Luke had taken from the storage shed with water.

"We'll need it for washing," he told her. "The

supply tank is on the roof, it'll be the first thing that goes."

They stacked the containers with their drinking water in the hall, which according to Luke was the house's strongest structural point.

"I'm going to mount the hurricane shutters over the windows," he told her. "Move the nonperishable food and whatever else we'll need for eating out of the kitchen. See if you can find where my mother put her candles, matches, and any battery-powered radios or flashlights."

Jade made several trips back and forth as she carried out his instructions. She collected canned food in an empty cardboard box she'd found in one of the closets. Her search didn't turn up any flashlights or batteries, but she did find a number of tapered candles, an ornate silver candelabra, and a box of stick matches.

Luke went outside to put up the large corrugated steel hurricane shutters over the windows, blocking off the sunlight. As he fit the bulky sheets of reinforced steel into the special slots built around each frame, he watched the sky.

Something told him this one was going to be bad.

From what Luke had told her, they would wait out the storm in the hall, away from the windows and doors. So Jade gathered together several changes of clothing for both of them, along with pillows, linens, and toiletries. By the time she was finished arranging everything, Luke came back in the house, carrying what appeared to be a small engine block, and a can of gasoline.

"This is the spare generator," he said as he placed it and the fuel at one end of the hallway. "We'll have to hook it up after the storm, if the others get trashed."

That reminded Jade of another piece of equipment. "What about the computer?"

"Damn, I forgot about that." Luke eyed the cramped space around them. "We can't fit much more in here. The monitor and printer are dispensable, but we'll need to preserve the hard drive."

"What about backing up and printing out the project data?" Jade asked. "You should do that, just in case something happens to the drive."

Luke agreed, and she went to the den to produce the report. During the night the program had finished calculating the massive amounts of input, and the screen was on standby, waiting for the next command.

Jade sat down and keyed up the final program menu. She selected each of the listed reports to be produced, and turned on the printer. It began to hum and feed out the final analysis.

It would take at least an hour for all the reports to be produced. She stacked enough paper in the feeder to keep the printer filled.

"Jade," Luke said from the doorway.

"This is amazing, you should—" Jade stopped

in midsentence when she saw him. The barrel of a large gun was pressed against his head.

"Hello, Miss Tremayne."

Yu-wei ordered Jade out into the front room as he kept his gun shoved tightly under Luke's jaw. She obeyed his command silently, her eyes flashing to Luke's only once.

I'm sorry, she thought, hoping he would understand.

I know, his eyes said. Me, too.

Jade looked at Yu-wei. "Please don't do this."

"I left some rope outside the front door, Miss Tremayne. if you'd be good enough to retrieve it for me?" Yu-wei asked, and stood waiting as she complied. "Excellent. Now, sit down, Dr. Fleming."

Yu-wei prodded him toward one of the straight-back chairs. Luke sat down slowly, his eyes never leaving Yu-wei or the gun pointed at his head.

"I advise you not to attempt what you are thinking, Dr. Fleming. I have no qualms about shooting you whatsoever. Miss Tremayne, the rope, please. Now tie him up."

She dropped the rope. "No."

Yu-wei raised the gun and tapped the business end of it against Luke's temple. "Tie him up, or he dies."

Jade slowly picked up the rope and looped it around Luke. Yu-wei told her how to tie the knots, and watched her closely. There was no way she could leave them loose enough for Luke to work out of. At last Yu-wei ordered her to step back and inspected the knots himself.

"Good. Sit down, Miss Tremayne. Yes, there, across from Dr. Fleming." Yu-wei waited until she had eased onto the sofa, then lowered the gun. "I see you have prepared to weather the hurricane. Have you been trying to contact Mr. Anderson? I'm afraid he wasn't able to answer your calls."

Luke tested the ropes with a jerk. "What did you do to Mike?"

"I instructed Mr. Anderson to stay off his radio and away from this island. He was most anxious to be cooperative. It is understandable. American men are extremely attached to their daughters."

Jade saw the disgust in Luke's eyes as he said, "Laurie. You're the one who took Laurie."

"A charming, if somewhat misguided, young woman. However, she made an excellent bargaining tool. I never married or had children, for precisely such a reason." Yu-wei sighed. "Much as I would enjoy conversing with you both, I am here to retrieve a specific item purchased by the People's Republic of China."

"SOAR was never sold to your government, Mr. Chang," Jade said.

"I regret to inform you that indeed it was. Among others. Where is the prototype, Miss Tremayne?"

"Go to hell," Luke said.

"Miss Tremayne." Yu-wei raised the gun again.

"Do you wish to watch Dr. Fleming die? I can make it a very slow, painful process."

"No," Jade said, and rose to her feet. "I'll give you the prototype. On two conditions."

"You will give it to me now," Yu-wei said, "or I will begin shooting your famous lover, one arm at a time, then one leg."

"Let Luke live, and tell him where Laurie Anderson is." Jade said. "If you do that, I'll give you the prototype."

"And if I do not agree to this?"

She was very calm. "Then you may as well shoot both of us."

Yu-wei bowed slightly. "Very well, Miss Tremayne. Anderson's daughter is tied under the pier at the Blue Reef Marina."

Luke's expression became frightening. "She'll drown in the storm surge."

Yu-wei merely leveled his gun at Luke's right kneecap.

"I have kept my end of the bargain, Miss Tremayne. Bring me the prototype. Now."

"It's not here," she told him. "Walter gave it to me for safekeeping before we left Miami. I'll have to take you to it."

Yu-wei hesitated, apparently unable to decide if he should trust her. Jade didn't blink. At last he inclined his head toward her. "Very clever of you. Go out to the beach now."

"Luke," she said, never taking her eyes from the

Chinese man's weapon, "after we're gone, you get loose and radio Mike, okay?"

"I'm afraid that will do no good," Yu-wei said. "Even if you could work yourself out of your bonds, your radio is useless. I have taken the precaution of permanently disabling your transmitter." He made a jerking gesture with his weapon. "Out to the beach, Miss Tremayne. Quickly."

"I want to say good-bye."

Yu-wei seemed amused by this, but nodded. "Keep your hands where I can see them."

Jade walked over to Luke, placed her hands on his face, and kissed him. "I'll be okay," she whispered.

"Do whatever you have to, honey," Luke murmured as he nuzzled her cheek. "I'm coming after you. Just hold on."

"I will," she said, then kissed him once more.

"That's enough, Miss Tremayne." Yu-weil's patience had evidently come to an end. "Go out to the beach."

Jade walked back toward the front of the house. The veins on Luke's arms stood out like cords as he watched her, then switched his attention to the Chinese man.

"You'll regret this."

"I doubt that very much, Dr. Fleming." Yu-wei yanked open the door and gestured for Jade to walk through it.

* * *

Once the front door had closed, Luke instantly strained against the ropes binding him to the chair. The knots were too solid, so he deliberately unbalanced himself. He fell over on one side, the impact cushioned slightly by the carpeting.

For once he was glad his parents had left all the original antique furniture in the house. His arms tightened, exerting pressure on the old wooden back they were tied around. Luke heard the aged wood groan, then crack. Blood ran down his arm from the bandage Jade had put over his wound. He ignored it, concentrating on breaking the turnings loose. At last something gave, and the chair back separated from the seat.

It took precious minutes to work his arms under his legs and feet. More to rid his wrists of the knotted rope. At last, bloody and aching, he stood up. He knew what he had to do first, and ran to the den.

"Always have a backup plan," Mike had said, as far back as calling plays in high school. They had agreed a radio and transmitter on Paradise Island was absolutely necessary.

What Chang didn't know was they had decided two would be even better.

The handheld UHF unit had a portable, lightweight transmitter that could be set up in a few minutes. The only drawback was its range, which was limited to one hundred miles. Luke only needed fifty, and prayed that Mike had kept the matching unit in his apartment switched on.

"WID714 to WAX237, over."

"Luke!" Mike was so distraught he forgot radio protocol. "I was praying to God you'd signal. That lunatic who has my Laurie, he's headed your way—"

"He's been here, Mike," Luke interrupted. "Listen to me. Laurie is tied under the pier by the Blue Reef, over." He listened to his best friend swear. "Mike. Go and get Laurie, over."

"I owe you big time, old buddy. You need help, over?"

"Keep the channel open, I'll let you know. WID714, out."

Luke took the precaution of hiding the radio unit before he raced to the front of the house. From the window, he saw Chang hoisting the anchor that had moored his boat in the center of the inlet. The engines were already humming.

No matter how fast Luke got in the water, he'd never make it to them by swimming.

Jade watched Chang secure the anchor and go to the helm. He hadn't seen what she'd dropped over the side. Now all she had to do was keep him distracted enough from spotting it.

"Give me your hands," he said. When she held out her wrists, he tied them together. Jade had to bite her tongue as he noticed her ring, then tugged it from her finger. "A lovely memento. Jade, isn't it? The same thing Dr. Fleming calls you?"

She nodded, swallowing hard.

"How sentimental." Chang carelessly fingered it as he went to the helm, then dropped it into a recess on the panel.

"I am curious, Miss Tremayne. Why didn't you accept Shandian's bid for the entire project?" he asked her as the boat came about. "It was an extremely generous offer."

"The SOAR processor wasn't perfected." Did he have any idea said technology was only three inches from his hand? "Your offer was premature."

"That is not true, you know. Your assistant Walter Carter supplied me with the design proposals. The theory was quite innovative. Given your talent, I had no doubt you would achieve your goal. I made seventeen million American dollars from my own government, simply by submitting copies of your abstracts. A group of Islamic freedom fighters in the Middle East were also most generous. My Muslim friends would like to have delivery of their merchandise."

She tried not to stare at the ring. "How could you sell it to the Chinese and the Muslims?"

"I merely embezzled the money from Beijing." Chang checked their position readings and throttled up the engines. He had to speak louder now. "The leader of the Muslim faction found your design to be the answer to a great deal of their current tactical problems. SOAR will make most of their current arsenal obsolete within two years. Which is when, I believe, they plan to invade several neighboring countries."

"You miserable, greedy son of a bitch."

He smiled. "You are quite naive, aren't you? Only a misguided idealist would develop such a unique approach to computer technology and then believe it would be used only for the common good. Do you know how many fighter pilots will benefit from SOAR's unlimited performance capabilities? How many targeting systems will be improved to deliver virtually pinpoint precise payloads? Thousands will experience your research firsthand, Miss Tremayne. Just before it kills them."

"Forget son of a bitch." Jade shot to her feet. "You're a monster."

"Yes, I am. A very wealthy one, for which I must offer my gratitude to you." Chang began heading out for the open ocean. "You see, in addition to the moneys provided by my own government, I will be paid seventeen *billion* American dollars by the Muslim terrorists. That will be of great comfort to me, while I am enduring my exile from the homeland." He smiled with anticipation. "Perhaps I will let you live. With your skills, you may prove to be an even more valuable commodity in the future."

"No." Jade gripped the side of the boat as it began to rock wildly. Waves were beginning to swell around the boat, and the sun disappearing behind a swift-moving sweep of clouds. In another moment they would be out of the inlet. "I won't let you."

Chang gave her a contemptuous smile. "You have no choice."

Jade looked at the water. "Yes, I do." Without hesitation she vaulted over the side of the boat and into the cold, deep water.

The wind slammed into the side of Mike's van, making it skid over the rain-slick asphalt. Jeff held on in the back. Juan swore as his dark head connected with the inner door panel. Again.

"*Jefe*, you got to slow down," he said as he rubbed the new sore spot.

Mike wasn't listening. Driving took up all his attention. He had to veer around the piles of debris already littering the road. He had the hand throttle pressed down as far as it would go. He'd be damned if he'd let up off the gas until they reached the pier. Every second counted now.

"Okay, kill us all," Juan said reasonably. "Then who will rescue *la niña*?"

"Shut up, Juan." That came from Jeff.

At last they reached the hotel parking lot. Mike drove through the abandoned guard gate, and back to the closest spot next to the beach.

"Get my chair out," he urged Juan, knowing it would take too long for him to clamber back, maneuver into the chair, and lower himself on the automatic ramp. With Jeff's help, Juan quickly unloaded the wheelchair and pushed it around to the driver's side, then hauled Mike out of the van.

"There." Mike pointed to the empty pier at the

far end of the private beach. "That's where Luke said she is."

"I'll go and find her," Jeff said. "Juan, you stay here with Mike."

Mike didn't care if he had to crawl. "I'm going with you."

Jeff nodded, then ran toward the pier.

Luckily the boardwalk extended to the end of the pier, and Mike was able to propel himself along the weathered planks. He and Juan both shouted Laurie's name several times along the way, but there was no response. Mike's dark eyes chilled as he saw the waves lapping just beneath the high tide marks on the pilings.

"Forget about me!" he shouted above the wind as Juan went to help him out of the chair. "Get down there and help Jeff!"

Juan jumped over the seawall and disappeared under the pier platform. Mike grunted as he hoisted himself from his chair to the wall, then dropped onto the sand. For once his useless legs infuriated him, but only for a moment. Then he started crawling toward the pier.

The churning waves were swelling now, rolling in steady, increasing progression. Mike's legs dragged behind him, leaving twin deep tracks in the wet sand. He peered into the darkness beyond the pilings, and thought he saw a flash of red hair. Juan surfaced on the other side, his head sweeping back and forth. There was no sign of Jeff at all.

"Laurie? Jeff? Juan, I think I see her." Mike pointed. "Back toward the support struts. Hurry!"

Juan dove under the water and swam back under the pier. Minutes passed, until Mike saw two heads surface. Juan, and Jeff. They staggered out of the water, carrying his daughter between them.

"Is she alive?" Mike shouted, frantically trying to get to them.

Juan helped boost Laurie into Jeff's arms, then stumbled over toward Mike.

"Hold on, *jefe*," Juan gasped.

Jeff carried Laurie up to dry ground, carefully lowering her to the sand. Then he started CPR.

Juan muttered in his native language as he tugged Mike's heavy body up beside his daughter's. As Jeff raised his mouth from Laurie's to do compressions over her heart, Mike peered at her. The sight of his daughter's still, white face and badly lacerated arms aged him twenty years in a second.

"Laurie?" he called to her, his voice torn with fear. "Baby, can you hear me?"

Jeff's hand cradled her chin as he sealed his mouth over hers and forced his breath into her lungs again. With a gasp he raised his head, and Laurie choked out a mouthful of water. Jeff rolled her to her side, and held her head as she coughed.

Mike watched helplessly, until the most beautiful blue eyes he'd ever seen finally opened.

Laurie gave her father a weak grin. "Hey . . .

handsome." She coughed, turned her face to Jeff, and sighed. "What . . . took you guys . . . so long?"

Mike swore and laughed at the same time as he pulled her and Jeff into his powerful arms. They were all wet and full of sand. He didn't care. With great tenderness, he pressed his lips to his little girl's brow, then saw the expression on Jeff's face.

Reluctantly Mike let his daughter go, and watched Laurie's supposedly best friend kiss her passionately. While he tried to fathom how that had come about, he silently thanked God for the second time that day.

Luke wandered back into the house, barely aware of his surroundings.

Jade had sacrificed herself for Laurie and him. No doubt she'd find a way to keep Chang from getting his hands on SOAR as well. Some way that would get her killed. Acts of incredible bravery and sheer stupidity usually did that.

He'd been so sure he could find a way to stop them before Chang took her off the island. Now the full hopelessness of the situation hit him. Jade was probably going to die, and there wasn't a damn thing he could do about it.

The supplies they'd put together for the hurricane filled the hallway. Jade had disconnected the hard drive unit, he saw, wrapped it in protective plastic and tucked it between two pillows. His life's work, pampered and protected.

He thought of the Chinese oil companies, eagerly preparing to punch through the ocean floor with their drills. A week ago it would have sent him into a bleak rage. Now he'd go and set up the rigs himself, if he could just have a boat to go after Chang and get Jade back. But he was stranded. He'd made sure of that, to protect his precious work.

She was never coming back.

He spotted the square marble paperweight from his desk, which Jade had tucked aside with the data files. He reached down and picked it up numbly. He recalled what he'd said to her. *When a powerful individual struggled against fate, they always suffered or died.*

He threw the marble block at the opposite wall, and it shattered into a dozen pieces.

Luke bent down again and took the drive unit in his hands. His invaluable data, stored and waiting to stun the U.N. Shuiba had cost him more than years of research, sweat, and money. It had taken the woman he loved from him.

He lifted the drive above his head.

"You're going to learn how to swim, Kathy."

After that terrible weekend at the lake, Gareth had insisted on teaching her. He had taken her to the YMCA every day for the rest of the summer. Forced her to repeatedly go back into the water. In her case, more was not better. Rather than easing, her terror grew to the point of hysteria.

"If I just had something to hold on to!" she'd wept after one fruitless session.

That had given Gareth a brainstorm. He'd bought a round inflatable float and had made her put it on before they'd gone into the pool the next day. Surprisingly, Kathy had been able to tolerate being in the water for a few minutes. Gareth encouraged her to kick her legs, and soon she was able to propel herself around the pool without assistance.

He'd tried to take the float away, naturally. Kathy had immediately reverted to her original terror, and sank like a rock.

"Okay, so you'll have to wear a float," Gareth said. "But at least if someone throws something to you, you won't drown, right?"

Jade recalled that as she clutched the seat cushion to her chest and steadily kicked her legs. She was as terrified as ever, but determined to make it to shore if she could.

When she'd jumped off the boat, she had deliberately snatched at the seat cushion she'd loosely tied to a mooring line and thrown off only minutes before. The weight of her body had made her sink for a moment, long enough for her to grab the cushion, kick her legs, and go under the bow of the boat. The engines' propellers had missed the back of her legs by inches, but she and the cushion had emerged on the other side of the boat.

From there she'd held on to the cushion and the trailing loop of rope, waiting until Chang had come about close enough to the curve of the island. Then she had untied the rope, thrust herself away from the side, and started kicking. The engines had covered the sound of her splashing, and within moments she was out of Chang's sight, headed toward the east side of the island.

It had taken every bit of her courage to move parallel to the shore rather than straight toward it, as fast as she could. She had to get far enough away that she wouldn't be seen. When Chang's boat disappeared from her own field of vision, she turned and started for shore.

It seemed to take forever, but at last her feet touched sand, and Jade lurched upright. She wanted to yell with triumph, but that would only alert Chang. She slogged through the surf up to the beach, and collapsed for a moment, still tightly clutching the cushion to her chest.

She'd made it.

"Thanks, big brother," she murmured against the vinyl beneath her cheek. A moment later she dragged herself up and began working the ropes from her wrists.

The wind had picked up, and the wild threshing it created made it hard to work her way through the undergrowth. Jade ignored the scratches from the saw-toothed leaves of the palmettoes as she struggled back toward the beach house. When she got to the fringe just beyond the outer curve of the beach, she saw Chang's boat was still bobbing on the swelling inlet waves.

She couldn't go in through the front of the house,

he'd see her. Carefully she crept around to the courtyard, and darted in a half crouch from the sea grape hedge to the porch door. She slipped in and silently eased the door shut.

That was when she heard the voices, and froze.

"I wouldn't do that, Dr. Fleming. Computer equipment is quite sensitive."

Luke's head snapped up. Chang stood at the other end of the hallway. "Where's Jade?"

Yu-wei ignored the question and scanned the crowded hallway. "I want the prototype."

"Where is she?"

"If you are fond of your right leg," Chang said as he pointed the gun at Luke's thigh, "you'll get what I want. Quickly."

Luke's eyes were narrowed to lethal slits. The son of a bitch had killed her. "Do it."

"The woman left the prototype here. I want it. Now."

Luke started advancing. "When hell freezes over."

Yu-wei took a cautious step back. "I will shoot you, Dr. Fleming."

"You'd be doing me a favor."

"I disagree," a calm voice said.

Both men turned. Luke grinned. Yu-wei sighed. "Ms. Tremayne. What an unexpected pleasure it is to see you again. Although I can't say I'm surprised. You are very resourceful."

"Sorry I can't say the same." Jade kept her hands

behind her back, and stood her ground as Yu-wei started toward her. "By the way, Luke, I can swim. Well, sort of."

"Glad to hear it, sweetheart." The leashed rage of the last several hours broke free, and he gave Chang a savage grin. "Go take a walk around the house for a few minutes so I can kill this stupid bastard."

"No. Mr. Chang wants the prototype, remember?" Jade smiled coolly as Yu-wei leveled his gun at her chest. "What he doesn't know is that he's already got it."

"Don't tell him," Luke said.

Jade lifted one hand to display her bare fingers.

"The ring!" Chang said. "Of course! Well done, Ms. Tremayne." He swung around, aiming the gun at Luke, who was very close now. "Stay where you are—"

With her other arm, Jade swung the heavy, cast-iron skillet she'd taken from the kitchen and smashed it into the side of Yu-wei's skull. A solid thunk preceded a low groan; then Chang sank to his knees. Luke lunged and took the gun. Yu-wei slumped over facedown on the floor.

"Jade."

His arms were around her, and Luke was kissing her face, her neck, her hair. She dropped the skillet, grabbed him, and squeezed with all her strength.

"Now I know how you felt," Luke said, and his brief, shaky laugh made her swallow a sob. He stuck the gun under his belt. "Come on." He let her go, and looked down at Yu-wei. "We have to try to radio Mike."

Jade took his hand and hurried to the den.

Luke retrieved the handheld UHF unit and activated it at once. "WID714 to WAX237, over."

Outside the house, the sound of the wind had risen to a shriek. Jade wrapped her arms around herself, cold and damp. Luke pulled her against him and repeated the transmission several times, until at last a garbled reply came over the unit.

"WAX237 here . . . happening . . . over?"

"Mike, if you can hear me, we're all right. Did you get Laurie?"

"Found her . . . Laurie's okay . . . there?" Mike's voice faded, and then there was nothing more than the sound of static.

Luke switched the unit off, then hugged Jade once more. "I've got to go tie Chang up."

"I'm going with you."

When they got to the front of the house, Jade just couldn't believe it. The door was flung wide open, and the wind roared in through it. A quick check of the hallway confirmed it.

Chang was gone.

Luke shook his head. "That jackass."

Jade hurried with him through the front door. They ran toward the beach just in time to see Chang climbing from the launch onto his boat. The surging waves were so rough he nearly fell in the water.

Luke lifted a hand and cupped it over his mouth. "Don't do it!"

They couldn't see his face, but even at that distance Chang's urgency was obvious. He started the boat's engines, and hauled in the anchor.

"He's out of his mind," Luke said. "There's no way he can make it through the storm."

"Let him go, Luke," Jade said.

"But the prototype—"

Her hand settled on his arm. "Let him go."

Yu-wei felt the wild jubilation of victory as he took the helm and pointed the bow toward the mainland. The storm was making the seas rougher than he'd expected, but he'd keep the boat at full throttle and outrun it.

The prototype was safely encased in plastic in his pocket, along with the promise of the billions it would bring to him from the Middle East. General Sung would be left behind to face the chairman's wrath, and all Yu-wei would have to worry about was which exotic hideaway he'd visit first.

The boat rocked, then began bouncing as bigger swells rolled in. Fountains of spray showered over Yu-wei as the bow was driven up then fell back to smash into the undulating water. The wind made a roaring sound in his ears as he fought to control the helm. He punched the throttle and pushed the engines to their limit.

As a boy he had heard stories of the great typhoons that sometimes came in over the South

China Sea; storms that sometimes swept away entire villages. Perhaps it would be better to turn around, and go back to the island. Yu-wei could circle the island, and anchor on the far side, away from the house. Fleming would never expect a third visit—

He looked back over his shoulder, but Paradise Island had disappeared. The sea had been transformed into a churning cauldron of dark water. The sun disappeared, and the wind tore at him with greedy fingers.

Before Yu-wei could react, a wall of water fell on top of the boat, and the engines stalled. He spat to clear his mouth and cursed. He'd have to go below and see—

The second wall was even bigger than the first, and flooded the deck with six inches of standing water. Yu-wei slogged his way to the cabin entrance, and had his hand on the door handle when the swell hit the starboard, and the cruiser began to overturn.

Not like this, Yu-wei thought in amazement, even as his hand was jerked from the door, and the boat rolled over like a great, floundering beast. His body was thrown into the cold sea, and before he could surface, the capsizing boat slammed into him. The last breath erupted from his lungs as the sharp disc of a propeller blade slid into his belly, ripping it wide open.

The sea turned crimson as Yu-wei sank, his eyes still wide with disbelief.

* * *

Luke carried the last of the supplies back to the hall. There he found Jade struggling to push the mattress from her bed in place.

"Here." He put his hands beside hers, and wedged it in place. The result created a small triangular niche between the wall and floor.

"Why do we need to do this?" Jade panted, collapsing on the floor beside it. Luke slid down next to her, and rested his head back against the wall.

"Protection against flying debris, in case the roof doesn't hold. The mattress will keep it off us."

"What if the mattress doesn't hold?"

"Then we don't make it, honey." His arm came around her.

"How much time do we have?"

Luke gave her a crooked smile. "Long enough."

Later, as they lay in his bed, the pitch of the wind climbed from howl to shriek.

Jade sat up. "It's here, isn't it?"

"Yeah." Something smashed into the front of the house, galvanizing Luke into action. He pulled her from the bed with him and set her on her feet. "Time to change locations."

In four minutes they were in their safe place in the hallway. Luke gave her a push toward the mattress. "Get in there, quick."

Jade didn't let go of his hand. "You're coming in here with me." She tugged.

There wasn't enough room for them to sit up, so Jade stretched out on the floor, and Luke eased in beside her. The sound of glass shattering made her jump.

"This is just the beginning." Luke tucked an arm around her. "It's going to get worse. But we'll make it."

"Then what's going to happen?"

"We get the hell off this island and get married." He bent his head to kiss her, then tucked her head against his shoulder. "You're mine. I want papers on it."

Jade thumped him with her fist. "I realize you're the sexiest man in the known world, but did you ever think about *asking* me first?"

"Yeah." Luke caught her hand before she could hit him again. "So what's your point?"

"Is that all you have to say?"

"You want to hear the rest of it? Fine. Do you have any idea what it was like, watching Chang take off with you? Knowing the whole time I couldn't stop him? Do you have the slightest idea of how scared I was, you silly twit?"

"And that's because"—she rolled her hand—"come on, spit it out."

"Fine." He looked ready to spit. "I love you."

"There." She gave his chest a couple of pats. "That wasn't so terrible, was it?"

He yanked her close. "When did you know?"

"When I realized staying with you was more important than finding out who I was." She rubbed her cheek against his shoulder. "You?"

"When I asked my best friend to find you if I got myself killed."

She started to say more, then a wrenching, tearing sound made her go still. "What's that?"

Luke's arms tightened. "The roof. It's starting to go."

Hurricane Deanna roared through the middle Keys and continued on her westerly track toward Mexico, sparing most of South Florida in the process. With wind gusts in excess of one hundred forty miles per hour, she left plenty of damage in her wake. Marathon was hit hardest, dead center in the storm as the eye passed over. The entire storm took less than twelve hours to wreak millions of dollars in damage.

Mike Anderson chartered a boat as soon as the all-clear was given, and notified the Coast Guard of the couple stranded on Paradise Island. He arrived shortly before the cutter, and had Jeff and Laurie help him into the launch.

From the inlet they could see Luke's house had been hard-hit. The roof was gone, part of one wall had collapsed, surrounding trees stripped or flattened.

Jeff carried Mike in through the front door, which had been blown in off its hinges.

"Laurie, grab that chair for me." Mike cursed his legs for the second time in a decade, and watched his daughter unearth one of the waterlogged chairs from the pile of smashed furniture. "Thanks. Luke?" he yelled as Jeff set him down.

The house was silent. Scary. Oh God.

"Go and find them, damn it!" Mike yelled at the two younger people.

Laurie and Jeff exchanged a glance as they ran toward the hallway, and spotted the mattress.

"Uncle Luke?" Laurie called out, and Jeff helped her pull the mattress to one side.

Beneath it, Jade and Luke lay motionless, in each other's arms.

"Are they alive?" Mike called from the front of the house.

"Uh, yes sir." Jeff grinned at Laurie with relief. "Just sleeping in this morning."

Luke opened one eye and surveyed the two people standing over him with surly dislike.

"You kids better have brought some damn coffee."

Epilogue

"The assembly has heard Filipino Senator Blas Ople's concerns regarding the possibility of China developing a strategic presence in the South China Sea, and the threat he believes this poses to freedom of navigation," the United Nations Representative said. "We will now hear from noted marine archaeologist, Dr. Lucas Fleming, on the historical importance of this disputed region. Dr. Fleming."

Luke approached the microphone, carrying a briefcase and a three-inch thick copy of the complete Shuiba project report. He wore a dark navy blue suit, and his normally untidy blond hair was slicked back away from his face. He scanned the seated members.

"Ladies and gentlemen, three years ago I was approached by the State Department to act as their consultant for a new project begun by the Chinese government in the South China Sea . . ."

Over the next two hours, Jade listened intently as Luke continued his presentation before the U.N.

Committee. Thanks to a cooperative effort between Dr. Fleming and Tremayne Systems, the Shuiba Project had been completed on time.

As he spoke, Luke had various maps and graphs projected on the overhead screen for the benefit of the committee. Using a pointer, he showed the original routes of Admiral Chêng Ho's expeditions, the vault in Shanghai where the bulk of the maritime records had been discovered, and the geological survey data performed over the year he'd spent investigating the sites.

Luke summarized the project's conclusions while copies of the project report were distributed, then answered direct questions from the representatives.

"Is this not yet another attempt on the part of American petroleum companies to prevent Chinese competition on the world oil market?" the representative from Beijing asked.

"Since most American companies like Amoco have sold their stakes in the Liuhua and other South China Sea oil fields, no, Representative, I don't believe that's possible," Luke said with a straight face.

Several members of the audience lacked his self-control, and laughed out loud.

"Dr. Fleming, do you believe your evidence deserves more consideration than that presented by the Chinese delegates?"

"The reported discovery has no serious scientific foundation, Representative," Luke said. "It's simply another bid to bolster Chinese claims of historical control." He scanned the dubious faces of the committee. "Ladies and gentlemen, if you will consult the summary pages of my report, you will find some interesting statistics."

Jade leaned forward in her seat. This was the part that was going to slam-dunk the Chinese delegation.

"South China Sea oil fields have produced over fifty-seven million tons of crude oil in the last eight and a half years. Exploration has yielded thirty oil fields to date, with more waiting to be tapped. The eleven fields currently in operation have a daily crude production of more than forty- five thousand tons."

The committee members exchanged surprised glances as the final map was projected. It showed the phony wreck sites superimposed on the immense oil reservoirs.

"Ladies and gentlemen, if the shipwrecks did exist, why would Beijing be at this moment preparing to erect twenty-six hi-yield drilling platform rigs in the South China sea? In the exact same sites? Surely not for purposes of historical preservation."

That set the Chinese delegate to ranting, while the balance of the committee exchanged significant looks.

A few minutes later, Luke left the presentation chamber and caught his new wife in his arms. They'd gotten married a few days after Mike had brought them back to the mainland, then had traveled to Jade's home in Atlanta to finish the project.

"You were great!" Jade said, and hugged him with delight. The cherry red suit she wore drew the eyes of two Arabs in flowing robes who passed by. Luke, still unused to seeing her in clothes that actually fit, frowned at them. "The bad guys never had a prayer."

"Thanks to you, Jade."

She grinned. He'd never gotten used to Kathy. "You can call me sweetheart."

He kissed her with frank, slow enjoyment before releasing her and loosening his tie. "Now, where were we?"

"On our way to the airport, if I remember correctly. I have the plane tickets." She patted the side of her purse. "Mike already stocked the house with everything we need. There's only one more thing I have to tell you—"

"Dr. Fleming! Dr. Fleming!"

"Ms. Tremayne!"

A mob of reporters ran down the hallway and soon surrounded the couple in a milling frenzy of cameras, microphones, and recorders.

"Is it true, Dr. Fleming, that you were targeted for assassination by the Chinese government?"

"Did the U.S. State Department hire you to act on the behalf of the OPEC cartel?"

"Do you have any comment on the allegations made by the two Americans recently apprehended for drug smuggling off the coast of Cuba?"

One short, perspiring reporter shoved his way

to the front with practiced ease and pushed a hand-held tape recorder toward Jade.

"Bartley Pearson with *The Investigator*. Is it true, Miss Tremayne, that you have proof you've slept with Dr. Fleming?"

The other reporters fell silent at once. Luke growled and reached for the man's neck, but Jade put a hand on his arm.

"Yes, it's true," Jade said. Cameras began popping everywhere. She threaded her fingers through Luke's. "I do have proof."

Luke stared at her in amazement. Then the implication hit him, and he went white under his dark tan. "You do? You are? We are?"

"I do, I am, and we are."

With a shout, Luke picked her up in his arms and whirled her around, scattering the inner circle of reporters. Flashes went off around them like strobe lights.

Pearson's voice rose a cracked octave. "Miss Tremayne? Miss Tremayne!"

Luke put Jade down and kissed her again. His head only lifted when a hand tapped his shoulder.

"Excuse me, Dr. Fleming." The reporter gave Luke a wary look before he turned to Jade. "You'll need to supply hard evidence, Miss Tremayne, if you want to qualify for the hundred-thousand-dollar reward being offered by my paper."

"Uh-huh." Jade gave the man holding her a mysterious smile. "We'll just have to deal with it, won't we, love?"

"I'm going to deal with you as soon as we get home," Luke said.

Pearson raised his tape recorder. "Do you have photographs? Video? A sworn deposition?"

Jade's shoulders shook; then she cleared her throat. "Not at the moment."

"Well then, Miss Tremayne"—his expression turned cynical—"how do you intend to prove you slept with him?"

"It's Mrs. Fleming." Jade smiled at the reporter. "Pictures will be available in about eight months."

With another shout, Luke picked her up in his arms and carried her out of the crowd.

"What does she mean, eight months?" Pearson said. "Why would it take that long?"

A female reporter smacked him on the back of the head with her notebook. "Think about it, dimwit."

Gareth Tremayne is alive.

But the bad guys at the Shandian

Corporation think he's dead.

Only one person can help Gareth—

a stranded restaurant owner named

Delaney Arlen.

Turn the page for a peek at

Gena Hale's next exciting romance

Dream Mountain

coming soon from Onyx Books.

That damn bear was digging through her garbage again.

Through the frosty kitchen window, Delaney Arlen watched the bulky silhouette hunched over her garbage cans. She wouldn't have spotted him, if not for the full moon. Despite the fact it was midnight and snowing hard, the pale light made everything outside plain as day.

And it was plain to see that damn bear was going to scatter trash from one end of the yard to the other. *Again.*

"That does it."

She'd just cleaned up the latest mess this morning. That was when she'd figured out the wind hadn't knocked the cans over. Wind didn't leave short black hairs and deep tracks in the snow. *Bears* did.

"Not this time." Laney pulled on her parka, then grabbed the shotgun from the rack over the doorframe. "Bad enough I'm stuck on this stupid mountain until Uncle Sean comes back—if he ever does—or someone clears the roads to Denver. And why do I get the feeling that might be next spring? No, I think I've got enough problems without having to pick up after you, Mr. Bear. Time for you to find a new hobby."

She was talking to herself again. Well, who could blame her? Stuck up here alone, no electricity since yesterday, thanks to the latest blizzard. The pile of firewood was disappearing fast. Her cell phone lay on the floor next to the wall where she'd thrown it, completely useless because she was too far out of range.

And *this* place. Laney had never built fires, or cooked on a hundred-year-old stove, or chopped wood. She was a city girl, born and bred, and she'd been very happy *not* knowing how to do all that stuff.

You're a dead man, Uncle Sean.

It was her own fault for getting into this mess. If Laney hadn't been so upset about other things, she'd never have fallen for Sean's story. She'd never have come up here with her uncle only to be abandoned.

For the last four days, when she wasn't thinking up ways to slowly torture her uncle or worrying about her other problems, Laney had been forced to deal with the realities of rustic mountain living. Cooking on the cranky, wood-burning stove. Keeping the pipes from freezing. Swearing at herself for being a trusting idiot.

Now this. Cleaning up yet again after Oscar the bear was, absolutely, the *last* straw.

She checked the load in the shotgun, pumped the slide, then pulled the door open. Icy wind and whirling snow slapped her face and stole her breath. Too furious to care, Laney stomped outside, where she had to slog through the foot-deep drifts to get to the side of the cabin.

"I should have loaded some real shells; I sure feel like shooting something. Lucky for you, Mr. Bear, all I'm packing is rock salt. That should convince you I am not a woman to mess with." Shouldn't it?

Her uncle's voice came back to her. *Never shoot an animal, darlin', unless you intend to kill it.*

Laney winced. She had trouble swatting flies. Even if she could get up the nerve to do it, what would she do with the carcass? Make it into a casserole?

Ragout of bear meat, yum, yum.

The falling snow made it hard to see, and that slowed her down. Her stomach knotted as it hit her—she was out here, by herself, with a real, live, hungry *bear*. That didn't make much sense when she thought about it. Oscar should have been curled up in his den, happily snoozing through the rest of Christmas.

What if it isn't *a bear?*

It's not Bigfoot. For God's sake, Laney, get a grip. She lifted the shotgun, wiped the snowflakes from her eyes, and yelled, "Hey! You! Oscar! Get out of there! Go home!"

Fifty yards away, the bear straightened, and the garbage can fell over. Trash spilled everywhere. The wind, of course, began its inevitable distribution process.

"Oh, for crying out loud—thanks. Thanks *a lot.*"

The bear shifted to the left, then started lumbering toward her, still on its hind legs.

Was it going to attack her? This wasn't good. She gripped the shotgun tighter.

"What are you doing? Don't you see I'm armed here? This is a *shotgun*, pal. Go on. Go hibernate or something. Don't make me shoot you, because I will. I'll do it. Do you hear me?"

The bear kept coming straight at her.

For a moment, she was too scared to breathe. Then she remembered how much she enjoyed breathing, and she put her finger on the trigger.

"Come on, give me a break here. I don't want to hurt you. Last chance. You don't really want to be a rug, do you?"

If she had to shoot it, the load of rock salt wouldn't kill it. She hoped. Still she hesitated. There was less than ten feet between them when she took aim.

"Please. Just go away!"

He kept coming.

"Oh, shit." Laney pulled the trigger.

A roar followed the shotgun's blast. The recoil made her stagger backward. The stench of gunpowder stung her numb, cold nose. Laney watched as the bear tottered to one side, then fell face-first with a *whomp* into the snow. He made one last sound, then didn't move again.

No bear in the world made a noise like that.

"Oh. My. God."

She tucked the shotgun under her arm and fought her way through the drifts to get to him. When she reached the big, dirty pile of fur, she saw blood on the snow.

"Oh God. Oh dear God. Tell me you're not dead. You can't be dead. It was only salt."

Laney knelt down in the foot-deep snow beside the hide. It slid under her shaking hand, as though separating from the body beneath it. It *wasn't* attached. She tugged at the fur, pulled it away, and stared.

"You can't be. This isn't happening."

She checked for a pulse. As soon as she touched him, a strange sensation shot up her arm. Where did that come from?

The flesh beneath the thick black hair felt firm and warm. There it was, she thought, pressing against the heavy beat. Slow, but regular. He was alive. She looked at his face, sat back on her haunches, and wondered what the hell she was going to do with him.

Laney hadn't killed the bear.

She'd wounded Bigfoot.

Later on, when "Bigfoot" awakens

While the woman was in the kitchen, he relaxed his guard. The pain he accepted as his due. It wasn't the first time he'd been shot, anyway.

He should have seen it coming. When he'd spotted her out in the storm, his first instinct had been to confront her rather than run. In spite of the shotgun she'd pointed at him. After all, there was the possibility that she was exactly who she appeared to be. And whether she was or she wasn't, she certainly wouldn't shoot him out in the open.

He'd neglected to take into account the low visibility caused by the storm. That, combined with the old hide he'd scavenged from the caves and wrapped around himself, had apparently convinced her to think he really was a bear. She'd yelled at him, but the wind made it impossible to hear what she'd said.

He'd started walking toward her, trying to catch the words, and then she'd shot him.

He savored the warmth of the fire for a few moments. Thanks to her, he'd been stuck in the cave for days. Nearly a week of freezing his ass off. Getting his chest peppered hadn't improved his mood.

Good thing Little Miss Chatterbox had only loaded the shotgun with rock salt. If she'd shot him at that range using standard cartridges, what was left of him would have been smeared over several yards of snow. He'd destroyed all his identification months ago.

Kathy would have never known the truth.

The trip to the bathroom had been informative. With one glance he'd seen the door to the back bedroom was shut, and the small scrap of paper he'd wedged at the top was still in place. His gear was safe, for the time being.

Or was it all part of the game?

The first time he'd seen her had been three days ago, when he'd peered through a window from the outside of the cabin. Courting frostbite to play Peeping Tom, he'd stood there for nearly an hour.

She'd been curled up in this very same chair, reading a book. The flames crackling in the brick hearth had nothing on that curly mop of hers. Childish hair but a ballerina's body. Long, graceful limbs. Narrow hips. Small breasts.

She was built for a gentleman's bed. Instantly he'd imagined touching that slim, silky female body with his big hands. A moment later she looked up as she turned a page, and lamplight fell over her face. Smooth, white skin. Butterscotch eyes. Full, rosy lips.

He'd already gotten hard, watching her, but seeing her face made him groan. She might be put together like a porcelain statuette, but that mouth of hers could bring a man to his knees in three seconds.

For a split second, he'd wondered if she was one of Richmond's women. No, the bastard preferred sleek, skilled blondes and wouldn't waste his time with a sweet young thing—even one with a mouth designed for sex.

The girl had shifted in the chair, rested her cheek against one palm, and sighed. The innocent, faintly troubled expression was the tip-off.

She was either bait or a player.

He silently acknowledged Richmond's shrewdness. She wasn't beautiful, not with that young face and Orphan Annie hair. Nor was she put together to tempt a discriminating man—too small and fresh. But she was vulnerable, and she was alone. It had been nearly six months since he'd gone near, much less touched, a woman.

So Richmond had thrown him a tender little morsel to lure him in. You didn't bait a trap better than that.

She couldn't belong to the house owner's family—he knew that. The Irishman had spent every summer on the mountain for the last twenty years, but never made mention of a daughter. No sign of a wedding ring or husband. She was too old to be a granddaughter; the old man's son was only in his early thirties. Even if she was related, there was no way in hell her family would permit her to stay on Nightmare Ridge alone, with no way out. Not this time of year.

He had even gone so far as to scout for an abandoned or broken-down vehicle. There wasn't a car within a five-mile radius of the cabin. Besides, how would she have known how to get here?

He'd nearly walked in on her four days ago,

when she'd first appeared. Coming back from his daily scouting expedition, he'd gotten within two hundred yards of the cabin before smelling the wood smoke. He hadn't lit many fires in the cabin, knowing the odor would give away his own presence.

Now he looked around the interior of the cabin. She kept things tidy. The garbage she'd thrown away had told him little about her, except that she didn't waste food and had already cleaned everything inside the cabin at least once.

Was she a player? If she was, why bother to drag him inside and treat his wounds? Had she meant to disable him, then interrogate him? The Florence Nightingale act could be a ploy to throw him off guard. Looking into those soft, candy-colored eyes, he'd almost fallen for it.

She didn't act like a player, but none of them ever did. He'd been down that route before, knew now he couldn't trust anyone. Least of all a friendly, compassionate woman who showed up helpless and alone in the middle of a snowstorm.

Gene Hale is the pseudonym for a nationally bestselling author in another genre. *Paradise Island* is her first work of contemporary romance. Readers may contact her at P.O. Box 9295, Coral Springs, FL 33071.